CURIOSI CASEBOOK

TIM WINTERMUTE

PRISMATIST PRESS

To Kathleen

Contents

1

PROLOGUE

They call Rome the eternal city and I spent an eternity in the coffin size elevator as it slowly ascended. Finally, it stopped abruptly with a lurch. Stepping out into the hallway I checked the instructions on the slip of paper then followed the corridor to the right. My footsteps echoed off the terrazzo floor and walls as I walked down the deserted hallway. Each of the doors I passed had the name of a business, except the one whose number was on the sheet I held. I hesitated, unsure if I was supposed to knock or just walk in. As I reached out the door opened. A middle aged woman wearing a rather stylish black pantsuit appeared. She greeted me using my name and without telling me hers she asked me to step inside.

The room was sparsely furnished with an oak table and one chair. Venetian blinds hung down over the two windows and only slivers of sunlight made it through the slats. Most of the light came from a florescent fixture on the ceiling. Facing me was another door that was closed. On the table was a thermos, a pitcher of water and some cups. There was also a briefcase.

After I sat down she opened the briefcase, pulled out five leather bound books and stacked them in front of me. Embossed on the cover of the top book was a Roman numeral. She told me that each book was a case and I would be left alone for four hours to read them. The outside door would be locked during that time, but there was a restroom behind the closed door facing me and I was, of course, free to help myself to coffee in the thermos and water. Then I was asked to empty my pockets and place the contents in the now empty briefcase. After closing the briefcase she picked it up and left the room without giving me a chance to ask any questions.

Four hours later the door opened just as I finished reading the last case book.

She placed the briefcase on the table. "Are you interested in publishing what you read?" she asked.

"Yes, but why did you choose the Prismatist Press?"

"Will my answer make any difference in your decision to publish what you just read?"

"No, I'll publish it, but..."

"That's your answer," she said, then opened the briefcase and placed the contents on the table. In addition to my cellphone, notepad, a couple of pens and the sheet of paper with the directions there was a thumb drive.

"The five cases you read are on this thumb drive," she said. "It is already formatted for publishing. Nothing on it can be altered and any attempt will result in the contents being automatically deleted. There are some minor changes from what you just read that have been made in order to maintain the level of secrecy that we require."

"Does that include the name of your organization?"

She gave me a bemused smile, "Knowing that we call ourselves the Curiosi won't help anyone find out who we really are." She paused and added, "Including you."

"I did look up Curiosi when you contacted me," I replied. "I didn't find any organization by that name, although I did learn that in Latin curiosi can be translated as spy or one who pries. There was also an odd historical reference I found that said the curiosi was the name of the Roman secret service under the Emperor Constantine."

"As I said, there's really nothing in the name that is helpful in finding out who we really are other than our members are curious."

"From reading these casebooks a reader could well conclude that your members are a diverse and, even eccentric, group who share a common interest in mysteries."

"The same could be said about the members of book groups that read Agatha Christie mysteries," she said as she lifted the leather bound books from the table and placed them in the briefcase. She closed the lid and said, "Now, it is time to leave."

After I stepped out into the hallway, I turned and asked her, "Do I use the same email address to reach you in the future?"

"That address is no longer valid, just like this office is listed as vacant."

"Then how do I get in touch with you?"

"You don't. We will contact you," she said, then shut the
door.

2

LOST AND FOUND

Paris, France - September 2015

It had probably been a garret where starving artists and hungry writers lived, but now it was just a hotel room on the top floor looking out over the rooftops of Paris. I stared at the long pane of glass that followed the slope of the roof where a dormer had once been attached. It had been lopped off when the hotel had been renovated. My eyes followed the street as it sliced through the rooftops until it ended at the row of plane trees, then skipped over the Seine and focused on the stubby towers and stolid flank of the Cathedral of Notre Dame. Its flying buttresses were as useless as a penguin's wings for levitation, but they kept the Gothic mass from sinking beneath the mud of the Île de la Cité. I reached for a pack of cigarettes but there was only my passport, my wallet, and my cell phone. I had given up smoking two weeks before and it wasn't like I was about to face a firing squad.

I took off the crumpled khakis and polo shirt I'd worn on the flight over and dropped them on the already rumpled bed. I know you're supposed to stay awake after a transatlantic flight until your normal bedtime so your biological clock would be reset to the new time, but I'd taken a nap anyway. After all, Paris was timeless. I showered, changed into a clean pair of khakis and a clean, crisp white shirt, then put on my only sport coat, a navy blue blazer that I took with me whenever I traveled. Its brand name was SuperSuits and the way it resisted stains and wrinkles it could have been the product of a sweatshop on the planet Krypton. After buttoning my blazer in the vain hope it would contain my paunch, I locked my room and took the elevator down to the lobby.

Since the first floor in Europe is zero, not one, I'd lost not only six hours coming over but a floor as well. When the elevator door opened I faced the front desk and the woman behind it gave me a cheerful "Bonjour." She was in her twenties and wore an expensive silk red and blue scarf wrapped elegantly around her neck, just the way you'd expect to see on a French woman. "Unfortunately," she said, in a more subdued voice, "the museums are closed because the workers are on strike."

"Then it's fortunate that I have to go to a business meeting and won't be able to go to a museum anyway."

She seemed disappointed in my response, but offered, "Perhaps tomorrow you will have time?"

"Will the strike be over tomorrow?"

She sighed and threw up her hands, "One never knows. Do you need directions to your business meeting?"

"It's not far from here."

"Even so, it is very easy to get lost in Paris." She reached down and pulled out a map and handed it to me. "In which case this carte de la ville will prove helpful."

No, I repeated to myself, one never knows, as I stuffed the map of Paris into one of the inside pockets of my blazer.

***

I didn't have to be at my meeting until after lunch and it was almost noon, so I turned left outside the hotel and walked the short distance to the Place Maubert where I picked up the Boulevard Saint-Germain to the Boulevard Saint-Michel which I followed until I reached the Jardin du Luxembourg. Inside the gardens I bought a coffee and a ham sandwich at a kiosk and passed up the rickety wooden folding chairs scattered under the trees for a bench next to the big pond in the middle of the garden. Sitting there I drank the coffee quickly, then slowly ate while I stared at the puffy clouds reflected on the still water. It could have been a Monet painting of lily pads except for the model sailboats that floated on the pond.

I took the long way back on the Boulevard Saint-Michel and just before the bridge over the Seine, turned right toward the Quai de Montebello, where I browsed the second-hand book-sellers with their open-air stalls. They are called bouquinistes, which sounds like the name of a terrorist group, only the kind that preserves books rather than burns them. Just before the intersection with the Pont de l'Archevêché, where the Quai de Montebello dissolves into the Quai de la Tournelle, I turned around, crossed with the light, and then turned left back onto the Rue Maître Albert. Framed in the window of a bistro were several men resting their elbows on the zinc bar while watching soccer on the television. Between the bistro and the hotel was a long, high wall with brick peeking through the cracks in the plaster and a wooden double door painted green. I rang the bell to the left of the door, and just before I was about to ring a second time, the door opened. The concierge, an elderly woman, dressed in black with a shawl around her shoulders, peered at me as if from another century, then motioned for me to enter the courtyard shutting the door behind me. I followed her across the courtyard to the front door of an 18th-century town house where she rapped the brass knocker several times and then turned and slowly retraced her steps across the courtyard.

"I am Leonard," announced the man who answered the door. He pronounced it lay-o-nahr, which was the proper way in French although his accent was Dutch. He had a long, thin face, black rectangular glasses, and wispy blond hair that could have been spun from gold.

"I'm Henry, Henry Scriviner."

"Of course you are," he answered. "I have been expecting you."

I followed as we walked past a sweeping staircase and several large rooms with parquet floors and fireplaces and chandeliers, but no furniture, until we reached the end of the hall where there was a closed door. He opened the door and ushered me into a room that was almost as large as those we had passed, with the same high, white ceilings. On the blue walls were faded rectangles and squares where paintings had once hung. The only furniture was a card table with several folding chairs. Beyond the table were glass doors that opened onto a garden with a fountain in the center. The smell of plants and the sound of trickling water filled the empty room. Leonard, who had not spoken since our greeting at the door, motioned for me to sit down in one of the chairs as he sat alongside. His long fingers tapped on a manila folder that rested on the table as if he were practicing a one-handed piece for the piano.

I was beginning to wonder if this was some sort of tactile torture when he stopped tapping and asked, "Did you have a good flight?"

"It was good and, even better, it was on time. However, the driver of the taxi I took from De Gaulle had a problem finding the hotel. He thought he knew where the Rue Maître Albert was but once we got to the Left Bank he couldn't find it and called the hotel on his mobile for directions. It's not easy for a Paris cabbie to get lost."

He nodded, "It is even more difficult for them to admit that they are lost. Many people think they know where the Rue

Maître Albert is, but when they look for it, they find that it is not where they thought it was."

"I've spent a lot of time here over the years, including the Latin Quarter, but I don't recall ever being on this street."

"You are not alone. Even though it is one of the oldest streets in Paris, most people walk past it without noticing it exists. It is hidden in plain sight. In the Middle Ages, Erasmus called it a cesspit, which, I believe, was as much a reference to its residents as to the refuse. It wasn't given a formal name until centuries later when it was named after Maître Albert, a famous teacher at the University of Paris in the 13th century. Now, even most people who know the street exists don't know who Maître Albert was."

"Speaking of knowing, how did you know I'd come to Paris, even though I don't know who you are and what you want me to do?"

"But, as you said, you have spent time here, so it seemed natural that you would want to come back at any opportunity."

"You know that I've been here before?"

"You are a published author so your biography is not a secret and I knew you have been here often. I have also read the novel you wrote that is set in Paris, which could only have been written by someone familiar with the city."

"You were actually able to find a copy?"

"I found it at Shakespeare and Company. I purchased a used copy."

"I'm surprised."

"That they had your book?"

"That they had a used copy. It means there was at least one person who read the book when it first came out."

"But you are being unfair. Your descriptions were very evocative. It made me feel as if I were there."

"But you are here."

"Yes, but rather there in the Paris you created. It made me see things in a different way. Your writing reminded me a bit of Hemingway."

"Unlike in Hemingway's novel, *The Sun Also Rises*, it only set on my novel."

"Really, you are too hard on yourself. After all, Hemingway committed suicide while you are alive."

I shook my head and replied, "If you think I'm hard on myself you haven't read what the critics who reviewed my novel wrote about me. In fact, I bet the used copy you bought at Shakespeare and Company belonged to a book reviewer who got it for free and sold it after he read it. Maybe he didn't even read it – you can never tell with reviewers. In any case, I took up nonfiction after that. Now I mainly do travel writing."

"It is your travel writing that caught our attention. I think you are very good at describing the people in the places you write about, if that makes you feel any better."

I gave him my 'aw, shucks' smile and said, "At this point just getting paid to write makes me feel better. You mentioned in the email that you wanted me write an article for you, but you didn't say what the publication was."

"Of course you must be curious."

"You sent me a round-trip, first-class plane ticket and paid my expenses for a week so, yeah, you could say I'm curious."

He took his hand off the folder and pressed together the tips of his long fingers, the kind that would look good on a concert pianist, and rested his elbows on his knees and leaned toward me, his blue eyes shining above the black frames of his glasses, "We want to retain your services."

"I know that much, but who is the 'we,' and what is the publication, you want me to write for?"

"We are the Curiosi."

"I've never heard of the Curiosi. Is it some new travel magazine?"

He smiled, "Although one could say that we are well-traveled, we are not a magazine and we prefer that no one knows of our existence."

"If you don't have any readers, why do you do you want a writer?"

He pulled his elbows off his knees and sat up straight, "The Curiosi are the readers. What we want you to write is only for the members of the Curiosi, and I can assure you that all of them will read it."

"If the Curiosi are like the National Geographic Society, I have to warn you I'm not much of a photographer. Also, even though I'm fluent in French, I'm a better writer in English."

He laughed. It was much deeper than I would have imagined. "The only resemblance between us and the National Geographic Society is that we both have members. Unlike them, it is our members who are the contributors to the knowledge that is shared. We need a writer who can write fluently in English because it is the only language our members have in common. Although your fluency in French is essential for gathering the information for this assignment, it is not for the writing."

"I guess it's a good thing for me that you don't communicate using some secret language."

He shook his head with an amused smile but didn't repeat the laugh this time, "We don't even have a secret handshake."

"Afraid you'll leave fingerprints?" I almost laughed, but didn't want to lose the job on account of a bad joke, so I quickly added, "No, really, how do people apply for membership if no one knows you exist?"

"Ah, well," he seemed intrigued by the question. "One doesn't apply to be a member of the Curiosi. One is asked to be a member. In any case, since we don't have a large meeting of the members, such as a convention, the primary way we share what we are doing is through written reports or papers that are circulated among the members."

"Not that I want to talk myself out of a job, but why don't your members do the writing instead of hiring someone like me, an outsider?"

Leonard nodded, "We could, but even for those of our members who have the requisite literary or journalistic skill, they find it difficult to write about an activity in which they are actively engaged, and there is also the bias that would enter into it since one would be imposing one's own point of view in some way. That's why we hire writers such as yourself."

"Sounds like you want a ghostwriter."

"No, not at all," Leonard shook his head vigorously. "We very much want a flesh and blood writer and not an apparition. In fact, you will be recognized as the author. We want you to tell the story however you wish in your own words, and you were chosen exactly because of your writing style. There will be no editing. The last thing we want is something academic and dry. Our one condition is that you cannot divulge anything about the Curiosi, nor can what you have written be shared with anyone other than our members."

"I've heard of limited editions but this is a bit extreme isn't it?"

"Limited, yes, but you will find that the compensation is quite generous." He took an envelope from the folder and handed it to me. I opened it and looked at the sheet of paper. "Half of your fee will be placed in your bank account once you sign the agreement. The remainder plus reimbursement for expenses, in addition to your lodging and airfare, which we have paid for directly, will be wired to you once you have submitted your report. You only have to sign."

I looked at the one page agreement that said whatever I wrote belonged to the Curiosi and that I was not allowed to share it with anyone or to disclose anything about the Curiosi, including their name. "What if you don't like what I've written?"

"We select our writers very carefully so we have rarely had a problem. As I said, what you write for us will not be changed in any way."

"It's nice to be trusted," I said, although I wondered how I would ever know if they did change what I wrote. I signed the agreement and handed it to him "When do I start?"

Leonard handed me a small card with an address. "You have an appointment at this address in thirty minutes."

***

The Rue Descartes was another ancient, narrow street, but most people recognized the great philosopher after whom it was named. Unlike the Rue Maître Albert, there were numerous restaurants and cafés, their tables thrust onto the sidewalk creating a gourmet gauntlet. Its philosophy seemed to be that as long as you can eat and drink, we don't care if you exist. The address I was looking for was barely visible, tucked between an Algerian restaurant and a Vietnamese one. As I approached the door it opened.

"Welcome to the Institute for Lost Things, Mr. Scriviner," said the man who opened the door.

Startled by his appearance and greeting, I answered. "This is a hard place to find – the address, not the street."

"Yes, the street is busy, but we are hidden in plain sight. In fact, we have no sign with our name or even a doorbell, as you can see."

"How do you know if someone is waiting outside?"

"Because all of our visitors are here by appointment, we always have someone wait for them at the door, just like I did for you. There is a very small peephole so we can see our visitors when they approach."

"And if they're late?"

He shrugged, "We wait longer."

After I entered he closed the door and told me his name was Gerard. He didn't give his last name. He limped slightly, swaying gently, as he led me down a hallway. Since he was shorter than me, I could look down at the bald spot on the top of his head where the strands of hair he'd combed over had slipped, revealing the shiny skull beneath. All of the doors we passed were closed except one slightly ajar, and I caught a glimpse of an arm with a hand cradling a pipe. The arm was in a tweed sleeve with a brown leather patch at the elbow and there was Cavendish in the smoke that drifted into the hallway. At the end of the corridor we entered a large room. There were filing cabinets against the walls and a sturdy library desk with six wooden, spindle-back chairs. Gerard motioned for me to have a seat and asked if I wanted coffee or tea.

"Coffee."

He went through a door and came back with the coffee in a mug that had the image of Rodin's *The Thinker* on it. As I sipped the coffee a petite woman entered. She wore a black dress and her long dark brown hair was pulled back over her shoulders with a few strands cascading down the sides of her olive cheeks. Gerard left the room, closing the door behind him.

We shook hands and introduced ourselves. Her name was Adriana Bellini. After we both sat down at a long table, she told me she was from Turin, Italy, "But I have lived in France for many years."

"You speak French like a native Parisian," I said.

"Only someone who is not born in Paris would give such a compliment," she laughed. "You speak French quite well yourself."

"I spent a several years here after I graduated from college and have been back quite often. I've written a number of articles on Paris and France for various travel magazines."

"Yes, Leonard sent me some to read. You are definitely no stranger to Paris."

"I know my way around, but I never knew there was such a place as an Institute for Lost Things."

Adriana smiled, "We prefer not to be found even though our purpose is to find lost things." She rose from her chair and walked over to one of the filing cabinets. "These files contain just some of the records of the things that we have found."

"And where are the things?"

"They are kept in another place that has much more room. As you can imagine, there are things of all kinds, shapes, and sizes. There are objects both big and small, and even places, which, obviously, have to remain where they are found. In a few rare cases they are living things, although if they are humans we have to return them promptly and without generating any publicity."

The door opened and Gerard stuck his head inside. "They have just arrived. You told me to tell you, even to interrupt you."

"Yes, you were right to interrupt." She turned to me, "You will want to observe. It has to do with the case you are reporting on. We told them to come now because we wanted you to be here."

I followed them out of the room through the door and down another narrow hallway. Gerard was limping faster to stay in front of Adriana. She asked him if the visitors were carrying anything. He said he wasn't sure. He didn't get a good look but they might be carrying something. He asked what she thought they would be bringing. She didn't answer Gerard as he opened a door. There were bookcases and, on the wall, a still life with apples and bananas in a bowl that looked like a copy of a Cezanne, and two men sitting in black leather chairs in front of a desk. There was a lamp on the desk and some books and papers stacked neatly on one side. The lamp was off but there was plenty of light streaming through a tall window behind the desk and it lit their faces as they turned. There was stained glass in the upper part of the window so half of their faces were tinged with scarlet and a bit of blue.

"Madame Professor," one of the men said as they both rose. He was the shorter of the two.

"You can call me doctor," she answered, coolly. "I have a PhD but I am not a professor. I'm not married either," she added. "So you don't need to call me 'madame.'"

"I'm sorry," the other, taller, man apologized.

"I'm not," she answered and told them to be seated. After introducing me as her assistant, she seated herself behind the desk. Gerard left the room and I sat in a chair against the wall. It was hard to see Adriana well because of the light. She asked, "Can we get in?"

The taller man answered, "Yes. Tomorrow it will be possible. No problem."

"But maybe the strike will be over tomorrow," Adriana said.

"No," the shorter man said. "It will not be over. We know this for a fact. Trust us." He leaned over the top of the desk as he spoke. The other man leaned with him but not as far. Adriana nodded and they both stood up straight.

"What time should we be there?" she asked.

"Early would be better," the taller man replied.

"Yes, early would be best," the other one added. "Maybe 10:00 a.m.?"

"Yes, and where?" Adriana asked. "Where do we meet?"

"Here," the taller man leaned forward and stabbed with his index finger at a sheet of paper he had laid out on the top of the desk.

Adriana looked at the paper, "Fine, okay. Then we meet there at 10."

The taller man looked at the other one, nervously, and then said, "You understand that while we have agreed to give you access to the museum, none of the works of art are to be removed."

***

The ceiling and walls of the restaurant were rounded like a barrel except this barrel was made of stone instead of wood. Adriana sat across from me, on the other side of a candle set on the table along with the two glasses of wine that we had ordered, as well as some bread and cheese. There were no windows because it was underground and we had entered by walking down a flight of stairs from street level. The room flickered in the candlelight making our shadows dance on the curved walls. It was only six o'clock and the restaurant was empty except for us, since this was Paris where no one eats dinner before eight o'clock. In fact, Adriana had asked Gerard to call ahead and ask them if they would serve us dinner this early.

"This place," she said gesturing with her right hand, "reminds me of the catacombs."

"Except that there are no skulls here and no food there," I replied.

She sipped her wine. "Are you making a joke?"

"Only an observation. It reminds me of a wine cellar."

"It might be a cellar now but it was not always a cellar. Where the stairs are there was once a door and if you had walked out through it you would have been in the street."

"Like dining in a sinkhole."

Her dark eyes sparkled in the candlelight. "Only it didn't sink. It has stayed exactly in the same place, but everything around it rose as one layer of Paris was piled on another until the door would no longer open and they had to use stairs instead. Many things are lost not because they are moved but because they stay where they are while everything else moves."

"So this cellar is maybe, what, a thousand years old?"

"Perhaps." She cut a slice of cheese that smelled as if it might have been almost that old. "But probably not. However, there may be a place beneath us that is that old or older."

"Another restaurant?"

"I can say with great confidence that if it is a restaurant, it is still waiting to be discovered."

"How did you end up here?" I asked her. "You don't have to answer. Biographical background isn't part of the assignment. I'm just curious how someone from Turin, Italy ended up in Paris directing an institute for the lost?"

"Lost things," she corrected me. "I will tell you this. I did not expect it. I was here, in Paris, in 1968. You know about '68?"

"Of course, the riots."

"The riots if you were on one side and the revolution if you were on the other. I had just graduated from the university in Turin and some of us came up together. We were in a Fiat 600. You know how small a car that is? Like a Deux Chevaux, which is very small. Somehow, four of us came up together in this small car to Paris to be a part of the revolution. We also had what we called a revolution in Italy, but the one here seemed, you know?"

"More revolutionary?" I offered.

She sipped some wine and stared at something over my left shoulder, or maybe nothing at all. "Yes, well, you know in Italy, it would just be another riot not a revolution. So we spend a week, maybe more, in the protests. We march here, we march there, we seem to march everywhere. Then, one day, we were in a very big march. There were thousands of us: students from all of the universities in Paris and workers. I remember especially the Metro workers because we were just behind them. There were banners and flags. We were carrying a red flag for revolution. The Italian brigade, we called ourselves. We were marching from the Bastille to the Gare de Lyon. Why there, I don't know. Maybe some of the people needed to take the train home afterwards. In any event, we stopped and the protesters in the front began to chant, CRS SS, CRS SS, and we knew that the CRS, the state security police, must have stopped us. So we began to yell as well."

Her eyes were larger now, reflecting in their darkness the flames of the candles.

"We still couldn't see anything, you understand? And then suddenly the people in front began to move forward and the people behind began to push us and we were carried forward. My feet could not even touch the ground because all of these people were pushing us forward and then there was a lot of smoke and tear gas and we were coughing and being pushed this way and then that way and people were running in every direction. The CRS were chasing us carrying those big plastic shields and they were wearing big black boots and they had batons and they were hitting people. And there were other people, demonstrators, who were throwing things at them: bottles, pieces of fruit, even shoes. They were throwing and running and throwing and everyone that the CRS caught they beat with their batons. I ran but I didn't know where I was going because I didn't know Paris very well at that time. I had lost my companions. Then I saw the entrance to the Gare de Lyon. There were people standing outside. They were people who were going to or coming from a train or the Metro and had stopped to watch all of this happen. I guess they would have called themselves innocent bystanders although for us to stand by was a crime. We all rushed into this group so the CRS had to stop because they didn't know who was who. I looked at them as they formed this line facing us as if they were trying to decide whether it was worth it to charge and just beat up everyone, and then the crowd, as if they knew what the CRS was thinking, turned around and rushed into the station. I suppose you could say that it was a moment of complete solidarity with everyone united in running away. And we ran inside and down the stairs to the Metro and through the gate. No one paid of course. Fortunately for us the Metro was running, even though all of the Metro workers were supposed to be on strike and part of the march. I was pushed inside a car by the crowd just as the doors closed and we left the station with a swoosh. You know how the Metro makes that swoosh sound as if all the air has escaped like you are in one of those pneumatic tubes that carry messages? It was like that. I will never forget."

"So, I stayed on the Metro until we reached Chatelet. It was only a few stops. I got out and walked across the Île de la Cité, past the police station, until I reached this side, the Left Bank. There were Che and Mao buttons still pinned on my blouse. I felt lucky that I had escaped, because as an Italian and a woman I would have been badly treated. But I also felt guilty for not having been arrested and beaten. I remember clearly that as I walked and thought this I took out my pack of cigarettes because I really needed a smoke. And then I noticed, as if it was the first time, that the cigarette pack was red, which is the color for revolution, but the cigarettes were Marlboros, which were the only brand I smoked, and on the pack was a picture of the macho cowboy Marlboro Man. It was the embodiment of false consciousness and yet I hadn't really seen it before." She stopped and looked at me. There were a couple of breadcrumbs on her lips that she wiped away.

"What happened then?"

"I stopped smoking," Adriana replied with a smile. "Then I decided not to return to Italy, and, instead, enrolled in a PhD program in philosophy at the Sorbonne."

"Why philosophy?"

"I suppose I wanted to search for the truth."

"And you ended up searching for things that are lost."

She laughed, "Many of which are hidden in plain sight, like the Marlboro Man."

***

After a breakfast of croissants and café au lait the next morning the desk clerk announced cheerfully that the museums were no longer closed.

"The strike is over?"

"No, there is still a strike, but they have gone back to work as a gesture of good will."

I decided not to ask how you could be on strike but also continue working. "I'm sure the tourists who want to visit the Louvre will be eternally grateful."

"No, the Louvre remains closed. Also, the Musée d'Orsay. They are the only exceptions since the workers feel that they cannot abandon their principles altogether."

"That means people won't be able to see the Mona Lisa at the Louvre."

"There will be no Mona Lisa, at least for today," she sympathetically, "I am very sorry, Monsieur."

"Don't feel sorry for me, I've seen her before. More than once, as a matter of fact, and I doubt she's changed."

"Ah, Monsieur, the Mona Lisa may not change but I think that whenever we look closely at a great work of art we see something new that we did not notice before because we have changed." She smiled and added, "At least, that has been my experience."

I nodded at the reproduction of the tapestry of the Lady and the Unicorn hanging across from the front desk. The lady looked more like a girl of fifteen and the unicorn could be a pony except for the horn. "What do you notice about the tapestry?"

"It is about love, Monsieur," she sighed.

"And if there was no horn on the unicorn?"

"Then it would be about a girl who loves her pony."

***

I settled into the back seat of the Citroën sedan, a car that reminded me of an armadillo although a hell of a lot roomier, so that my knees didn't jam into Gerard's back in the driver's seat. It began to rain again as we pulled away from the hotel. Soon it was a torrent and the Citroën moved slowly through the water that had accumulated in the narrow street. On the Quai de la Tournelle, Gerard took the first turn and we were on a less congested street. The rain attacked the windows and was barely beaten back by the windshield wipers. This, combined with the constant turning from one street to another, made it impossible for me to figure out where we were. Gerard gestured with his hands as he spoke, although he managed to get them back onto the steering wheel in time for the next turn.

They were arguing.

"I think we should have turned there," Adriana said.

"I don't think so."

"Are you certain?"

"No. Anyway, it doesn't matter. We can turn at the next street."

"But we are losing time."

"Only if I am wrong."

"Yes, I suppose you were right," Adriana looked back at me and smiled as she said, reassuringly, "Don't worry, Gerard will get us there with time to spare."

"Where?"

"You don't know?"

"You never told me."

"But I thought you knew. I mean, you never asked."

"I thought you would tell me but then you never did."

"There is no point in telling you now because we are almost there," she replied and turned to face the front.

The car stopped. Gerard announced, "It is only a block from here. It would be better to walk so that we are not noticed."

We got out and waited as Gerard opened the trunk and re-moved a suitcase with two wheels on the bottom. It looked small enough to fit into the overhead compartment of a plane.

"Is that what you brought?" Adriana asked him, as he rested the suitcase on the sidewalk and closed the trunk. "It will look very suspicious."

"People will think we are tourists. You see, I have even placed an Air France baggage ticket on the handle." It hung limply, already waterlogged. "And the rain will keep people from looking closely at us in any case."

"If it continues," Adriana scanned the murky sky. "Anyway, we have no time for an alternative." She turned and began walking. I quickly caught up with her but Gerard was slower and we stopped at the end of the block to wait for him. Gerard was wearing a raincoat that was much too large for his small frame and made him look even smaller than he was. I realized that we were approaching the rear of the Musée d'Orsay and the two men who had met with Adriana the day before were standing next to the back entrance. The tall man had on a black trench coat and the shorter man was wearing one of those plastic raincoats that you could see through. Somehow the tall one had managed to keep his cigarette lit even though he was not wearing a hat. They looked at Gerard and the suitcase he was wheeling behind him.

"Why do you have a suitcase with you?" The shorter man asked.

"Gerard thinks it makes us look less suspicious, like we are tourists," Adriana answered.

Both men looked at each other and then the tall man said, "I guess you will need to bring it with you then. We can go in this door. Bertrand will go in first and turn off the alarm, then he will open the door and signal to us. If no one is looking, we will go in. If not we will wait."

"Won't we look suspicious waiting here?" I asked. "Three people and a suitcase?"

"Yes," the man said. "You have a point."

"I have a map," Gerard said, taking out a map of Paris and unfolding it. "You can be showing us directions, you see. After all we are pretending to be tourists."

The man looked at the map and the suitcase. "Okay, I can see that it might work. We will talk loudly and gesture. You will say you are angry the museum is closed and want to know how to get to the Eiffel Tower."

"Why do they have a suitcase if they are going to the Eiffel Tower?" Bertrand, the shorter of the two, asked.

"Because we are not going to go there after all," Gerard answered. "Instead, we are looking for the Hotel Proust. They will believe that because it is only a few blocks away. Some friends of mine from Lille stayed there when they were visiting." Gerard turned to me and added, "As I recall it was really a very pleasant hotel and was quite reasonable for the Sixth Arrondissement."

Bertrand opened the door and entered the building, while the tall man began talking loudly as we huddled together pretending to be tourists looking for the Hotel Proust.

A minute later Bertrand opened the door again and motioned for us to enter.

"No one is looking," the tall man said. "Let's go. Quickly."

Gerard folded the sodden map. He had trouble folding it back the way it was originally. Instead it was like a sandwich with too much salami and not enough bread.

"Could you carry the suitcase?" Adriana asked me. "Gerard has his hands full."

I pulled the handle of the suitcase. It felt empty. We entered a room with a video camera mounted near the ceiling. Bertrand unlocked another door using a card that he slid into a slot and we walked up a flight of stairs with me carrying the suitcase by its handle. At the top of the stairs there was another room that had a console with closed circuit television monitors. On one of the screens was the street outside. It was still raining and the street was deserted. The other screens were filled with the empty galleries.

We walked through another door, but this one was not locked. There was something like an airport metal detector on the other side that we passed through before emerging into a vast space with a high vaulted ceiling of glass spanned by iron girders. I was familiar with it from past visits to the museum. This was where trains and people and baggage, all of them just arriving or about to depart, once waited before the Gare d'Orsay was closed years before it was renovated into a museum.

"You can leave us now," Adriana told the two men.

"But it would be better if we accompanied you," the tall man replied. "We are responsible if anything should happen."

"We have permission from the Ministry so you are not responsible," Adriana said.

"Still, they will know it was Bertrand who was here because he used his code to enter, and if anything happens he will be held accountable because the Ministry will deny everything as they always do. And then I could not let Bertrand take the blame by himself so I would also be held responsible. You see, it is not so easy."

"What do you think will happen?"

He looked at the suitcase.

"We are searching for a lost item. If we find what we are looking for we need to carry it in something and, as Gerard said, a suitcase won't arouse suspicion."

"Because you are pretending to be tourists," Bertrand added.

Before they could ask another question Adriana said, "You won't find any of your artwork missing, if that's your concern. Besides, isn't there something attached to each piece of art that will set off an alarm if we walk through the detector?"

"Yes, you are right. The alarm will go off," Bertrand nodded.

The tall man looked at Bertrand, "But the alarm system is monitored at all times, and someone will have to come and find out what has happened if it goes off. How will we explain our presence if that happens?"

Bertrand shrugged, "That we caught the crooks?"

Adriana looked at both of them sternly. "As I said, we have permission from the Ministry so you won't get into any trouble. Now, why don't you go somewhere, perhaps the bookstore, and we will find you when we are done?"

The tall man had taken out a pack of Gauloises while she spoke, doing this slowly, as if he was going nowhere fast.

"I thought there was no smoking in the Musée," Gerard said.

Ignoring Gerard, the man lit the cigarette with one click of his lighter and exhaled a fat yellow cloud. "By that clock," he pointed to the large clock set into the glass above the entrance at the far end that was the original one from the train station. "It is 10:45 now." I looked at the giant hands that almost cut the face in half. "No later than noon. That should give you enough time to find this thing that has been lost."

***

After they left, we moved quickly. Adriana led, followed by Gerard, whose coat billowed behind him. I gave him a couple of paces as I pulled the suitcase so that I didn't step on the coat's trailing edges. We walked through the galleries, catching fleeting images of the beginning of Impressionism until we stopped in front of a nondescript, unmarked door. Gerard pulled something out of one of the deep pockets of his coat and fiddled with the lock. It opened. We descended a flight of stairs and entered a long room filled with pipes and electrical lines and mechanical equipment bolted to the floor. At the end of the room was a metal door. It had been painted many times and its current color was black. Gerard used the same device he had used on the other door, jiggling it while turning the door's knob. It was dark behind the door. Adriana found a switch on the wall. The room was bathed in the feeble light of naked bulbs. The room was large and there were boxes and pieces of office furniture and empty picture frames stacked against the walls.

We stood silently for a minute. I was about to ask what they were looking for when Adriana whispered, "There it is."

"Yes, I think you are right." Gerard answered.

They began pulling stacked boxes away to reveal a gray door. This door needed to be painted. It was wood and there were cracks in it. Gerard turned the knob and pulled. The door didn't move.

"Is it locked?" Adriana asked, a trace of anxiety in her voice. "We don't have a key."

"No, it is just stuck. Who knows how long it has been closed."

"We hope as long as the railway station, some sixty years."

"Let me help," I offered and took out my Swiss Army knife. I ran its blade inside the crack between the door and its frame. "Now try."

Gerard pulled on the handle and the door opened half an inch. Adriana and I slipped our fingers into the gap and pulled together. With a loud groan the door opened a foot and then with me pushing and them pulling it opened halfway before it stopped and wouldn't budge any farther.

"It's warped pretty badly." I remarked. "I don't think even a Swiss Army knife has a tool for that."

"That's okay, we have enough space," Adriana answered.

Gerard pulled two flashlights from somewhere in his voluminous jacket and handed one to Adriana. She switched it on and slipped through the opening in the doorway with Gerard following. He turned to me once he was inside. "Please, could you pass me the suitcase?"

I picked up the suitcase by its handle and handed it to him. Then I started to squeeze through the opening, but was stopped by his raised hand. "No, it is better that you stay on the other side and keep watch."

"Yes," Adriana added. There was a slight echo in her voice. "There is not much room in here in any case. Also, please let us know what the time is every five minutes, okay."

"It's 11:15," I answered.

"That does not give us much time before they will come looking for us," Gerard noted.

"We know what we are looking for."

"Yes, but where is it exactly?"

"It is exactly where we will find it, so just begin looking."

I could see through the opening, in the beams of their flashlights, that they were in a room packed with all sorts of stuff. It looked like a Goodwill store donation bin. There was scraping and bumping and an occasional thud as objects were moved around.

"11:45." There had been no conversation except Gerard's grunts and sneezes, a few profanities, and a couple of monosyllabic observations coming from the space behind the door.

"We are running out of time," Gerard announced.

Adriana did not answer. There was more scraping and bumping.

"Here!" She exclaimed as if she had found the needle in the haystack. "Shine your light here." Immediately there were two beams pointed in the same direction. One shone almost directly down and the other, slanted from a greater distance. In a second, both had converged. Adriana's face appeared and then disappeared. Gerard had moved between us. His tent like coat blocked my view completely. It was silly that he was still wearing it. Something opened. It sounded like the suitcase.

"11:50," I called out.

"Finished," Gerard said, then handed me the suitcase through the opening in the doorway. "Be careful, it is heavier now."

When they both emerged from the room, they were smiling. Gerard took a tube of something and squeezed it onto the edges of the door and then closed it again.

"A little glue," he explained to me. "It should stick just like it did before."

We moved the boxes back in front of the door.

"What time is it now?" Adriana asked.

"11:55," I answered.

"We don't want anyone to come looking for us," Adriana said. "Can you carry the suitcase? Gerard is a little tired."

Gerard was hunched slightly and his coat now dusted the floor whenever he shifted his weight to his bad leg. I pulled on the handle of the suitcase. It was much heavier and whatever they had put inside shifted slightly.

The two men were waiting just where we left them, both of them looking at the clock, whose hands were pointing at one minute to twelve. The tall man seemed disappointed that we had made it just in time, but Bertrand smiled. "Ah, you found what you were looking for?"

"Yes, it was not difficult," Adriana answered matter-of-factly.

"And what was it that you are now carrying in the suitcase?" The tall man asked. He was smoking another Gauloises.

"Nothing that is of value to you or the Museum."

"How do we know that is true? Perhaps you should open it and let us see what you have found."

"But we have permission from the Ministry."

"Ah yes, but you do not have permission to take anything that belongs to the Museum. We have a duty to assure ourselves that no crime is being committed."

"Believe me, this does not belong to the Museum. And we are not stealing anything. We are taking something that was left here when this was the Gare d'Orsay, long before it became the Musée d'Orsay, and taking it to another location."

"Lucas," Bertrand said, saying the tall man's name for the first time. "It is true that the instructions were that they could not take any artwork from the museum, but if this is something from the old train station then they can take it, just as she said."

"How do we know that they are telling the truth unless we inspect it?" Lucas asked. He flicked some ashes on the floor. "There is nothing in our instructions that denies us the right to inspect what they are removing."

"I protest," Adriana said.

"Of course you do. We will make a note of it. Now I will open the suitcase."

Adriana looked at Bertrand. It was an appeal. He shrugged. Lucas took the suitcase from me, laid it flat on the floor, bent down and unzipped. Bertrand and I looked over his shoulder.

Adriana and Gerard stayed where they were a few feet away. After all, they knew what was inside.

"Ha!" Bertrand laughed. "It is nothing, just as they claim."

"No, it is not nothing," Lucas replied.

"What is it then?"

"I don't know. It looks a bit like an old typewriter. I don't think its art, whatever it is." He got up. "However, there are many things here that I don't think of as art. I must ask you to tell us what it is."

"Tell them Gerard," Adriana said.

Gerard looked at her and then into the suitcase. He was sweating and wiped his forehead with the floppy sleeve of his coat.

"Go on, Gerard, it is okay to tell them," Adriana urged.

"It is...," he paused and looked at Adriana again.

"Yes, Gerard, please tell us what this mysterious thing is that you claim is not art but is so important the Ministry has given you permission to remove it?" Lucas asked.

"It could be a typewriter."

"Why would you go to all this trouble to recover an old typewriter? That makes no sense."

"Perhaps it isn't a typewriter," Gerard added.

"If it isn't a typewriter then what is it, exactly? If you can't explain then we will have to ask one of the curators to look at it to make sure it isn't a work of art that belongs here."

"Have you ever heard of the SIGABA?" Adriana asked, walking over to the suitcase and looking into it. She looked up at

Lucas, who clearly had no idea what she was talking about. "It was the most famous cipher machine used during World War II. It was even more complicated than the Enigma. You have heard of the Enigma, haven't you, the German device that was used to encode secret messages?"

"Of course, the Enigma," Lucas replied, looking at Bertrand and then at me. He wasn't a good liar.

"Then you know that the Enigma's rotor could only turn in one direction, while the SIGABA had rotors that could turn in both directions."

"Ah, yes." Lucas nodded, still trying to conceal his complete bafflement.

"The SIGABA was invented by the Americans and the Germans never broke the code."

"And this is one of them?" Bertrand asked.

"Not really. You see there was another cipher machine invented by a Swede named Hagelin in the late 1930's and there has been a theory – never proven – that Hagelin developed another machine. That machine was also lightweight and easy to operate but utilized a technology that was even more advanced than the Enigma or even the SIGABA. The machine was never put into production and, according to the theory, the plans were destroyed to keep it from falling into the hands of the Nazis. However, it was possible that a prototype was constructed and if the Nazis had been able to get their hands on the prototype they would have been able to construct a working machine and you can well imagine what the result would have been."

"What?" Bertrand asked.

"Stupid," Lucas cut him off. "It is obvious. If the Nazis had such a device instead of the Enigma, they might very well have won the war."

"I see."

"But how would the prototype end up here, in a museum?" Lucas asked Adriana.

"Remember this wasn't a museum, the Musée d'Orsay then, but a train station, the Gare d'Orsay. That's why it doesn't really belong here now that it is a museum."

"Yes, we all know that it was closed as a train station in 1939 and was just sitting here until it was made into a museum in 1986. Still, how would this code machine be left at the Gare d'Orsay?"

"A possible scenario would be that the prototype had been stolen and, while being transported to Germany, at the Gare d'Orsay it was stolen from the Nazi spies by an agent working for British intelligence. It was then hidden. According to this scenario, the British agent who hid it was killed before he could disclose the location. That may or may not be true. However, we do know that the Nazis invaded France soon after the time this would have occurred, which would had been just after the station was closed, making recovery difficult if not impossible. In any case the important thing was keeping it out of the hands of the Nazis."

"Ah, yes," Lucas said. "You see, Bertrand? Look, it is all very clear. And now, we have found it."

"But how did you know where to find it?" Bertrand asked.

"Yes," Lucas added. "If it was lost for a long time, a half century, how was it that you knew where to look?"

"Some things are better kept a secret for all concerned," Adriana answered. "Besides, who is to say that this is actually the prototype since we have not had a chance to examine it in detail."

Lucas said, "Anyway, I have seen enough to know you are telling the truth. You have found the famous spy machine that everyone has been searching for."

Adriana smiled as she stooped down and zipped up the suitcase. She looked at me, "Please?"

I took the suitcase from her. Gerard stood apart, hands stuffed in the pockets of his raincoat.

"We must let them go," Lucas said firmly to Bertrand. Then he turned to us and whispered, "Your secret is safe with us. You can tell the Minister that we know nothing."

***

We walked through the detector and the room with the monitors and into the rain. Outside, on the sidewalk, after the door closed behind us and we were alone, Adriana said, "I wish we had time to look at the artwork. With no one around they would look so different, as if they existed only for us."

"Which one is your favorite?" I asked.

"Monet's paintings of the Rouen Cathedral," she answered without hesitation. "But don't you find it a bit boring that he painted the front of the cathedral over and over again?"

"No, because each one was done at a different time, with different light, so they were all different. Every time he painted it, and every time I look at them, I see something new that I didn't notice before, not just because the light is different, but also because Monet, the painter, is seeing something he didn't see before. Monet isn't the only one. Think of Cezanne painting the same mountain again and again or Rembrandt's many self-portraits."

"Sounds a little like what a travel writer does," I replied. "We keep going back to the same places and writing about them."

"Exactly, and would you describe that as boring?"

"To write or read?" I laughed.

"Personally, I like anything by Toulouse-Lautrec or Van Gogh," Gerard interrupted as we approached the car. "No one can accuse them of being boring. Crazy, maybe."

It was still raining as we climbed into the Citroen but sunlight had begun to fall through the cracks in the clouds, collecting in the puddles in a pool of colors, the beginning or end of a rainbow, depending on your point of view.

"We were lucky that it rained after all," Gerard said putting on a pair of sunglasses.

"Yes," Adriana answered. "The weather forecast was right. I'm glad it's over, though."

"I didn't realize that you needed the rain that much," I said.

"Without the rain, Gerard would not have had the opportunity to wear his very chic, new raincoat."

The car swerved as Gerard started to laugh, his shoulders rose and fell in great heaves, as if they were beyond his control.

"Maybe you should stop the car, Gerard," I suggested.

"Yes, Gerard, we wouldn't want us to die laughing," Adriana added.

Gerard didn't stop the car but his shoulders settled as the laughter subsided. Adriana patted him on the top of his head, covering the bald spot that was still wet. She looked at me out of the corner of her eye as she did this.

***

We parked on the street and walked to the Institute. It was a short walk. The buildings on both sides of the street were now drenched in sunlight pouring down. I felt part of a big secret as we walked past people, none of whom had a clue as to what I was pulling behind me in the small suitcase. It felt like the world I was a part of had one more dimension that was hidden from them. I wondered if they sensed this at all as we passed just inches from each other.

As soon as we were inside the Institute, in the room that I first entered only yesterday, I lifted the suitcase and began to put it on the table.

"No," Adriana said. "You can just put it over there in the corner. Somewhere out of the way."

I held it there suspended a few inches or so off the ground. "Weren't we going to open it now so you can examine it?"

"Why would we do that?" she asked.

"Because you went to all the trouble to get this cipher machine."

"No, I didn't say it was a cipher machine. I only presented it as a possibility, a theory, a scenario, and that idiot..."

"Lucas," Gerard answered.

"Lucas. He and the other guy, Bertrand, they decided for themselves. They thought they saw something. But what they believed they saw wasn't really what was there." She stopped and looked at me. "I'm sorry, I guess you also decided."

"So if it's not a cypher machine, what is it?"

She shook her head, "It looks more like an old typewriter to me – a portable – one that probably doesn't work because of all the rust on it. But who needs even a typewriter that works now?"

Gerard added, "It was something I found back there that I put in the suitcase so it would feel like there was something in there when you carried it. You believed it was in there, didn't you? I thought you were convinced, anyway, the way you carried it. We hoped they wouldn't ask us to open it. But just in case they did, we couldn't put the real thing in there, you understand?"

"Yes, Gerard, now he understands. But next time please put something in there that is easier to explain."

"It was all a lie?" I asked.

"Nothing I told them was a lie. But the conclusion that they, and you it seems, drew wasn't the truth."

I put the suitcase down. It fell over on its side. I picked it up and moved it into a corner of the room, sliding it between a filing cabinet and the wall. When I returned to the table Gerard was standing with his coat unbuttoned. He had pulled the front back and exposed six bulging pockets sewn into the inside. Adriana began to take from each pocket a large plastic envelope and placed each one on the table. When she finished, Gerard took off the coat with a sigh and draped it on a chair.

I watched as they opened each envelope and placed the contents carefully on the table in stacks. They were pieces of paper, hundreds of pieces, and all of them were the sort of yellow, jaundiced color that afflicts paper when it ages. When they were done, Adriana motioned for me and I walked over to where she was standing. I saw that some of the pieces had handwriting on them, some were typewritten pages and others carbon copies. There was a name I recognized on the page in front of me, beneath the title.

Overcoming my shock, I asked, "How on earth did you know it had survived for all these years and where to find it?"

"It was really Gerard who first made the discovery. You know there is a central lost and found office where they kept a record of everything that is found at any of the stations. Gerard has been looking through their archives. To tell you the truth I think it is as much a hobby as research, isn't it Gerard?" He looked up from the stack where he had been stooped, pretending that he was not listening, and nodded. "He discovered an entry in the book for the Gare d'Orsay for 1922, in December a few days before Christmas. People seem to lose a lot at that time of year. The entry described a valise with the name Hemingway written beside it, only it was spelled with two m's."

"But," I interrupted, "didn't his wife, Hadley, report she had lost it while taking the train from the Gare de Lyon?"

"Yes, you were right. She was on her way back to Switzerland where they had been staying for a few months. It was either lost or stolen when she left it alone for a few minutes in the car before the train departed. In fact, Hemingway came back immediately and looked everywhere for it but concluded it had been stolen."

"What happened?"

"I don't know exactly what happened. I think it was stolen but Gerard believes that Hadley misplaced it. In any case we were able to trace the number of the railway car where it was found in the Gare d'Orsay to a train that had been in the Gare de Lyon two weeks before when Hadley lost the valise. Whether it was the same car that Hadley was sitting in or one on the same train where a thief might have hidden it we will never know since we don't have a record of her ticket. In any event, what was significant was that it was a valise that had been taken to the Gare d'Orsay's lost and found and had never been claimed. Obviously, that's because everyone was looking a couple of weeks before in another train station."

"If they knew his name since it was on the entry, why didn't they contact him?"

"Ah," Adriana answered, the forefinger of her right hand traced an invisible line across the top sheet of the typewritten stack. "We had three possibilities. The first, that because his name was misspelled the clerks at the train station were too bureaucratic to consider looking for a person with only one m. A second possibility, and this is Gerard's favorite, was that they opened the valise and found the manuscript, but because it was written in English they decided that it could not possibly be important and was promptly forgotten by those very same clerks. However, my own favorite is that Hemingway was simply a nobody at that time, so when no one claimed it, the whole thing was forgotten. When the station was closed, the lost and found was forgotten. We were able to locate the original plans of the Gare d'Orsay and compare those with the ones used when the station was renovated into the museum. Out of the spaces that were not part of the renovation plans, this was the only room that seemed likely to have been used for the lost and found storage. Of course, we had no way of knowing for sure until we were there. It was possible that the room where the lost and found articles were stored was part of the renovation, whether called for in the plans or not, and the contents simply discarded as garbage."

"But," Gerard interrupted, "I was confident as soon as we found that the door was stuck. It was like being the first ones to enter King Tut's tomb. Except there weren't any mummies."

"Or any curse," Adriana laughed. "At least none that we know of."

"I'll tell you what's a curse," I said. "That you've just discovered something that has been lost since the 1920's. Something that people don't believe exists, and weren't even looking for, but if they knew it was still out there, they wouldn't stop looking for it, and you can't tell anyone you've found it, you can only catalog it."

She looked at me and smiled, "On the contrary, I consider it a blessing. But if you do think it's a curse that we can't tell anyone, you must do nothing to try and remove it by telling anyone. You must send your report to Leonard, but only the members of the Curiosi will know."

"In other words, this," I waved at the yellow sheets of paper, "was never found."

"If it is found it will be by someone else, by accident, probably."

"How will anyone else ever find it if you've got it?" I said, wishing I had some sort of Enigma machine to decipher what she was saying.

"We left a receipt, a claim check, where we found the valise with the information on how to contact us if they are searching for this particular item. If they read the claim check and are really looking for the lost manuscript then they will understand what it means and will contact us. We are only keeping it safe until then."

"And if they never find it? What if the building is torn down?"

"They would never tear down the Musée d'Orsay."

"Then maybe there'll be a fire, or a flood. It's in the basement, anything could happen."

"Then it will be safe with us."

"Will you read it?"

"Of course."

"Lucky you."

"Lucky you, as well. If you wish you can read it. However, you will have to do it here and now, and you cannot tell anyone what you have read."

"Too bad because it would make a hell of a book review."

***

At the end of Rue Mouffetard is the Place de la Contrescarpe. Cafés surround the square, and when you sit at one of their small round tables you might also think that you were somewhere else: maybe a Norman village or an ancient town in Burgundy. This is especially true if you have never been to such places.

On one side of the square is the wall that once surrounded Paris, and on the other side the road that connected it to Rome. The road from Rome is now Rue Mouffetard and Rue Descartes is on the other side of the wall that is no longer there. The backfill from the moat in front of the wall is called the

Contrescarpe, and if you are in one of the cafés, you could be sitting where there was nothing once except the space inside the moat. You would also be very close to where Hemingway lived when he first came to Paris. It was here that he wrote the stories and here that Hadley packed them, before she took them to the Gare de Lyon and lost them, and it was here that Adriana and I sat at one of the cafés after we had found them.

"Now that you've read the lost manuscript do you think the books that Hemingway wrote after it were better?" Adriana asked me.

"He claimed that he had written six true sentences and they were in the lost manuscript that you found. I wonder if Hemingway were still alive and you returned the manuscript to him, if he would still believe that those sentences were the true ones? Maybe he would find others that are true now and the ones he thought were true then are now false."

Adriana smiled and said, "Or that none of them are true."

"Maybe what's true is that Paris is a *maybe* kind of place," I said and sipped my wine. Then I asked her, "What did you write on the claim check that you left in the valise? You said that it was written so that someone who understood the importance of the papers would understand."

"It was a baggage claim with our phone number and the lines, 'If you are lucky enough to have lived in Paris as a young man, then wherever you go for the rest of your life, it stays with you.'"

"That's from *A Moveable Feast*. Appropriate, since it's Hemingway's memoir of his first years in Paris when he was writing the book that was lost."

"It is the only book by Hemingway that I have read," she said. "By the way, the museum strike will end tomorrow, so you can visit the Musée d'Orsay again and have the time to appreciate fully Monet's paintings of the Cathedral at Rouen."

3

SECOND CHANCE

Paris, France - September 2015

French filled my hotel room. After punching the top of the clock radio several times, I finally hit the right button and the Gallic rush hour chatter from a morning show was replaced by soft rain against the roof. I got out of bed and faced a window that streaming water had transformed into an impressionist's canvas. I kept staring until the rain stopped and the romantic Monet it had painted was replaced with the reflection of an Edward Hopper lonely man looking out the window of a hotel room in a big city. Sometimes the City of Light shines a bit too harshly. I went to the desk under the window and turned on my laptop. When I opened the file labeled *Romantic Paris* there was a blinking cursor on a blank screen. I'd forgotten to save what I'd written the day before.

When Curiosi offered me a free ticket to Paris, I'd signed up to write an article for a travel magazine called *Globe Trots* just in case the Curiosi, whoever they were, didn't pan out. Now, even though I'd apparently struck gold with the Curiosi, I had to write the damn article and start from scratch. I recalled Hemingway's opening lines from *A Moveable Feast* about trying to write when the bad weather arrived after the fall was over, and how he had to shut the windows in the night against the rain and the cold wind that blew across the Place de Contrescarpe. But it wasn't that bad; it was the beginning of the fall, not winter, and the rain had stopped and it was still a week before the deadline.

I took the stairs instead of the elevator. A little exercise before breakfast would be good for me, even if it was a dash down the stairs rather than a run up them. After flipping the timer switch for the lights in the stairwell I took off as it ticked a countdown to darkness and managed to reach the lobby door just as the stairs went black. I wondered if the amount of electricity I'd saved by beating the timer and not using the elevator was more than the energy I'd expended.

The young woman at the front desk looked at me in surprise as I entered the lobby from the dark stairwell, "Is something wrong with the elevator?"

"No. I just needed a little exercise."

"It is very good exercise," she replied with a smile. "You will also be taking the stairs when you go up to your room?"

"I barely made it down before the lights went out so I think I'll stick to the lift. Sort of like downhill skiing," I said.

Maybe she didn't get the ski lift analogy or maybe she did and decided to call my bluff, because she responded by telling me that I could always flip the light switch at each landing and that would reset the timer and I would be able to climb to the top floor without being plunged into darkness. "I always try to walk up the stairs," she said, and then unhooked the pedometer from her belt and held it up. "Unfortunately, this counts each stair as only one step when it really should be at least two because of the extra effort."

"C'est la vie," I said with a shrug and a smile then headed for the room off the lobby where breakfast was being served.

***

It started raining again while I ate the usual petit déjeuner of croissants washed down with a bowl of café au lait. Even though I borrowed one of the umbrellas in the stand near the hotel entrance, the wind had picked up and the lower half of my body was wet by the time I finished walking the short distance to my meeting with Leonard to discuss a second case. This time the old woman opened the gate as soon as I rang the bell. She was wearing a yellow waterproof slicker and she peered at me from under the brim of a large rain hat. The hat was struggling to take off in the wind with its brim flapping like a duck, but it was tethered to her chin by a thick strap. She wore pontoon-size galoshes and she could have used the broom she was holding to paddle around the lagoon-like puddle that had formed in the courtyard. After closing the gate behind me she resumed sweeping the water toward a drain in the center of the courtyard.

Leonard stood in the doorway of the house watching me wade toward him. Somehow he had managed to stay completely dry except for the tips of his shoes, which left a wet imprint on the floor as I followed him. My hair was damp from the rain, the shoulders of my coat were soaked, and my shoes squeaked. In the room at the end of the hall, the French doors were closed. The rain was streaming down the glass set into the doors. Leonard was standing behind the desk with his back to the windows and motioned for me to sit in one of the two folding chairs facing him. I noticed on what had been a bare wall when I was here the first time, there was now a poster advertising a new art exhibit called *Second Chance* at Centre Pompidou. On the table between us there was a manilla envelope and a copy of the report I'd turned in the day before. "Did you get a chance to look at it?" I asked.

"Of course," Leonard answered. "I spoke with Dr. Bellini and she said it went very well. Of course, she hasn't read the report and won't until it is sent out to all of the Curiosi."

"You mean she doesn't have a chance to review it first?"

"It would be pointless since, as I told you, we publish exactly what you write without any changes. Your style, your point of view, what you decide to include and exclude, are all part of the report. She will write her own report, of course, which will no doubt be quite different and will not be nearly as interesting to most of our members as yours."

His fingertips pressed on the table as he looked down at me. I waited for him to continue. Finally I reminded him, "You wanted to discuss another case?"

"Yes," he replied sitting down. "It would be the same arrangement as the one you just completed and should only take several days at most."

"I'll do it," I answered, figuring that I could still fit in the travel article. "When does it start?"

"Not until 4 p.m. I will notify you at your hotel where to meet the Curiosi with whom you will be working. That means you will have most of the day to enjoy Paris. Do you have anything in particular you would like to do?"

"Nothing really." Except, I thought, to find something romantic to write about.

"There is a concert at Saint-Julien-le-Pauvre at 11 a.m. that might interest you. You know it is one of the oldest churches in Paris? It is even older than Notre Dame. Of course, you could fit the entire church into the nave of Notre Dame. As I recall, the Sorbonne used to meet there in the 16th century until the students made a mess of the place. I think it was a barn for a while after the revolution. The French Revolution not yours."

"Who is performing?"

"The Quartet Apollinaire."

"Never heard of them."

"I'm sure you won't forget them once you have," he replied.

"Maybe after the concert I'll have time to see this show at the Pompidou?" I said nodding at the poster on the wall.

"Yes, it is well worth seeing if you have a chance afterwards," he said without a trace of irony.

***

Okay, I was curious about the music. I sat in the last row. The chair had a wicker bottom that I could feel through my thin khaki pants. I sat four rows back in Saint-Julien-le-Pauvre facing the transept with three arches flanked by saints that separated the nave from the choir. The rainy afternoon filtered through the stained glass windows set high in the stone walls and mixed with the light from the candles along the walls to illuminate the Quartet Apollinaire as they sat in front of the arches filling the place with Mozart. There was a woman with a cello between her legs. Her legs looked pretty good but her face was hidden by her long, thick hair as she bent over the instrument. Unlike the woman, the faces of the three men were all visible as they sat on either side of her with two violins and a viola tucked under their chins.

As they began to play I noticed the couple in front of me. The man's gray hair was combed over a bald spot and his right arm was around the woman's shoulder. His arm was thick and seemed about to burst the sleeve of his sport coat. Although her hair had a few strands of gray, it was in a style that was more Mademoiselle than Madame. He whispered in her ear in English. Had they come to romantic Paris to revive their marriage or to escape their spouses? The music wrapped around his words so I couldn't understand what he said. She tilted her head slightly toward him so that her right ear touched his lip. Her shoulders jumped up and down, as if she were laughing. There was a smile on the right half of his face. Beyond his face, behind the musicians, a screen, hidden in the darkness inside the center arch of the transept, began to glow. Projected on it were men in black ties and women in long evening gowns. They made their way into an ornate, gilded theatre where an orchestra sat on a stage. The audience settled into velvet chairs and then began to applaud as a conductor in black tie and tails strode to the podium in the center, bowed, and raised his baton. Then the screen flickered, went blank and turned from color to black and white with the audience and orchestra replaced by scratchy scenes of bombs being dropped from waves of planes followed by aerial shots of the ground – a tapestry of buildings and houses vanished behind puffs of smoke and were replaced, when the smoke cleared, with bomb craters, burned shells of buildings, and dead bodies. The woman in front of me buried her face in the man's shoulder. When I looked back toward the screen it was blank and the arched opening was dark again. The quartet stopped playing. There was only stone-cold silence from the audience. I glanced at the glowing face of my watch and decided to join the couple in front of me and most of the rest of the audience in heading for the exit.

***

It was just past noon when I returned to the hotel. The afternoon desk clerk, a man who never smiled and looked like his only form of exercise was walking outside for a cigarette break, gave me an envelope with a note from Leonard that told me to meet my contact at 4 p.m. at the Hotel Aragon, room 17, in Montmartre near the Place du Tertre. He didn't give a name for the contact person, so he must have thought we could just introduce ourselves when I got to the room. After the concert I was in no mood to write anything romantic so I had time to see the art exhibit at the Pompidou that had been advertised on the poster in Leonard's office.

The outside of the Pompidou is covered in a glass skin so that you can see the inner structure, the skeleton of the building from the outside. It made me think of a body with the skin peeled off, exposing the skeleton, while the vital organs, which are the artwork, remained hidden and protected by the steel ribs. You needed to buy a ticket to see those. After I paid, I took the escalator that glides up the outside of the building to the fourth floor and the Musée National d'Art Moderne. Would I mislead my readers if I described the Pompidou as romantic? There were couples, but none of them were exhibiting any affection except two men. It took me fifteen minutes to find the exhibit whose name was on the poster: *Second Chance – Works From the Penny Geldhart Collection*. At the entrance to the exhibit there was a crowd encircling a black rectangular box. It was about three feet wide by three feet high and maybe a foot more than that in length and it rested on a four-foot pedestal. One end was almost completely open except for an inch thick frame. There was a door on two hinges that has been pulled back flat against the right side.

Next to the box, a slightly built man in a sharply cut black suit was speaking. "So, you can see why it was considered a pivotal work because it influenced not only the surrealists but the abstract impressionists and the entire modern art movement. As you look at this work of art I suggest you take the time to meditate on what I have just told you. Think about how Berthold flipped a coin to decide whether to place the depiction of the dead cat or the live one in the box and how that embodied the *Chance* exhibit at which it, as well as his other work, was to be shown for the first time. Then fate intervened and all of his work was destroyed by the Nazis except this one. And ponder how Berthold died tragically before he could continue his work and how his widow, the heiress Penny Geldhart, was able to save only *Schrödinger's Cat* and spirit it out of France just in front of the invading Nazis. This act of devotion on her part was the beginning of a life dedicated to art that led to what is acknowledged as one of the world's greatest private collections of modern art. Some of the most important pieces from the Geldhart collection are in this exhibit beginning with this one that was the first piece she collected, and is considered by most experts to be the greatest."

The crowd took the guide at his word and everyone seemed to be meditating on what they saw in the box. I realized that I didn't have time to see the cat in the black box and still make my four o'clock appointment in Montmartre so I decided I would just have to take the guide's word for it. However, I made a note of the story he told about Penny Gelhart's devotion to the artist, which sounded pretty romantic and worth including in my travel article. I wouldn't mention that I didn't actually see the cat, dead or alive.

***

As the funiculaire climbed the Butte Montmartre toward Sacré-Cœur I remembered going to see it with a girlfriend years ago on a trip to France. It was her first time in Paris and Sacré-Cœur was one of the places she wanted to see. When we stood outside looking at the domed, white edifice, she told me it reminded her of the Taj Mahal that she'd seen on a trip to India, although not as beautiful. I wondered if every place we visited was going to elicit a similar memory of something else she'd seen that was even more beautiful, although she reminded me of Brigitte Bardot so I was prepared to put up with a lot. Still, I told her that I didn't see how the two could be compared since the Taj Mahal was built by a man as a memorial to the woman he loved while Sacré-Cœur was a church. She answered, with a smile parting those puffy Bardot lips, that she didn't think it was strange at all since both were places of worship.

After exiting the funiculaire I took the Rue du Cardinal Guibert that passed between Sacré-Cœur and Saint-Pierre de Montmartre. Saint-Pierre had been renamed a Temple of Reason during the French Revolution and wasn't quite as romantic a place of worship as Sacré-Cœur. Next to its back wall was an alabaster bust of a man wearing a Roman tunic that rested on top of a thick, black pedestal. As I passed, the bust's eyelids flipped open and black spots on a whitewashed face stared at me. I dropped some coins into the bowl at the base of the pedestal and the dark eyes peered down at the bowl, then the face softened, its lips parted and a red tongue licked them. Although there were plenty of people who would have been turned on by what I'd just seen I figured they weren't likely to be reading the magazine where my article was going to be published so it would be better to describe Sacré-Cœur as a place that evoked the romance of the Taj Mahal.

The Hotel Aragon was near the Place du Tertre but I passed the Espace Montmartre Salvador Dalí on the way. I'd heard that there were more than three hundred works of art by Dalí in the Espace while the Place du Tertre looked like it had about three hundred artists trying to sell their work to tourists. It was probably a good bet that my readers would find more romance in a self-portrait painted in five minutes at the Place than looking at Dalís for five hours. I scribbled a description into my notebook then stuffed it into my jacket pocket and walked on to the Hotel Aragon. It was a narrow building wedged in the middle of the block. Each of its six floors had four windows. The stone façade looked thick enough to be the walls of either a fortress or a prison, and might be both depending on who occupied a particular room. There was a glass door with a plate glass window next to it on the ground floor through which I could see a small lobby that was empty except for a desk clerk behind the counter. I told him I was supposed to meet the person staying in room 17. He replied that they had gone out, so I said I'd wait. He didn't seem to want anyone sharing the tiny lobby while he read the pornographic magazine I'd seen him slip under the desk when I'd walked in so he handed me the key.

***

Room 17 was on the third floor. Opposite the double bed there was a wooden dresser with three drawers and a mirror. On top of the dresser was a crumpled handkerchief, an open box of cherry cough drops, and a well-thumbed paperback copy of *The Selected Poems of Federico García Lorca*. There was a night table on the left side of the bed, the side closest to the window, with a black phone but no clock or radio. There was also a framed photograph of a golden retriever although the picture was in black and white. A large, wooden armoire, heavily shellacked in black, stood against the wall on the other side of the bed near the corner. Next to the armoire was the bathroom door. Through the opening I could see half of a bidet, a pair of running shoes and a blow dryer tucked into a pink vinyl bag on the floor.

I sat down in the only chair to wait. The upholstery was worn and the padding lumpy. Beside me was the room's single window. A gauzy white curtain was drawn across it. In the mirror a billowing whiteness brushed past my image and into the room.

There was a rustle of wind and the curtain billowed, stretching toward the bed then collapsed back against the window, sucked into the opening at the bottom. Through the thin cloth I could see the vague form of the city spread out beneath Montmartre. I felt as if I had been in this room before even though I knew I hadn't, so maybe it was only the memory of the Edward Hopper painting I'd recalled that morning. I picked up the book of poetry.

"I sat down

in a space of time

It was a backwater

Of silence,

a white silence,

a formidable ring..."

The phone in the room rang, so I answered.

"Is this Scriviner?" a man asked in English, with a New York accent.

"Yes."

"There's been a bit of a screw up. The address Leonard gave you is where someone who's working with me on this project is staying."

"Who are you?"

"Max Beck." There was a sigh from the receiver and I could hear the wind against the pane of glass, the curtain shifted, the city rippled. "We're supposed to meet here not there."

"Where's here? I mean where you are?"

"On the left bank, in the building next door to Shakespeare and Company on the Quai de Montebello across from…"

"I know where it is."

"Good. We're on the fourth floor, first door on your left when you get off the elevator. If you take the stairs it's the second door on your right but our office is on the top floor so why would you do that? The name on the door is Palimpsest Press. It'll take you a half hour but don't worry we'll be here. I'll even buy you a drink."

***

There was no "we" at the Palimpsest Press, at least not at the moment. There was only Max. I walked through the outer office and found him sitting behind a desk that was covered with loose papers. The desk was surrounded by stacks of books and more papers except where a clearing had been carved out for the chair in which I sat. On the wall to my right there was a floor-to-ceiling bookcase. The books were jammed together so tightly their spines were cracking. Along the left wall was an uneven line of black cabinets. Behind Max was a high window and I could see the Île de la Cité and Notre Dame and the trees along the banks of the Seine. It was like the scene from my hotel window only the Seine was no longer hidden from view. It flowed hazily through the tobacco smoke that hung in the air over the desk where Max rested his elbows, both cushioned by the leather patches sewn into his Harris Tweed jacket. His right hand cradled a pipe. As he looked at me, furrows appeared on his bushy eyebrows and continued on across his hairless head, reminding me of a freshly plowed field.

"Scriviner. Hell of a name for a writer." Before I could answer he continued, "As I said on the phone there was some sort of screw up. Sorry. Anyway, I read some of your stuff. Pretty good. Leonard filled me in on you as well."

"You seem to know more about me than I know about you."

"I'm from New York." A Bateaux Parisiens drifted behind his broad, tweed covered shoulders as it passed beneath us on the Seine. There were tourists on the long narrow upper deck craning their necks and taking photos. Hopefully, the sun reflecting off Max's bald head wouldn't spoil their shots. "Came over in '55 after college. I was from Brooklyn so naturally I wanted to be a famous writer but I was too young for the Second World War and spent a year in Korea instead. No one wanted to read a whole hell of lot about that one. So, while Mailer and Jones were becoming famous, the only alternative for guys like me seemed to be Paris. It turned out that a lot of other guys had the same idea or they wanted to be famous painters or famous jazz musicians. A few guys were actually lucky enough to get one out of the three and a few of them actually had some talent."

"Were you one of the lucky ones?"

"I wasn't lucky and I wasn't, to tell you the truth, all that talented. I was also a lousy intellectual but I did become fluent in French from listening to all of the BS. I was more successful at picking up girls who thought I was smart because I kept my mouth shut and smoked a pipe," he held up the pipe. "But it didn't pay any better than a writer or painter and even if you became famous you were still poor. I went back to New York and did some teaching but that didn't pay either so I got into publishing and made some money. At least I made enough so I could afford to move back to Paris and buy the Palimpsest Press," he waved an arm at the room. "Buying might be too grand a word, since what I really did was assume the debt."

Max pushed himself away from the desk and stood up. He was almost as tall as me, which was more than I expected given his fire plug chest. He looked out the window. Instead of looking at the boat just before it disappeared beneath the Pont au Double, he seemed to be staring at the gargoyles of Notre Dame. "What do you think people were really looking for inside a gothic box?" The question bounced back at me from the window pane. He half turned. It was an oblique angle and I couldn't tell if he really wanted an answer.

"I don't know, but some people call churches god boxes," I answered. "Although, I have to admit a god in a box doesn't sound very omnipotent."

He completed his turn and looked at me, the furrows appeared as if he were giving my reply serious consideration, but then they disappeared and he said, "I'm doing some research for a book that Leonard thought might be worth writing about for the Curiosi so he sent you."

"What's the book about?"

"Haven't got that far. In fact, there might not even be a book, but if there is, the title will be *What You Get Is What You See*," Max replied, sitting down on the edge of the table.

"What are you researching, the getting or the seeing?"

He laughed, "Hell if I know. Like I said, I haven't gotten very far yet. Have you heard of Henri Berthold?"

"The painter."

"Have you seen his work?" Max asked, then puffed on his pipe.

"As a matter of fact, I saw *Schrödinger's Cat* at the Pompidou earlier today. Actually, I only saw the black box, because there was too much of a crowd and I was supposed to meet you at 4 p.m. Not that I knew who you were and, as you know, I ended up in the wrong place."

He grunted and took the pipe out, "For some reason Leonard gave you the address of the place where a colleague of mine is staying. You'll meet him later, in fact."

"Anyway, that's all I know about Berthold. Is the book about him?"

"Can't say at this point if he'll be in it or not. That's part of the research. First, though, I promised you a drink, didn't I?"

***

We took the stairs down at a leisurely pace. The stairwell was brightly lit and there was no timer, which was a good thing, since the stairs were marble and a tumble in the dark would have done some serious damage. Outside we turned right but walked only a few yards before stopping in front of Shakespeare and Company. "How's it going?" Max asked a man in his twenties wearing faded blue jeans and a red T-shirt sitting on a bench beside the door. He looked up from the book he was reading and grinned. There was a stack of books on the bench beside him along with a spiral notebook. On the front of his shirt was a picture of Jean-Paul Sartre but with the big ears and lopsided grin of *Mad Magazine*'s Alfred E. Neumann. Printed underneath the picture was the caption, "Why worry when there's nothing at all?"

"I'll catch up with you later," Max said and began walking away with me in tow.

"Who's the kid with the existential sense of humor?" I asked.

Max laughed, "Ned Nordley. He's the guy who is supposed to be helping me out on this."

Max didn't say anything more about Nordley as we crossed the street and walked along the quai. The wind was blowing, tugging at our clothes and sweeping the leaves in front of us. We continued past the Pont Au Double on the Quai de Montebello to the Pont de l'Archevêché where the Quai de la Tournelle began. Beneath the bridge, next to one of the restaurant barges moored to the quayside, a group of painters were spread out along the flat stones.

Max paused and we both leaned against the railing of the bridge. I squinted at the painters. "You'd think they'd get tired of painting the same thing over and over again. I mean, there's a million paintings or photos or postcards or whatever for sale in Paris of the Seine and Notre Dame as seen from the Left Bank," I said in an effort to demonstrate my keen powers of observation.

"I see what you mean but maybe it's the first time for them. And then, again, every moment is different, what with the light, the clouds, the shadows, and whatnot, always changing, each painting has to be a little bit different because what they're seeing is different. And here we are just rushing right past it without noticing a damn thing. Even the people taking photos or videos, I bet most of them are missing this as well. Instead, they're thinking about what a hell of a picture it will make for their friends back home. Not that they're the only ones. Take me, for example. The window of my office looks right out on this scene but most of the time I've got my backside to it. I'm looking at a pile of papers instead. Maybe if I were to try painting it like they are I'd really see it."

"Maybe you'd be famous," I replied.

Max laughed, "Fat chance. I tried painting once. The choice then was between trying to be a writer or a painter. But this time if I tried it would be just for myself."

I looked at the painters. They were young and old, men and women. Some were standing behind easels and some had the paper fastened to boards resting on their knees. From a distance I could only make out splashes of color. So much for my powers of observation.

"Don't you think it's kind of strange," Max continued, "that Notre Dame was built as a place to find God, but it's big enough to get lost in? "

"Maybe that's why they say the last place to find God is in a church," I replied, but Max didn't hear because he was already halfway across the bridge.

When I caught up with Max, he was on the Quai de l'Archevêché. He had stopped at the edge of the Square Jean-XXIII behind Notre Dame. A brass band was seated under the trees. Their instruments glinted in the sunlight that drifted through the orange-tinted leaves. A conductor raised his white-gloved hands. There was a pause as he looked from side to side at the row of blue uniforms with gold braid looped through stiff epaulets. Horns were lifted to lips and with a broad sweep of the conductor's arms they began playing. It was a waltz, Strauss, I guessed. Passengers from two tour buses that had pulled up to the curb pointed their cameras and cellphones. A man and a woman on roller blades stopped beside us and several young women with small children sat down under the trees. Within minutes the band was surrounded by a crowd of people.

"I wonder how many of these people would ever buy a recording of this music," Max whispered.

"None of them, probably."

"Damn right. It's being here, now, that's everything."

"It's also free so they don't have to buy it."

"Yeah, you've got a point," he chuckled.

Halfway across the Pont Saint-Louis a man in a long robe with a turban stood completely still. He was painted white so that he looked like the statue of a swami. His eyes were closed and he didn't move and there was a bowl at his feet half-filled with coins and banknotes. Max tossed a euro into the bowl and the statue's eyes blinked but the tongue stayed hidden.

***

We took a seat at a sidewalk bar on the other side of the Pont Saint-Louis and ordered two glasses of red wine. As we sipped our wine, a man at the table next to us was typing on his laptop. The typing was energetic. Suddenly he stopped, pulled his shoulders up from the hunched position and inhaled deeply from a cigarette while looking at the screen. Then he placed the cigarette on the lip of a plate next to a half-eaten croissant and began typing again.

"You can see his fingers move but it seems like some sort of prestidigitation," Max said. "You know, sleight of hand? You can see what is going in and coming out, but does anyone really know what the hell's happening inside the thing?"

"Don't tell me you still use a typewriter?"

Max raised one bushy eyebrow and then looked at his watch, "Time to go and see a man about a painting."

I picked up the glass of Bordeaux from the table and as I quickly finished it off I looked back at the bridge and noticed that the statue had vanished.

We walked down the Rue Saint-Louis en l'Île. Max moved quickly against the stream of pedestrians on the narrow sidewalk. I followed in his broad beamed wake, jostled slightly by the turbulence he created. We walked almost half the length of the island, which wasn't very far, before Max turned right onto the Rue des Deux Ponts. I wondered if he was going to cross the Pont de la Tournelle, taking us in an arc back to the Left Bank, but he stopped in front of the Restaurant Les Yeux Enchantés. A restaurant named the enchanted eyes might be worth mentioning in my piece on romantic Paris. Max opened a door next to the restaurant and entered. I followed him up a long flight of steps. At the second landing he knocked on a door, and after waiting a minute or so, a man opened it.

"I'm Max Beck."

"Fred Loswell," the man answered. He was tall and thin and the skin on his face was stretched tight over high cheekbones. If it weren't for the sagging skin of his neck, he would have passed for someone in his fifties.

"Thanks for agreeing to meet me. I mean us," Max said. "This is Hank Scriviner. He'll be sitting in, maybe take a few notes. Hope you don't mind?"

"Not at all. Although I'm not sure if I have anything that will be worth taking note of," Fred replied, firmly shaking our hands.

We followed him down a short hallway and entered a large room. Taking up most of the left wall, facing the Seine to the south, was a window. Set back from the window was a long worktable. Its top was splattered with color and there were cans with brushes in them and big tubes of paint. Many of them were partially squeezed so that they looked like half-eaten sausages. Paintings of different sizes, some framed but most of them not, were stacked against the wall opposite the window with other paintings hanging on the wall above them. In the center of the room were several wooden easels and a couple of stools.

Fred asked us to take a seat at the end of the room where there was an old easy chair with dried paint stains on one arm, an uncomfortable-looking straight-backed chair with its cane seat slightly unraveled, and a couch that sagged like a hammock. The upholstery was faded and worn. Max plopped into the easy chair so I took one end of the couch with a firm grip on the arm to avoid sliding into the depression in the center. Fred, who had left us, returned carrying a tray with a pot of tea and three cups. He poured us each some tea. "It's tea time so I hope you don't mind There's some milk and sugar if you care for any," he said as he settled into the straight-backed chair. His ramrod posture made me try to sit up a little straighter on the sagging couch.

Max put some milk in his tea followed by a couple of spoonfuls of sugar. "Quite a spectacular view you got here Fred," he said as he swirled the tea with a spoon. "How'd you manage to get a place like this?"

"This is my studio but I support myself primarily by teaching painting. I moved here in 1946. It was right after the war and everything was pretty cheap, at least for Englishmen – cheaper still for Yanks. I'd had my eye on this area along the Quai d'Orléans. When I was here as a student before the war I stayed on the other side, on the Rue de Poissy. The place where I lived then is now one of those posh little Left Bank hotels that I couldn't afford to spend one night in. Back then, though, I spent a lot of time looking out the window of my tiny cell of a room thinking that the light would be so much better on this side because it faces south and there's the river so nothing gets in the way and it would be quieter as well." He sipped tea as he talked, sometimes chuckling, his shoulders shaking, especially when recounting how he thought that he would be able to work so much better if he only had a studio over here. "Of course, when I finally got this place and put the window in all I did was spend my time looking across the river at the other side. It seemed to me like the Seine might as well be the English Channel. Gradually though I got used to the quiet over here and the light really was so much better. And then, after I'd painted the view of the Left Bank from here hundreds of times I stopped noticing it so much." As he looked over toward the easels and the window, he told us how his students love the place. "For them, the view isn't a distraction at all but rather the chief attraction. It's probably the one thing they'll remember about me – the view from my flat." He shook his head and sighed. As he held his cup I noticed it trembling slightly. "Would you care for some more tea?"

"Not for me," Max answered. "Mind if I smoke?"

"No, go right ahead. I've had to quit but I suppose I'm ad-dicted to second-hand smoke. Are you smoking Gauloises?"

"Just a pipe. Is that okay?"

"Certainly. I don't think there's too much difference between the two. At least from a second-hand perspective. You can use your teacup for an ashtray."

Max tapped the tobacco into his pipe and lit it. The old man inhaled deeply as Max exhaled. "You told me on the phone that you're with Palimpsest Press. I don't believe I've heard of it. It's a rather odd name isn't it since a palimpsest is a piece of paper that's had the original writing scratched off and something else written over it. Do you print your books on used paper?"

"You're right about the name. You might say we like to get beneath the surface of a subject."

"In this case I suppose you might say you want to get under the paint," Fred answered with one of his gray eyebrows closing in a wink.

"Yeah, I guess you might put it that way. I'm just doing a little background research on the surrealists and I thought you might help fill in a few blanks."

"Fine, but just because I'm an old artist doesn't qualify me to be an art historian."

Max and I laughed politely, then Max said, "As I mentioned over the phone, Palimpsest Press is considering a book on the surrealists in the 1930s before the Second World War. Since you were here before the war you were sort of an eyewitness and we were hoping that you knew some of the surrealists and could help us."

As a matter of fact, Fred did know a number of the artists and most of them were surrealists at one time or another, including himself. "However, I would never claim to have been a truly committed surrealist because I never quite got it. Breton was always talking – but then he was a poet and they all seemed to talk so much that you wondered when they had time to write – about how surrealism revealed the unconscious and the imagination."

Max said, "He wrote in the Manifesto of Surrealism that surrealism was the actual functioning of thought but without any aesthetic or moral concerns."

Fred nodded in agreement, "Breton and some of the others were always writing manifestos. I thought all the manifestos and proclaiming this and that and the other seemed awfully pushy, but then it might be that being English I was just more reserved. However, I think that Breton was actually convinced that this unconscious world was more real than the real world, and that, through surrealism, you could make contact with it, or it with you."

"It's like a wormhole," Max said.

"A wormhole?"

"Yeah," Max flipped through the pad he'd been using to take notes and read, "'A wormhole is an opening in the time and space continuum that leads to another universe.' Somebody just told me that and I wrote it down because you never know when something that sounds like nonsense might end up making sense when you see how it connects to something else."

"I have to admit I never would have thought about such a connection, even if I'd known about such things as wormholes. I wonder if they look like Van Gogh's *The Starry Night*?"

"You can't see them since they're black holes, and since no light can escape from a black hole, they're invisible."

"Ah, well, painting something that is invisible is what surrealists loved and showing these wormholes as a bunch of gaudy, whirling objects in a black sky would be just about perfect. Some people even claim Van Gogh was a surrealist. He was a bit before their time, of course, but he was considered crazy. Speaking of crazy, as I recall Breton was quite enamored with Freud because of his theories about the subconscious and all of that. It really upset him that the only surrealist Freud seemed to admire was Dalí, and that was because he met him once."

"Freud isn't the only one," Max pointed out. "Dalí is usually the first person a lot of people think of when they think of surrealism, right?"

Fred rolled his eyes, "A lot of us called him Avida Dollars because what really interested him was money. Even Dali began referring to himself by the same name. He was outrageous but cunning. He would do anything to be the center of attention, the star attraction, and he knew exactly what to charge for admission to the show. No one worked harder at looking exactly like what everyone imagined a surrealist would look like, which was actually the antithesis of surrealism; most surrealists looked disgustingly normal. One always got the sense that Dalí was trying to make himself the piece of art that everyone else should admire. He would have been happy if he could have hung himself on a wall and, of course, being immortal he could enjoy everyone looking up at him and he could look down on them for eternity." Fred paused and sipped his tea. "Perhaps I'm too harsh. But he did support that Fascist dictator, Franco, you know? Anyway, I'm sure you didn't come here to listen to me gossip about a dead Dalí."

"But you do seem to believe that Dali was someone who took advantage of the true surrealists, the real artists?" Max asked as he hunched over the table reaming out the bowl of his pipe with a Swiss army knife.

"Oh. Dalí was an artist, don't misinterpret me. He was quite good, at least in his early work. It's just that he wasn't really original, in my opinion. He watched what others did and then he added a few flourishes and embellishments and that, together with the contrived eccentricity of his persona, made his work seem daring and different."

"They say the people we often think of as leaders are just people who see which way the crowd is moving and then rush to the front of the line," Max observed, relighting his pipe.

"Shoving aside anyone who gets in their way, I imagine," Fred laughed. "But Dali ended up repeating the same themes over and over. It eventually became clear that the only creativity he exhibited was in the way he disguised the same old thing, just like the way he wore outlandish makeup and clothes. In my opinion he ended up being pathetic rather than prophetic. He wasn't the only one, of course, just the best at it."

"Being pathetic?"

"No, well, yes that too. I meant he was the best at the other part as well."

"Who was second best?" Max asked.

"There may be a tie for that."

"What about Berthold?"

"Henri would have been a contender. He certainly looked and acted the part of the great surrealist, the genius artist, but he managed to get himself killed before he became pathetic."

"It does seem that a primary requirement for being a famous artist is to be dead. The only people who seem to make any money from an artist are the collectors. It's really pretty amazing, isn't it?" Max asked. "I can't think of any other line of work where that occurs, can you? A Marxist might call it the ultimate example of alienation from one's labor."

"So that explains why I'm not famous; it's because I'm not dead," Fred chuckled. "Still, that might explain why so many artists were fond of Marxism. That was until Stalin decreed Soviet realism as the only true art. He shared that artistic taste with Hitler, by the way. For both of them true art had to be some heroic illustration. The super real rather than the surreal."

"Sort of ironic that both Stalin and Hitler lived in Vienna at the same time as Freud."

"Too bad they didn't get psychoanalyzed by Freud. Think of how much human suffering might have been prevented," Fred answered.

"Who were some of the artists that you feel embodied the true principles of surrealism?"

"Oh, the usual suspects – Max Ernst, André Masson, Tanguy, Picabia, Duchamp...the photographer Man Ray...let's see there was also de Chirico and Magritte and Miró."

"But not Berthold?"

"Henri's great work was *Schrödinger's Cat*. At least the only one we can judge him by, since of all his other works were destroyed by the Nazis according to his widow, Penny Geld-hart. You know it was his widow, Penny, who really made him famous? The Cat was what she built her collection on. Considering how much he cheated on her it's sort of poetic justice that the only thing he left her was a passionate love affair with modern art. But, as I was saying, Henri did look and play the part of a great artist, I suppose that was why so many people were attracted to him, including Penny."

"Did you know him well?"

"At one time, of course. But then I hightailed it back to England just as the Nazis invaded France in May of '40. Of course, when I got to London, I immediately found myself much in demand as a private in his Majesty's Army. Just before the Nazis entered Paris on June 14, Henri got himself killed in a stupid car wreck. Penny never should have bought him that sports car. She must have known he'd go and smash the damned thing straightaway. It wasn't until later that I found out Penny had managed to smuggle *Schrödinger's Cat* out when she returned to the States after burying Henri. Frankly, I was astonished when I finally saw it after the war. What I had seen of his work gave me no idea that he was that bold and original or even any good, for that matter."

"So, you think it was truly a one of kind?"

"I can only speak about the work I saw, and, as far as the other works of his that I saw were concerned, if the Nazis hadn't destroyed it, I imagine Penny would have. She certainly wouldn't have wanted any of it to show up later and ruin the reputation she'd built for Henri. But, as I said, I can only speak for the work I saw and I never saw the work that was to be shown along with *Schrödinger's Cat* nor had anyone else except Henri and Penny. It was to be part of a show that Penny was bankrolling for Henri called *Chance*. So maybe it wasn't one of kind, but we'll never know now."

"Was anyone else going to be part of the show?"

"Not that I know of. Of course, the show never took place so who knows?" He paused and knitted his brows. "Now that I think of it, Jacob Sternlieb might have been involved in some way. Jake and Henri were great chums. Unlike Henri, though, Jake looked and acted more like a clerk than an artist. He sort of blended into the background. In fact, I can't recall what he looked like or much of anything else about him. He did have a mistress. I do remember her because she was quite pretty. She was Canadian, I think, named Harriet something. Harriet Baker, that's it. How could I forget since Sternlieb joked that the only dough he ever made was with Harriet Baker. He didn't make many jokes so you remembered things like that. Anyway, he died in a camp and the Nazis destroyed all of his work as well. As far as the Nazis were concerned, being both a Jew and a surrealist was the worst possible combination. Unlike Penny, poor Harriet wasn't able to save any of his paintings."

"Sternlieb you say?" Max said, leaning forward. "Do you remember anything about his work?"

"I only saw his paintings once and that was at his studio in a flat he shared with Harriet. It was in the Marais, which is the old Jewish quarter. I thought they were very good, the work of a serious surrealist, if that term exists. He seemed to be someone who was really searching and not just showing off. It's funny, but I was reminded of his work when I finally got a chance to see the *Cat*. The fact that he and Berthold were friends and were going to do a show together might explain it. I suppose Sternlieb was a positive influence because from what I saw, his previous work was much better than Henri's. As I said, unlike Henri, none of his work survived so we will never know whether he painted something that was as good as the *Cat*. It reminds me of what Breton said about Picabia's work. He called it the emotion of the never seen. Well, I can tell you I'm getting a little teary-eyed just thinking about Jake Sternlieb and other artists who were pretty damned good, but the world will never know it because of the Nazis."

Max nodded and tapped the embers of his pipe into the teacup and put the pipe in his jacket pocket. "It's not just the artists whose work was destroyed by the Nazis; great work has been destroyed by stupid people who felt threatened by it since the beginning of history."

"Yes, you're right. Somehow, I find that hard to forgive, even though I suppose I should. But I'm a lapsed Anglican and I'm not sure if the Golden Rule applies to the destruction of art."

"I don't know either," Max said getting up. "But I know the Ten Commandments apply to the destruction of people."

"Did you get what you were looking for from Loswell?" I asked Max as we walked across the Pont de la Tournelle at a more reflective pace than earlier. It was now late afternoon and the autumn sun and shadows covered the trees along the quai in an oily light, like vinaigrette on a salad. I wondered if Fred Loswell was watching us from his window, perhaps including us in another of his paintings. We might possibly be famous someday even if totally unrecognizable.

"More than I expected," Max answered.

"What do we do next?"

"I'm going back to the office to do some thinking. It's 5:30 now, so why don't we meet for dinner at 8:00 at the café next door?"

***

There was a cellist playing outside the café, beyond the fringe of the awning that stretched toward the Seine. It was early and the evening was warm so I sat down at a table. The green canvas above me seemed to inhale and exhale with the breeze. The cellist was playing Eleanor Rigby. I couldn't see her face but only her long black hair that swayed with the swing of her arm drawing the bow across the strings. There were several other customers sitting outside but they didn't seem to be paying attention, so when she stopped I walked over and tossed a euro into her cello case. She looked at me and smiled. There was something about her that looked familiar. "Were you in the string quartet that played yesterday at Saint-Julien-le-Pauvre?"

She answered, surprised, "You were there? What did you think?"

"Of the music or the bombing?"

"I apologize for that. It was a surprise for us as well. My boyfriend put that whole thing together. I got the others to agree to let him but I didn't know what he had planned to show on the screen. In fact, I couldn't see it because the screen was behind us and, anyway, I look down when I play."

"I noticed."

"How could you not? We finally saw it after everyone left and then we understood why so many people in the audience walked out."

"I mean, I noticed that you look down when you play," I replied. "If you hadn't looked up I wouldn't have recognized you just now."

She blushed, "I almost wish you hadn't. I am so embarrassed. My boyfriend shouldn't have done that. He said he couldn't tell us because it would have ruined it since it was supposed to be unexpected. I told him he made us look like fools, particularly me, and ruined the musical experience completely. Of course, he's not a musician or he would have understood." She held up her bow and asked, "Would you like to hear something? Eleanor Rigby was going to be my last piece, but I feel like I should play another one for you just to help erase that awful memory."

"It was a surprise."

"You don't think bombs being dropped was awful?" She seemed horrified that I wasn't.

"I meant it was an awful surprise," I reassured her. "But you were quite good."

"It was one of my favorite pieces by Mozart and now I think it's ruined for me."

"Could you play it again now, at least try a few bars?"

She smiled and nodded her head, "But of course. Perhaps in this setting it will make me forget the awfulness." She began to play but stopped and looked up at me, brushing the hair away from her face. "I forgot the beginning, sorry." She said, then fingered the strings at the neck as she hummed softly and began again.

The young man I recognized as Ned Nordley arrived before she finished. He sat down in the empty chair beside me and began to say something but noticed that I was listening to the cellist. When she stopped after four or five minutes, he clapped louder than me. She stood up and bowed. Ned went over and talked to her for several minutes. She seemed upset with him as they talked. I signaled the waiter for another glass of Bordeaux. When I turned around she had packed the cello in its case and placed it on a wheeled luggage carrier, securing it with a red striped bungee cord and was leaving.

"See you later back at the hotel," Ned called out to her as he sat down at the table.

She stopped and mumbled a reply that I couldn't make out. Then she gave me a quick look before walking off, pulling her cello behind her.

Without introducing himself, Ned began talking as if we were in the middle of a conversation, "You see in physics, the theory of quantum mechanics says that one thing, at least on a subatomic level, can be in two places at the same time. It only becomes a fixed point in space and time when it's observed. Einstein had trouble with that. Supposedly, Einstein said if that was true then why weren't there moons all over the heavens?"

"I thought he said God doesn't roll dice," I replied with the only answer I could think of.

Ned stared at me, his eyes half-closed as if he were taking my reply seriously, then took a drag on his Gauloises and replied, "Yes, he supposedly said that as well." He was now wearing a black sweatshirt. Stenciled in white letters across its front were the words, "Art is a three letter word." The bottle of Kronenbourg next to his right elbow was a third empty and the ashtray beside it a quarter full.

"Do wormholes and black holes have anything to do with these theories?" I asked. "Max mentioned them today."

"Really?" he smiled. He squashed the stub of his cigarette in the ashtray. "I didn't think Max listened to me when I mentioned them the other day."

"I don't see what art has to do with physics and this theory you mentioned?"

"You don't know about Schrödinger's Cat?"

"Do you mean the piece by Henri Berthold, that's in the Pompidou?"

He sighed, "No, the real Schrödinger's Cat, which was the name given to a thought experiment that Erwin Schrödinger, a physicist who helped develop quantum physics, devised in 1935 to illustrate one of the theory's most perplexing aspects. You're sure you haven't heard of it?"

"Never. I was never very good at math...or physics. I don't even know what a thought experiment is. Is that something like Descartes' 'I think therefore I am'?"

Ned lit another cigarette and leaned toward me across the table. "That's a hypothesis not an experiment. Let me explain Schrödinger's thought experiment. First off, a live cat is put in a box. The box is then sealed so nothing can get in or out, and no one can see in or out. In the box there is also a device that holds a small amount of a radioactive element. There is a fifty-fifty chance that the atom will decay and if it does the device will break a container containing poison that will kill the cat. If the atom doesn't decay the cat lives."

"That doesn't sound like something that would get a seal of approval from People for Ethical Treatment of Animals."

Ned laughed, snorted, then coughed, "Maybe that's why it's a thought experiment. He didn't want to piss off PETA. But, seriously, the real point is that according to quantum mechanics, which is what they call this type of physics, and doesn't have anything to do with the mechanics who fix your automobile by the way, is that as long as the cat is in the sealed box both of these outcomes are equally possible, neither outcome can be predicted and, in fact, neither of them has occurred. The cat is suspended in a sort of half dead-half live state. However, when the box is open and the cat is observed then it is either dead or alive. Of course, quantum mechanics deals with the behavior of subatomic particles not cats, how these particles can be in multiple locations and can act as particles or waves at the same time and only become fixed at a single location or in a specific position when they are observed."

"In other words this cat has nine lives and nine deaths when it's in the box," I said, wondering if Ned had any sense of humor.

To my surprise Ned laughed, "Anyway, Berthold named his painting after Schrödinger's Cat because of this thought experiment. People think he was being hip, and Berthold was quite hip from what I understand. You know, the surrealists were fascinated with science so it would have been a sort of an inside joke. For most people then who didn't know anything about Schrödinger or quantum mechanics it was just a strange looking cat in a box. But now it's considered a masterpiece." He stopped abruptly and ground the butt of his Gauloises onto the tabletop.

"It's something to think about," I said then snuck a peak at my watch. It was after eight o'clock, and beyond the reach of the electric light bulbs strung beneath the awning, Paris was glowing and Max was late. "I couldn't help notice that you know the girl who was playing the cello?"

"You mean Clare? She's my girlfriend, although right now she's quite angry with me."

I was tempted to say that it sounded like a love-hate relationship, but was saved by the chirping of a cricket coming from the small backpack that he had set on the chair between us. He thrust his right hand into the pack and took out several books before he finally pulled out the chirping cell phone. "Bloody mobile," he said pressing it to his left ear. He listened, said cheers and flicked it off. "That was Max. He won't be able to join us after all. Said he was looking for a bakery or something. You wouldn't think that would be very difficult in Paris, would you? Anyway, he said to meet him here tomorrow morning at 9 a.m."

***

After I left Ned sitting at the café, contemplating cats or Clare or both, I walked into the Latin Quarter hoping to find some romance I could write about. I passed a half dozen clubs pulsing with electronic music and lights before I found a night club, a Paris boîte de nuit, with a dark interior and no vibration. The middle-aged man who greeted me at the door was dressed in a slim black suit, crisp white shirt, and thin black tie. I was decidedly unhip in my wrinkled khaki pants, blue shirt, and Navy polyester blazer, so I was seated at a table just inside the door. Everything was dim with candles flickering on the tables and a solitary light, cloudy with smoke, covering the back of the man sitting at an upright piano. When the door opened the light from the street came flooding across the floor, like the tide, washing over the soles of my shoes and then receded just as quickly when the door slammed shut. Occasionally the pianist looked sideways. He, at least the left side of his face that I could see, looked a lot younger than he sounded. The small tables that filled the room formed a semicircle behind the back of the piano player. Most had at least two people. The waitress asked what I wanted. I wanted a cigarette, one of Ned's Gauloises, and something with vodka or gin and a stick to swizzle it with, but I ordered a coke.

A couple was dancing. They were very close, moving in a constricted circle in the center of the small space between the piano player and the tables. Her face was buried in his shoulder. A cigarette glowed on his lip. His hand moved up and down her spine. They were both wearing black. How would one of my readers see the image in their mind? Would it appear to them romantic? I took out my notebook and opened it. Then I realized, I'd been here years before. Instead of a piano player there was a folksinger sitting on a stool with a guitar. He'd sung Leonard Cohen, Cat Stevens, and even Bob Dylan. I remember the singer did "Like a Rolling Stone" and I was alone then as well. I closed my notebook.

***

The next morning Max was sitting outside at the café. It was the same table where Ned and I sat the night before. After I left Ned and spent an hour at the night club, I went back to my hotel room, turned on my computer and wrote up my conversation with Ned and my trip to the night club. I could use the night club for the article and maybe Clare playing her cello with Notre Dame lit up in the background before Ned arrived, but there was no way to spin Schrödinger's cat into something romantic.

"What did you think of Ned?" Max asked after I sat down.

"Opinionated."

"He sure as hell is," Max said and immediately launched into a story "A couple days ago Ned got into an argument with some college kid from the States who's majoring in art history. Ned and I were looking at some books on aesthetics and art criticism at Shakespeare and Company, and Ned started telling me that they were all rot because they were full of half-baked philosophy and that what was good and bad art could be understood logically. Well, this kid was standing nearby and muttered that what Ned said was bullshit. Ned calmly told the kid to imagine a box that had an opening on one side that you shove the art into, the input so to speak, and on the other side there was another opening where the piece of art comes out, but with a grade attached. That would be the output. He said that most people, and there was no doubt that he was including the kid, think that making an aesthetic judgment about art is a process that's as mysterious as what goes on inside the box, so they insist you can't really talk about it in a logical manner. But Ned said that just because you can't see inside the box doesn't mean that you can't figure out what's going on inside. He contended that by knowing all the types of art that go into the box and all of the types of aesthetic judgments that come out the other side you could figure out the process of aesthetic reasoning that went on inside the box and that you could reveal everything that was going on inside the black box even if you could never open it up and observe it directly. Then Ned told the kid that this was his theory of aesthetic taxonomy because all judgments about art could be understood scientifically once you put everything you knew into categories so you could compare what came out with what went in."

Max shook his head and smiled, "Of course, the kid didn't agree at all with Ned's opinion and said that deciding what was good or bad art wasn't something you could understand through logic and that was the whole point. It was a poetic, spiritual, even mystical sort of truth. You just knew what was good and bad by looking at the stuff for a long time. Those who were really good devoted their lives to communing with art. Sort of ascetic aesthetics, I suppose is what he was getting at. Then he said that he didn't understand how Ned could compare art to displaying dead animals. Ned told him that he hadn't thought about the connection until the guy had confused taxonomy with taxidermy, but that maybe they did have a lot in common."

Max stopped and puffed on his pipe before continuing, "That's when the kid got really pissed off and told Ned that since he felt art was explained by a black box he would certainly want to see Berthold's *Schrödinger's Cat* at the Pompidou since it's inside a black box."

"Obviously the kid didn't understand a thing I was saying," said Ned, who'd approached without us noticing.

"Who does?" Max laughed. "Anyway, now that we're all here, we need to get going."

We caught the Metro at Saint-Michel and got off at Bastille, or where the Bastille had been before it was torn down after the French Revolution. As we stopped so that Max could unfold and look at his street map, a young couple holding hands skated directly at us on roller blades. Just before a collision they let go of each other's hands and glided past us on either side.

"I'm glad those two managed to untangle themselves in time," Ned said.

"Who's doing the tango?" Max asked as he looked up from the map.

"Those two, and I said tangle not tango," Ned pointed at the couple skating into the distance, their hands clasped together once again, their hips swaying in unison as they skated. "I don't understand why you don't use a map app on your phone instead of that thing that makes you look like you're playing an accordion."

"Because I'm too dumb to use a smartphone, so I have this instead." He pulled out an old flip phone from the inside breast pocket of his tweed sports coat, held it up, and then jammed it back into the pocket. "We need to take the Rue Saint-Antoine toward the Rue de Rivoli." He folded the map and put it in the other side pocket. We walked quickly along Saint-Antoine past the Rue de Birague, a narrow street running into the Place des Voges, and then turned north onto the Rue Malher that runs diagonally into the twisted streets of the Marais.

"This is the Rue des Rosiers," Max announced as he stopped and pointed to a slab of beef hanging in the window in the building we faced. "And this must be where Marjorie lives since she told me it was above a butcher shop."

***

Marjorie sat in the middle of a couch while Max and I sank into two easy chairs that had the firmness of quicksand. Her short auburn hair and slight figure made her look like a child, although the fine lines around her mouth and eyes, and the pitch of her voice as she spoke in American-accented English revealed her to be closer to my own age. The rear room was quiet except for the ticking of a clock and a scratching against one of the windows. Two windows looked out onto a courtyard and the yellow-leafed fingers of an oak pressed against their panes. Ned sat at a desk in front of the windows, and on the desk were stacks of papers under which there were more stacks forming an archipelago from the end of the desk to the bookcase that was set against the wall behind the couch. It reminded me of Max's office except that this was not the natural order, but some new chaotic creation.

"As I explained on the phone last night when you called, my Aunt Harriet died last month and I'm still in the middle of sorting things out," Marjorie turned her head slightly toward the desk. "This is where I do the sorting, obviously. Usually where you're sitting would be piled with these papers." She pointed at the stacks on the floor.

"I can see that you've been hard at work. How's it going?" Max asked, sympathetically.

"As long as I keep the piles separate I'm okay," she answered, then rolled her eyes, "I thought it would only take a week. So far I haven't found anything of more than sentimental value, although some of the furniture might be worth something. But, you never know, so I've spent a lot more time than I thought going through everything."

"You didn't know your aunt very well?" Ned asked.

"No. We live in Toronto. Lived, I mean since my parents are both dead. I grew up there, but now I live in Windsor. That's just across the border from Detroit. Aunt Harriet came over here when she graduated from college in 1938, before the war. She came over to study art and never returned to Canada except to visit a couple of times. I hardly knew anything about her. My mom and she weren't particularly close even though there aren't any other sisters or brothers. She didn't talk very much about herself and when she did, what she said seemed pretty dull," she sighed, and gave a tired smile, "at least to me, but I wasn't paying attention, I have to admit. She left everything to me and my brother and sister. I volunteered to do this – to be the executor since I don't have any family obligations and I'm not teaching this term at the college where I'm a professor of sociology." She looked out the window as if she were searching for something. She turned back to us. "I mean it is Paris, supposedly the most romantic city in the world. So now you know about as much as I do."

"Mind if I smoke?" Max asked holding up his pipe.

"If you don't mind if I do?" Marjorie said, walking over to her purse and extracting a pack of Marlboros.

"I guess I've got the all clear as well," Ned said tapping his pack of Gauloises.

"Do you want one?" She held the pack toward me.

"No, I quit a few years ago."

"Oh, I'm sorry," she answered. "Will the smoke bother you?"

"No."

"She lit her cigarette, and said to Max, "You told me on the phone that you're doing some research for an article on surrealists. What does that have to do with my aunt?"

"Your aunt's name came up in our research. Apparently she knew some of the surrealists we are interested in writing about, in particular Henri Berthold. We were hoping she might have some information on him and, although it's a long shot, maybe something he did. We're sorry that we won't have an opportunity to speak with her."

"I think she would have preferred that as well," Marjorie said.

Max responded quickly, "We certainly don't want to intrude on your grief."

"You're not intruding. I didn't mean it that way when I said that she would prefer to be here. It's just a bit of black humor on my part. Wasn't Berthold a famous artist?"

"Famous for *Schrödinger's Cat*, which happens to be one of the most famous surrealist works," Ned said.

"Oh, well I don't know much about art, not to mention the surrealists. In fact, I probably wouldn't know a surrealist from an impressionist. In any case, I really don't think any of the paintings here would be one of his or by anyone with talent," she pointed the red end of her cigarette to the wall behind Max and me. "They're awful if you ask me. I can't imagine her wanting to look at them once, much less have them on her walls. I don't even want to get near them."

We looked at paintings on the wall behind us that she was pointing at. "Well, I have to agree," Max said. "They certainly don't look very good although they're painted in the surrealistic style. Certainly nothing like Berthold's work. We do know that your aunt knew a painter named Jacob Sternlieb. When I say knew, they were apparently quite fond of each other from what we've been told."

"You mean romantically?"

"Yes."

Marjorie smiled and shook her head, "And we all thought Aunt Harriet was an old maid, the virgin aunt. It seemed particularly tragic since she lived in Paris of all places. When she visited us she never said anything about artists and all of that. We thought she just taught English. We knew she loved the French language and culture, but you're saying that she had an artist named Jacob Sternlieb as a lover."

"He was a surrealist painter," Max answered. "He was also Jewish."

"That must be why Aunt Harriet didn't mention him. Lovers would have been quite a shock but a Jewish lover would have probably been too much for the family. I mean the older generation, not mine. What happened to him? Is he still alive? It would be great if he could tell me about the Aunt Harriet I never knew existed."

"He was rounded up with other Jews during the Nazi occupation of Paris and he died in a concentration camp."

Marjorie looked at the paintings, "How tragic. That would explain why these ugly painting are on the walls. They must be by him and they reminded her of her lover." She paused as if she was weighing whether she would do the same thing, then said, "There are a lot more of them in the back room. I mean the front. This is the back of the apartment. It's a bit confusing to know which is which. In any case, it's in that direction overlooking the street and the sign for the butcher shop."

Max pulled himself out of the overstuffed chair and walked over to the wall. He looked at several of the paintings, touched their frames and then lifted the side of one of them away from the wall. "Do you mind if I take this one down?"

"No, go right ahead. I haven't taken any of them off the wall. I sort of think of them as my aunt's homemade wallpaper," Marjorie said. "I've been leaving them for the last. It doesn't seem right to just toss them now that they seem to have been painted by her lover and they meant so much to her, but, as I said, who else would want to look at them?"

Max pulled one of the paintings off its hook, leaving a patch of faded paint behind with a black smudge of the nail in the center. He carried it over to the desk and bent over the canvas.

Max grunted as he looked at it. Finally, he announced, "That's his signature."

Ned bent over the painting and looked at the signature, "It's his name alright. It could be forged, of course, but there wouldn't be any reason since they weren't for sale, so it must be his work."

"A brilliant observation, my friend," Max answered.

"You said his work, so it is his?" Marjorie rose from the couch, a movement that created a small avalanche of papers from the piles on either side of her.

"Not your aunt's lover, Sternlieb, but Henri Berthold's."

Surprised, Marjorie said, "And I was about to toss them in the trash. Shows you how ignorant I am about art. I thought they were horrible and here you're telling me they were done by a famous artist."

"It's his, but it is pretty bad," Max said as he held the painting up so we could all get a better view of the signature. Then, as we gathered in front of it, he announced from behind the painting,

"I stand corrected they're only half bad – the side that you're looking at, but not what's painted on the back." He turned it around and on the other side was another painting, one that was of the same subject but vastly superior, even to someone like me with an untrained eye.

"But why would he paint another one on the back?" Marjorie asked in astonishment.

"He didn't. It's a different canvas that's fitted in the frame and it says J. Sternlieb down in the corner along with the date of the painting." Max placed the painting on the table so we could all look at it more closely.

"Really?" she held it up and examined both sides closely. "This is all so amazing. I mean, my aunt having a lover and now this and...You say he was a surrealist as well?"

"Yes," Max answered.

"Like Salvador Dali?"

"Indeed. There were a number of them. Even Pablo Picasso was one for a bit."

"I guess that it reminds me of one of them then." She put it down. "Do you think there are any more?"

"Let's see," Ned said, removing the other paintings from the wall and turning them over. "They're all Berthold on the front and Sternlieb on the back. Same subject or theme, but a hell of lot better."

"It appears that your aunt's paintings have a side to them you've never seen," Max said with a wry smile. "Is it okay if we examine all of them?"

"Go right ahead. As I said, this is a real mindblower. First, to find out Aunt Harriet had a lover and then that she was hiding his works and that these ugly paintings are by a famous artist. Sort of bizarre, well you know, it's..."

"Surrealistic?" Ned suggested, with a grin.

"You say there are more paintings in the front room?" Max asked.

"Yes, they're hung from floor to ceiling, I'll show you," she walked quickly toward the hallway and we followed her past the entry door, then the kitchen, a bathroom, and a bedroom. She opened the door at the end and we entered a large room with a high ceiling and white walls covered with paintings.

After asking again if it was okay to take down the paintings, Max took each from the wall, verified Berthold's signature on the front and then turned it around to reveal another painting by Sternlieb. As he did this, Ned photographed the paintings on both sides with his smartphone. Even working quickly it took an hour to examine and photograph all of the paintings on the walls.

As we stood looking at the walls with only the Sternliebs facing us, Ned asked, "I don't get why your Aunt Harriet would leave them hanging with Jacob Sternlieb's paintings facing the wall? The Nazis are long gone so it couldn't be because she was afraid they would see them and destroy them."

"Oh, now I understand," Marjorie answered. "It's the opposite of what I originally thought when I assumed that the ugly paintings facing out were Sternlieb's. You see, she wasn't just hiding his paintings, she was hiding the side of her that she hid from everyone, including herself. She was probably afraid of what would happen if she ever looked at them."

"Is that all?" Max asked, breaking the silence that followed Marjorie's observation.

"Isn't it enough?" Marjorie answered.

Ned pointed to the corner and asked, "What's in that black box over there?"

"I don't know, I haven't gotten to it yet. Go ahead and look if you want."

Ned and Max examined the outside of the box. It was about three feet high and wide by four feet long and it was secured with a padlock. "Do you have a key?" Max asked.

"No."

"Can we break it? We'll pay to fix it."

"Well, I guess. I mean I'll have to look inside myself at some point."

Before she has finished, Ned had pulled out a Swiss Army knife and was prying at the clasp. It broke free and he pulled the lid up. We circled the box as he opened it. Inside was something wrapped in heavy brown wrapping paper. He pulled it out and placed it flat on the floor. Gingerly, Max unwrapped the brittle paper to reveal a framed blank canvas. Ned knelt beside Max as he turned it over so the other side faced us.

"No wonder Aunt Harriet locked this one away," Marjorie gasped. "She loved cats. To put such a horrible picture of a cat as this on her wall – at least I think it's supposed to be a cat –

would have been too much for her, even if the other side had a painting by her lover."

"There isn't another side," Max answered turning it around, "although there's a slot for the canvas of another painting to be attached to the back. There's only the painting of this dead cat and it's signed by Henri Berthold."

***

"Monsieur Beck? I am a very busy man so please get to the point."

"You bet." Max said as he walked quickly across the Turkish carpet to the Armani-clad man with a note in his hand. The man sat behind a Louis-the-something desk, while we settled into several gilt encrusted chairs. Behind him the gold curtains were drawn back from the windows revealing the Ritz on the opposite side of the Place Vendôme.

"You told my secretary that you wish to return something that belongs to the Geldhart Collection."

"I told her to make an exchange."

"Yes, I see that is what you have written, but if it belongs to the Geldhart Collection why should we have to give you anything in return? I warn you if this is some attempt at extortion I will call the police immediately."

"Although I agree, Monsieur Gaspert, that it most definitely belongs with the Penny Geldhart Collection, when you see it you'll realize that you have in your possession something that belongs to someone else's collection. I call it an exchange, although I will agree it's not an equal exchange."

"I don't see what the problem is then? We certainly do not wish to have anything that doesn't belong to us."

"I'm glad you see it that way, Monsieur Gaspert. Mind if I smoke?" Max held up his pipe.

"Yes, I do mind. Do you have any idea what smoke does to these priceless antiques?" Gaspert replied pointing at the furniture. "Please, could you just show me what you have?"

"Okay then," Max shoved the pipe back into the pocket of his tweed coat. "Ned, would you be so kind as to show Monsieur Gaspert the painting that belongs with the Geldhart Collection?"

Ned stood up and slid a long cardboard cylinder from his backpack. He opened the top and pulled out a tube and unrolled a canvas on the table.

Gaspert bent over and looked at the painting. "But this, this is preposterous," he said spitting out the word. "It's a very bad imitation of Berthold's *Schrödinger's Cat*. It's not even correct in its depiction of the cat's state. The cat shown here is most definitely a dead one and everyone knows that Berthold's Schrödinger's Cat is alive. This is an insult."

"I agree it's an insult but it's not an insult to Berthold. It's one of his originals as you can clearly see by his signature at the bottom and the date, which was just a week before his death."

"Yes, well anyone can forge a name. This is really of no interest to anyone," he said waving his hand dismissively.

"On the contrary, we think there will be a good deal of interest in this discovery. Particularly, when we explain where we found it and they get a look at all of his other works."

"His other works? Everyone knows that they were destroyed by the Nazis. It is one of the great tragedies of the art world."

"It turns out his work escaped the Nazis unscathed, although that might still be a tragedy depending on your point of view."

"But if that's true, then those works of his belong to us and I demand you turn them over."

"Turn them over. Why, that's exactly what we did when we discovered them and guess what we found," Max smiled. He looked over at Ned, who then placed a number of photos on the desk.

"Ah," Gaspert sighed with relief. "Just as I said. These are the true works of Berthold. One can clearly see the genius and no one can mistake that they are the work of the same artist who painted the Cat. What a magnificent discovery. I demand you hand them over to us immediately."

"Oh, you'll get all of Berthold's works," he nodded to Ned. "But, like I said, you can't have Berthold's paintings unless there's an exchange for something you have that belongs to someone else."

"You keep talking about an exchange. What is it, exactly, that you want in exchange for Berthold's paintings?"

"Look at the photos more closely, Monsieur Gaspert, particularly the signatures," Max said.

"They're smaller and at the very bottom so here's a magnifying glass in case you need it," Ned said pulling out a magnifying glass from a pocket of his jacket and handing it to Gaspert.

Gaspert examined the photos with the magnifying glass in silence. Finally, he unbent himself. "But the signature on all of these is that of J. Sternlieb not Berthold."

"Now if you want to see Berthold's signature we have those as well."

Ned quickly removed the first set of photos and replaced them with others showing Berthold's work.

As Gaspert bent over and examined the photos his hand began to shake. Finally he dropped the magnifying glass on the desk and collapsed onto one of the gilded chairs.

"Those are your Berthold's," Max said. "and as such they most definitely belong with the Geldhart Collection and I imagine you will want them if for no other reason than to make sure no one else ever sees them. However, you have to give us the Jacob Sternlieb that you have or there will be quite a public exhibition of Berthold's collected works."

"But why would we have something by Jacob Sternlieb?"

"I guess technically you don't have it since it's on loan to the Pompidou. You'll find his signature if you remove the painting of Schrodinger's Cat from the black box. Unlike Berthold, Sternlieb signed his paintings at the very bottom and the frame in the box covers it up. Of course, if you want to replace it with this Cat by Berthold, the signature will be quite clearly visible for all to see. On the other hand, if the Pompidou doesn't believe that is a fair exchange I believe the new owner of the one that is on display there will agree to let it remain for the exhibit provided the real painter, Jacob Sternlieb, is credited." Max stopped and gave an amused smile. "Here's another alternative, you could show both paintings of the Cats. Every time someone looks into the box one or the other would be randomly displayed just as Berthold and Sternlieb intended for the original show."

Gaspert glared at the photos of Berthold's work as if that would make them disappear then sat heavily in one of the delicate chairs. "Merde," he whispered.

"I take that to mean you don't like that idea," Max said, "I have to say I agree with you since I think his work looks like 'merde' as well."

***

Max had a chance to light his pipe after we left Gaspert's office. He cupped his hand against the swirling wind of the Place Vendôme until a white cloud escaped from the bowl. I thought of the smoke from the Vatican for the election of a new pope.

"Why did Harriet Baker hide the paintings in her apartment?" I asked. "You'd think she would have shown them to Penny Geldhart."

Max shrugged his shoulders, "Yes, everything would have been different. But she knew that Penny Geldhart wouldn't have been interested in promoting the work of Harriet Baker's dead lover, and without Geldhart's fortune and power behind it, what were the chances that it would have gotten anywhere near the recognition it has now? Great art and genius aren't always recognized on their own. In fact, from what I've seen that's the exception rather than the rule. By saying nothing, Harriet, assured that Sternlieb work was seen and recognized as that of a genius even if they thought the genius was Berthold. Even though someone else got the credit, Harriet knew who really painted it and that was enough for her. On the other hand, maybe she didn't want to risk what she thought was true by opening the box in the back room, I mean front room, and finding out whose Cat was really inside."

"I have to say that of the two reasons you gave, I prefer the first. It's certainly more romantic," Ned said. "Speaking of which," he added, hoisting his pack onto his shoulder, "I've managed to mess things up with Clare, so I better get back to the hotel before she decides to split."

With that Ned loped off down the Rue Saint-Honoré, the pack slung over his shoulder bouncing up and down with each stride.

"When do you think you'll have this written up for Leonard?" Max asked me as we strolled toward the Rue de Rivoli Metro stop.

"I hope to have it done within 24 hours. After that I've got this other piece to finish that I agreed to write for a travel magazine. It's on romantic Paris. Too bad I can't include this."

"Yes, it is unfortunate that your account will only be for the Curiosi." Max sucked on his pipe some more, his arms crossed, the seams of his tweed jacket about to burst and knitted his bushy eyebrows. "However," he said, his eyebrows lifting, "we will need an author of the book that my Palimpsest Press is planning to publish on Jacob Sternlieb, the famous surrealist artist."

"I didn't know you wanted to publish a book on him."

"I didn't either until now. I'm pretty sure I will be able to get the exclusive rights from Marjorie who, by the way, will soon be the center of attention in the art world. Given all the publicity, this could be the chance for our first best seller."

4

CATHARSIS

Languedoc Region, France - October 2015

A 'spectral summer' is what they call it here in France. That makes more sense to me than calling it an 'Indian summer.' There's nothing about it that is Indian or Native American. In fact, I would have considered the orange and yellow leaves floating in the Seine on a balmy day as a spectral apparition if it weren't for the ones on the sidewalk that were stuck to the soles of my shoes in a most down-to-earth manner. I scraped them off on the curb and headed up the Rue Maître Albert toward my hotel, just past the house where I met with Leonard. A row of men sat at the bar next to the large double doors that hid the courtyard and the house. They reminded me of *Nighthawks*, that Edward Hopper painting of three people sitting at the counter of a New York diner late at night. Only these guys were drinking pastis and it was the middle of the afternoon and it was Paris. I went in and sat down on the one empty barstool.

***

"She was, well, you know, a bit odd," the bartender leaned toward me as he answered my question about the old lady who had greeted me at the door when I visited Leonard. "I have not seen her for several days and she used to come in here and have a glass of vin rouge every afternoon. Then she would sit over there in the corner as far from the bar and the window as possible. She only had one glass. But before she sat down with her wine, she would sweep the floor with the broom she brought with her. Strange, no?"

"Filthy," the man next to me said after the bartender moved to the other end to refill a glass. "This is a filthy place. I hope the old lady comes back soon because the place has not been clean since she stopped coming. Soon it will be unhealthy to drink here." He sipped the pastis. "But still, all in all, it is a safe place. Out there, you could be sitting at the poshest brasserie and," he slapped his hand on the bar causing the bartender to stop the conversation he was having at the other end, "boom! Just like that a terrorist bomb. But who would want to blow up this place? Nobody would even notice that it was gone. They wouldn't notice that we were gone either. We are nobody and this is a nowhere. It would be a big waste of their time, not to mention the terrorist who would have to blow himself up. I don't think he would become quite the martyr that he imagined. Instead of getting one hundred young virgins in heaven he would get that old woman in hell." The man laughed and shook his head.

The bartender walked back to our end, "We gave them back their countries, didn't we, so why do they want to terrorize us?"

The man beside me sighed and finished his pastis, "Maybe they just want to get even."

"But you can never get even," said a man next to him with a five o'clock shadow and sleepy eyes who had been drinking in silence. "Anyone who knows anything about history knows that. Why just look at our own Revolution. Where is the equality that was promised? It is only an illusion. The reality is that there are only those who are ahead and the rest of us who look at their asses."

"If that is the case," the bartender suggested, "perhaps they should have chopped off Marie Antoinette's ass instead of her head then it would have been a true revolution."

The man looked into his half empty glass and then answered with a straight face, "I agree that it would be good to have fewer asses in the world."

***

Having finished my report for the Curiosi and sent my article on romantic Paris to *Globe Trots* magazine, I was about to turn on my laptop and book a return flight to New York when my cell phone started vibrating. I grabbed it before it bounced off the desk onto the floor of my hotel room. A man's voice asked if I was Henry Scriviner? When I told him I was, he asked me to hold for Trish Barrett Greenberg. I'd never heard of Trish Barrett Greenberg. When we were connected she told me she was the editor-in-chief of *Travelux*. I understood why I hadn't heard of her, as I'd never heard of *Travelux*, either. She wasn't surprised and, in fact, seemed pleased at my ignorance. She explained that it was an exclusive travel and leisure magazine for the very rich, making it sound like it was so exclusive that you had to inherit a subscription.

"You've been selected to write a feature article for us," she said, as if I'd just won a jackpot. "You have been highly recommended as having the credentials in French culture and art that we look for in a writer. You can imagine that our readers are quite discriminating." Unlike the readers of the magazine where I'd just sent my romantic Paris article, I thought.

I thought about asking her to whom I owed the honor for the recommendation but figured I should act like I didn't care, to give the impression that it happened all the time. "Is there any particular area of art and culture in Paris that you want me to write about?"

"Oh, we don't want you to write about Paris. No, we want you to write about some off-the-beaten-track place in France. It should be a place that requires some adventure but must also be safe. Our readers like to flirt with danger while avoiding any commitment, you understand? They are particularly concerned about terrorism so please avoid any place where that might occur and, in fact, don't even mention the subject in your article."

"Not even a rumor of the war on terrorism?"

There was a pause at the other end before she replied. "Rumors and gossip are okay, in fact we encourage it, but not about war or terrorism or anything political. Of course, it goes without saying that it should be expensive and exclusive. Do you know of such a place?"

"I know the perfect place," I lied, but there had to be plenty of expensive and exclusive places in France outside of Paris where I'd like to spend a few days and, after a bit of creative writing on my part, would be perfect for her readers as well.

"Where?"

"Telling you before I write the story would spoil it. You've heard about athletes leaving their game in the locker room, haven't you?"

"Locker room? Our members don't want to read about things that make you sweat unless it's a spa."

"That was just a figure of speech."

"Okay, I'm sure you will pick the right place but just remember to avoid what I told you such as war, terrorism, politics and..."

"Got it," I cut her off.

"And remember there must be some beautiful scenery for the photographs."

"You want me to take photographs?" I asked. Instead of just using my imagination, I'd have to find something that actually looked like what I described and take pictures of it.

"Of course not," she replied. "We will send a professional photographer after you have submitted the article. A picture is truly worth a thousand words because they cost a fortune to print so we will decide what we want photos of after we have read your copy."

I agreed to the generous fee, with half in advance and half on completion. After I hung up, I was about to go out to an expensive celebratory lunch where I could peruse a map of France while sipping an expensive Bordeaux when my mobile chimed again. This time it was a text message from Leonard.

***

An hour later I stood beneath the rose window in the rear of the upper chapel of Sainte-Chapelle. The oval window was the last of sixteen stained glass windows that began with scenes of the Garden of Eden. Leonard provided the narration as we walked past each window in a clockwise direction until we reached the final one, which depicted the apocalypse as seen through rose-colored glass. Leonard explained that the rose window was a late addition – a gift from Charles VIII two centuries after Louis IX had constructed Sainte-Chapelle in the 13th century. The fifteenth window depicted. the journey of the relics – splinters from the 'true cross' and the nails of crucifixion –

to Sainte-Chapelle, which Louis had built to house them. Although the relics had cost him three times what it took to build the chapel, they had been removed long ago and consigned to storage in Notre Dame across the street. I made a note not to invest any of my meager savings in relics futures. Still, whether the relics had arrived after a divinely inspired reverse pilgrimage from the Holy Land or through grand theft, I was indebted to them for being bathed in beauty and light. As I began to float away in the sea of color there was a tug on my jacket. I reached down and felt an envelope that Leonard had slipped into my pocket. He told me it contained train tickets on the next morning's TGV express to Montpellier.

"We have another assignment for you."

"But I already have an assignment," I answered.

"Ah, yes, for *Travelux*. I believe you were highly recommended?"

"You're saying that's just a cover story?"

"I don't know if it will be on their cover, but it will most certainly be published. However, the reason why you have an assignment with *Travelux* is to keep the one you have with us a secret."

"But I have to pledge to keep what I do for the Curiosi a secret, so why is a cover story necessary?"

"Because in this case, we need to be particularly careful not to raise any suspicion. There are certain forces that would do anything to prevent the success of the case you will be reporting on. Because of this it is of particular importance that no one suspect that you are engaged in anything more innocent than an assignment for an exclusive travel magazine. While the article that you write for *Travelux* will be quite different than the account that you submit to us, both will satisfy the expectations of their respective readers."

"I get it. I'm getting paid to write two completely different versions, one based on what I see and the other based on what *Travelux* wants their readers to see."

Leonard looked at me, his eyes hidden behind the reflection of the Rose Window on the lenses of his glasses. He smiled and replied, "Some people see Saint Chapelle as a gateway to heaven, but most see it as a place where they can be immersed in beauty. They are all happy with what they see, just like your readers will be happy with the version they read."

***

It was only after we parted that I began to think about Leonard's reference to malevolent forces whose suspicion I was to deflect with my cover story, and soon I was suspicious of everyone: the salesman in the men's department at the Samaritaine department store who asked me what I was going to be doing when I told him I was looking for some really nice clothes that would be appropriate for the south of France this time of year; the woman, too beautiful to be alone, sitting at the table next to me at the Brasserie Lipp that night; the old man playing the accordion in the Metro car on my way to the train station who seemed to know only one song and that one not very well; and, finally, the young woman who sat down across from me on the train as it pulled out of the Gare de Lyon. Her high cheekbones, blue eyes, a nose with a small diamond stud in her left nostril and short, blond hair with a faint streak of purple were a perfect disguise. Her name was Liv something or other that sounded Scandinavian but that was because the young conductor slurred it badly as he read her ticket out loud. He was trying the usual phonic foreplay that Frenchmen are known for, but he couldn't handle her last name and it petered out into guttural Gallic. Instead of puckering her lips in a smile at his attempt, she turned away and looked directly at me, shrugged her shoulders and placed a set of headphones over her ears. The conductor shifted his eyes from her to me as if he was trying to figure out if I had been the reason why she had resisted his charm, then quickly dismissed the idea and turned his attention to the passengers in the next row.

Unlike Liv, I was not interested in attracting attention so I stuck my nose into the Michelin guidebook on southern France that I'd purchased before boarding the train. I figured the more stars next to the hotel or restaurant, the more likely an alignment with what *Travelux* readers were searching for. It would help if I knew exactly where in southern France I was going so I could check out what places had the most stars twinkling over them. My ticket was for Montpellier, but was that my final destination? Leonard told me only that I should look for a Claude Tremblay. There was no description of Claude, though, so I could only assume he knew what I looked like. The book described Montpellier as the historic capital of Languedoc, which is now part of the Occitanie Region of France. I looked at the map and saw that it was only a few kilometers from the Mediterranean coast and just to the west of Provence, where I'd visited both Arles and Avignon. The first was where Van Gogh went to escape his madness, and the second was where the Pope went to escape from his Church. I'd also been to Marseille and the Riviera. To the southwest of Montpellier were the Pyrenees and beyond that, Spain, where I'd also been a number of times. Then, over to the far west was Bordeaux. I located Biarritz on the Atlantic coast, and recalled an especially memorable week there a couple of years ago. I'd never been to Languedoc, which was the space between the places I'd been to before. Although it was off my beaten path, was it on one that the *Travelux* reader would want to tread?

The train stopped at a station. Outside on the platform a man walked by in a chalk-striped suit carrying a briefcase. He was followed by a woman in high heels pulling a red suitcase. They both headed for the stairs passing another man who was leaning against a pillar. He was wearing a short black leather jacket that was as weathered as his face. Just before the train began moving again he pocketed the mobile that was glued to his ear, picked up a small leather valise and boarded the train. Liv was also watching him, but when he disappeared out of view she returned to the book she was reading and her music. I figured the book must be something light, some romantic fantasy even though I couldn't see the title. I was surprised that it had a hardcover. She lifted it slightly, tilting it so I could read *The Mays of Ventadorn* by the poet W. S. Merwin. She looked up and caught my eyes and gave me a "got you" look before returning to her reading.

Languedoc. I pronounced the name several times to myself, each time trying a different pronunciation. It sounded like a comfortable easy chair. A chaise Languedoc off in the corner of the French provincial living room. Instead of plush and lush though, the first picture I looked at in the Michelin guidebook showed a land of right angles and sharp edges with mountains and plateaus sliced by deep gorges. It appeared to be either scoured by sunlight or hidden in shadows. The next photos were of a ruined medieval fortress perched on a rock and a village barely clinging to a steep hillside. Other pictures showed a softer side: serpentine rivers between leafy banks, hills covered with vineyards, plump grapes, and ruddy-faced villagers eating cheese and sipping wine. My mouth began to water. One can't live on bread alone, especially the crusty carbohydrates I had with jam for breakfast at the hotel. Now this was more like *Travelux* country. I could even smell the food.

The source for the smell wasn't my imagination; across the aisle from me, a family I hadn't noticed before was preparing to eat breakfast. The grandmother unpacked not only the ubiquitous baguette, but several different cheeses, a couple of jars of jam, hard-boiled eggs, and an assortment of oranges and peaches. She arranged them neatly on the table, which the mother had set not with plastic but gleaming silverware and china. The father poured steaming coffee from a thermos into three cups, while the young son popped a straw into a carton of fruit juice. I reached down and grabbed my small backpack on the floor next to my feet and rummaged around until finally pulling out a notebook. Not edible but something I could write on.

"One begins not with the breakfast of champions but a breakfast with champignons on the train heading south," I began my *Travelux* article. Then I described the omelet and champignons that I imagined in front of me on a white linen tablecloth in a luxurious dining car. After that I paused, stumped, tapping my pen on the sheet of paper while staring out the window. The country was getting more mountainous. A new aroma overpowered the scent from across the aisle. Liv had placed a number of containers on the table between us. It looked and smelled like a mini smorgasbord. The strongest smell was a fish that looked as if it had just been reeled in from a barrel of pickles. There was an equally odiferous aroma from a wedge of cheese on a hunk of bread that looked as grainy as a two-by-four. Finally, there was a cardboard container filled with what was either a virulent yogurt or a biological weapon. She didn't look like a terrorist, but, then again, neither do the terrorists. Liv mixed whatever it was with a plastic spoon and slipped a glob into her mouth, licking the spoon afterward. Then, looking at me, she smiled, again, gesturing with the spoon, inviting me to have a bite.

I shook my head as if I'd love to but I'm full. That's a lie, of course. I am hungry, but not for that. I won't include this in the article but I will alter the description of the mother to make her a little more Liv-like.

***

Dinner is six courses stuffed with deliciously, malevolent cholesterol. I can't wait to get it past my lips. Instead, someone shook me and I dropped the fork and opened my eyes. I looked up at the young conductor instead of a waiter. His face was the face of someone who'd been jilted before he'd had a chance to prove what a great lover he was. "Montpellier, Monsieur. You must leave now." He spat the words out as if he held me responsible for his failure with Liv, who had apparently disembarked along with everyone else. I grabbed my bags and got out of the empty car as fast as I could.

As soon as I reached the top of the stairs that led up from the platform, a middle-aged man approached. He was tall and trim and wore a dark blue suit with a yellow tie. I had imagined Claude as stouter and a bit of a slob. Before I could say bonjour, he veered to the left and embraced a woman young enough to be his daughter, but was more likely someone else's. Just above me the large black arrival and departure board reshuffled with letters and numbers, spinning like a slot machine, before snapping into place, announcing that the train to Monte Carlo, with stops at Nice and Cannes, was now boarding. Passengers pushed me aside as they rushed past, down the stairs. Those who were still in the waiting room sat reading newspapers or dozing. I walked over to the information desk and told the woman that I was late and had apparently missed the person who was supposed to meet me. "I wonder if he left a note. His name is Claude Tremblay."

"But Claude Tremblay is just outside the main entrance," she waved her hand toward the far end of the waiting room. "You must hurry though."

The only men waiting outside were a line of cabbies standing next to their taxies. One of them opened his passenger door and motioned to me. Claude must have given up on me and already left. Perhaps he's assumed the worst and called Leonard. I should call him as well and tell him that I'm okay, except I don't have a phone number, only an email address. Then I saw "Claude Tremblay." It was printed in large red letters across the side of a blue bus. I walked past the expectant cabbie and crossed the roadway to the bus stop. The full name on the idling bus was Claude Tremblay Tours.

"Monsieur Scriviner." The man greeting me had broad shoulders, a big belly, and the forearms of a major league slugger. "I am Claude Tremblay." He said then grabbed my suitcase and shoved it into an open cargo bay. After slamming the door of the bay closed, he motioned for me to enter the bus.

"I don't have a ticket."

"Ticket? Of course not. The ticket is already paid for," he answered, pushing me gently up the steps. "I hope you aren't hungry, because I am out of box lunches. Of course, you probably ate on the train." Inside, the bus was filled. All of the passengers were probably mad at me for keeping them waiting. I jammed myself into the vacant aisle seat kitty-corner from the driver's, scrunching down as much as possible. At least I don't have to run a gauntlet to sit at the back of the bus.

After a quick survey of the passengers, waving a fat index finger as he made his tally, Claude settled into his seat and pulled the handle that closed the door. "Merde," he cursed, and opened the door again. He quickly descended the steps and out of my view. "But this is a private tour," I could hear Claude protest. "Well, of course, if you are willing to pay extra, I have one seat left, Monsieur, the one behind the driver, who happens to be me."

A moment later the man boarded, wearing the black leather jacket and the same tired face I'd seen on the platform of the train station outside Paris. He took a newspaper and magazine out of his valise before shoving it onto the rack overhead and settling in across the aisle from me. Claude quickly closed the door, released the air brakes, ground the gears and turned the steering wheel. After a short descent down a ramp from the station entrance we squeezed into traffic.

"Welcome ladies and gentlemen," Claude's voice boomed, amplified by a microphone at the end of a silver cable snaking out from the dashboard. "You have taken the plane and the train and now you are on the bus," he switched to heavily accented English, "and are leaving the driving to us." After waiting for the laughter to subside he switched back to French. "Of course, as you can see, there is only me, although some people might say I am large enough for two."

The man opposite me took a pack of cigarettes from the inside pocket of his black jacket and tapped it against the palm of his left hand. "Also, for your information," Claude announced, "we are an eco-friendly bus, so please no smoking." The cigarette lingered on the man's lip as if he was contemplating whether this was a request or an order. Claude added, "Violators will be transferred to a self-guided walking tour." With the cigarette still riding his lip the man looked around, as if he was conducting a quick poll of faces. He caught my eyes for a second and then shifted his eyes farther back. After completing his tally of stony stares or, in my case, diverted eyes, he pried the still unlit cigarette from his lips and carefully slid it back into the pack.

Claude returned to his spiel as he maneuvered the bus through the narrow, congested streets. "We are now in the city of Montpellier so if you were expecting some other city, then I am sorry to inform you that you took the wrong train. Montpellier is a very ancient place going back to before the Romans. In the 13th century it challenged Paris as the biggest city in what is now called France. I believe Montpellier was actually bigger, but Paris wished to erase us as much as possible from the history books. The university here is one of the oldest in Europe and its medical school was the very first. I am afraid we are to blame for your doctor bills. Montpellier is the unofficial capital of Languedoc. It is unofficial only because Languedoc is no longer an official government region but part of Occitanie. Again, one can see the hand of Paris at work. The word Langue- doc means language of the Oc or Occitan. It is also sometimes called Provençal by those people who live on the other side of the Rhône, but they are ignorant, of course, and we must pity them. It is said that the word Occitan came from Aquitaine. You have heard, no doubt, of Eleanor of Aquitaine, that beautiful queen of the English King Henry who locked her in a dungeon for years? A peculiarly English way of making love."

I was somehow relieved that I wasn't named after King Hen- ry, but a very nonroyal uncle who I'm pretty sure never locked my aunt in the basement. As we entered a traffic circle, I pressed against the arm of the seat, pushed by centrifugal force as the bus entered a tight orbit before suddenly veering off onto a street marked by a sign for the A9.

"Speaking of love, Occitan is the true language of love. You probably think it is French that has always been the language of love, and Paris the place for romance, but they learned every- thing about love from us. This is the land of the troubadours after all, of romantic poetry and song. Unfortunately, we were too loving, which is why the Parisian French conquered us. You see, until the 13th century, France was divided into two separate realms: one in the north that spoke French and one in the South that, of course, spoke Occitan. In the 12th century there was a war and the north conquered the south. Even though we have had to give up our beautiful language and speak French, we will never agree that the north, Paris, is the true capital of love and romance."

"He makes the Albigensian Crusade sound like the American Civil War," a male voice muttered in English from the seat behind me. He sounded like a don. Not a mafia don, but a professor at Oxford or Cambridge. "But without the slaves. It was much more complicated than that."

"He's just giving us a tour," a woman answered, in the same accent at a higher pitch.

"Still, some people might believe the prattle he's spewing and think it's fact," the man said.

"Not everyone wants to hear a lecture when they're on a bus. He's talking about romance. Since it's probably the only subject you're not an expert in, you might actually learn something for once."

After pausing at a tollbooth, we merged onto the N9. Claude moved the microphone closer to his lips as the whine of the tires increased and the wind began to thump the windshield. It made him sound a bit more intimate, like a lounge singer. The man in the black leather jacket pulled apart the newspaper and unfolded the sports section with a crack that sounded like a pistol shot.

"As you can see we have now left Montpellier," Claude said. "We have come a long way from the Roman road that used to connect Montpellier with Narbonne. The autoroute is much faster and I can assure you that the bus is much more comfortable than a chariot."

Faster and more comfortable maybe, but the four lanes, the overpasses, the entrances and exits seemed indistinguishable from the German autobahn, the English motorway, the Italian autostrada, or the New Jersey Turnpike. There was no romance on this road.

"Over there to our left is the Mediterranean. You can't see it, of course, but if you could see the Mediterranean you would also see the town of Balaruc-les-Bains, which is the third most popular spa in all of France. And if you could see Balaruc-les-Bains, you would also be able to see the beach town next to it, Cap d'Agde, that was constructed in 1970. Although it was built on sand, it has managed to become one of the most popular seaside resorts in all of France. In fact, it was a finalist for the best children's resort. I would personally give it first place as the best resort for parents to lie on the beach drinking piña coladas so they can forget about their kids."

"Somehow that doesn't surprise me," the man behind me said.

"Not everyone's favorite place is the university library," the woman answered.

"We are passing the exit for the city of Béziers," Claude boomed. "Not only is Béziers the wine capitol of Languedoc, but it is also famous for its many festivals such as the summer festival and the festival of Aphrodise, which, I'm sorry to inform you, does not celebrate Aphrodite. It celebrates Saint Aphrodise who is the patron saint of Béziers. Saint Aphrodise gave Béziers its heraldic symbol, the camel, perhaps confusing sandy beaches with the desert. My favorite Béziers festival is the wine festival, which will begin next week. It is a shame that the good Saint didn't choose wine as his heraldry. After all it is a much better aphrodisiac than a camel."

"Very funny," the man behind said. "Why doesn't he mention that in 1209 crusaders massacred everyone in Béziers and burned it to the ground? And it wasn't just the Cathars who were slaughtered, it was also the Roman Catholics who were the majority of the inhabitants. They made the mistake of trying to defend their neighbors."

"Not everyone enjoys the dark side," the woman replied.

"We are approaching the city of Narbonne," Claude started again. "It has a quaint medieval center with the Canal de la Robine running through it. Next to the Canal is an outdoor market where you can buy everything from clothes to cover your outside to food to fill your insides. What many people don't know is that it is also a city with a terrific nightlife. Speaking of night spots, if you have a chance to visit Narbonne, why not visit my favorite, the Why Not Café?"

"Why not?" the man behind me grunted. "That sums up Narbonne. After all, as soon as they found out what happened to Béziers, the good citizens turned their back on the Cathars and welcomed Simon de Monfort's crusaders. Then, five years later, they switched sides again, only to change sides once more as soon as it was advantageous. They even agreed to demolish the walls of their own city. Finally, as their crowning achievement in duplicity and cowardice, they welcomed the Inquisition and threw out all the Jews and closed the famous Jewish university."

"But remember they were punished with the plague and then they were sacked and put to the torch by Edward, Prince of Wales during the Hundred Years' War," the woman said. "That should cheer you up."

We had left the autoroute and were on a two-lane road. At first, we followed the river Aude, crossing several times before leaving it behind and climbing up from the river valley. Vineyards appeared on the right side with most of the vines ending in a stump with two branches stretched out at right angles. Globs of purple hung from the branches. Claude called the vines 'podiums' although they reminded me more of empty crucifixes. The leaves on the trees had begun to change color, so the landscape was a mottle of yellow and red leaves, brown vines and green grass. We drove past a vineyard with a grove of trees in the middle that surrounded a small stone building with a crusader's cross carved into its face, just below the peak of its red-tiled roof.

I asked Claude if he knew what it was. "A private chapel or something like that, or maybe a shrine that marks a place where something important happened, but that was a long time ago so everyone has forgotten what was so important about it. Now it's a barn. There are many such places around here."

We entered a village where half a dozen old men were playing bocce in the town square. Claude honked his horn and waved at the men and they tipped their straw hats in reply.

"They must not be serious about bocce," the man behind me said. "Otherwise, they'd be pretty upset at us for interrupting their game."

"Perhaps they're too relaxed to be angry," the woman answered. "It's an example of pastoral tranquility."

"More likely they're paid by Monsieur Tremblay to be part of the tour."

We stopped at a traffic light. A motorcycle pulled up beside us. It was one of those sleek Italian jobs, without an ounce of fat on its frame. Its leather-clad rider looked up as if searching the windows of the bus, his face hidden by the tinted visor of the black helmet that covered his head, then revved the engine. The light turned and he pulled away in front of us and quickly disappeared. A few minutes later we left the village behind, crossing the Canal du Midi on a humpback bridge. Trees stretched into the distance on either side of the canal forming green palisades. A barge floated toward us.

Claude told us the canal was over 250 kilometers long, connecting Toulouse in the west to the Mediterranean Sea near Agde. "You can take canal boats, like the ones you see here, for cruises. They are better than being on those big cruise ships because you can eat every night at the captain's table. In fact, you can rent one and be your own captain."

The word 'eat' only aggravated my hunger. If I'd been booked for a cruise on a barge rather than a tour on a bus I'd be having lunch. It wouldn't have to be at the captain's table, either. A sandwich with a deckhand would be enough. I heard the rustling of paper behind me followed by the smell of fresh baked bread.

"It's just bread and cheese," the man said.

"It's not just any bread and cheese, it's French bread and French cheese," the woman replied.

There was a chorus of chewing by unseen passengers. The man across the aisle pulled out a candy bar. I closed my eyes and tried breathing through my mouth and thinking of something else. Ingrid Lindstrom floated into my mind. We were in my parents' decidedly uncool station wagon, driving down Minnesota Avenue in Kansas City, Kansas on a Friday evening. The avenue was lit up by neon signs of fast-food restaurants with long forgotten names like Griff's and Peter's. We pulled into a place called Zesto's and bought a 'buzz ticket' for twenty-five cents from a young kid wearing a white Zesto's hat. The place was so popular that they charged for the right to cruise through and check out who was and wasn't there, refundable if you actually parked and ordered something.

We would look for a vacant spot in the row of cars facing out at us. Girls in black skirts and white blouses and bobby socks scurried between the cars. They carried trays of burgers and French fries and milk shakes that they attached to the driver's window. Faces stared out through the windshields of the GTOs, Malibus, Barracudas and Mustangs as we passed. Everyone is looking at Ingrid instead of my pathetic set of wheels. After the waitress attached the tray with our order of burgers, fries, and shakes to my rolled down window, Ingrid and I look at each other, filled with anticipation, and as I inhale the heady mix of burgers and perfume, my eyes open and there's only the leftover scent of a dozen box lunches and one chocolate bar. We had left the valley and were climbing into what Claude said was the Haut-Languedoc. The road curved, switching back and forth as it rose, and the curves were sharp. Although the narrow, deepening valley was green with shrubs and stunted trees, above it there were outcroppings of bone white rock.

We were approaching the 'Causses,' Claude informed us, mountains of limestone with deep gorges. The limestone soaked up the water that collected in underground lakes, and fed the rivers that had carved the gorges. We passed two white crosses shrouded with dried flowers; Claude stopped talking; a flaming red convertible sped past. Our brakes hissed as we slowed, leaving just enough space for the car to slip in front of us before we crossed a narrow bridge over a spring that gushed out of the rock. The driver was hunched over the steering wheel, his head covered by a plaid cap, one of those jaunty flat ones whose front snaps to its brim, but the woman in the passenger seat, her blond hair streaming behind her, looked back. She said something. Although lip-reading isn't one of the languages I've mastered, I translated it as an apology.

"Crazy driver!" shouted the woman behind me. "Doesn't he know that those crosses mark the spots where someone died in a terrible accident? Even if he doesn't care about himself, what about his wife?"

"Wife?" her husband answered. "She can't be his wife. His wife would never let him drive like that. In fact, he wouldn't buy a car like that if he were going to use it to transport his wife. Therefore, she is most definitely his mistress."

"How romantic, Donald."

A few minutes later we pulled off into a gravel parking lot. The stop was abrupt, as if an elevator has suddenly stopped between floors. Claude set the brake and pulled the handle opening the door. White dust swirled up the steps of the bus. "Ladies and Gentlemen, we have arrived at our destination, or, at least, as far as I can take you in the bus. No motor vehicles are allowed in the town so you will need to walk the rest of the way, unless you can persuade someone to carry you. You can wait for me or you can proceed on your own. Your luggage will be taken directly to your hotel."

I stepped down from the bus. No longer protected by tinted windows, the brightness of the sun almost blinded me until I put on my sunglasses. Next to the bus was a wagon hitched to a large draught horse. From the back of the bus, Claude had begun unloading the luggage and handing it to another man who stacked it onto the flat bed of the cart. On the other side of the cart, at the end of a row of parked cars, was the red convertible and next to it the motorcycle.

"What a relief," I heard the voice of the man who sat behind me. I turned around. He was tall and gaunt and, I suspected, bald under the floppy, white sun hat that was pulled down to his ears.

Before I could answer, I heard his wife, who stepped out from behind him, "Yes, you won't be subjected to Monsieur Tremblay's version of history anymore." She was a foot shorter and a bit broader than her husband with a face that followed the same curve as her large round sunglasses. Unlike her husband, her head was uncovered, revealing gray hair, cut in a no-fuss style.

"What I was referring to was the lack of leg room, although you're quite right on that score as well." He turned to me and added, "You know what I mean, we tall men suffer, particularly in the land of the shorter races, don't we?"

"I was lucky to have the front seat. There's more leg room."

"I thought about taking it," he said.

"But he gave it up to sit with me. Donald can be such a martyr."

"Even martyrdom has its limits, Lavinia, when it comes to the kind of torture Monsieur Tremblay subjected us to with his twaddle. Only a moronic martyr could put up with."

I watched them stride off, the thick soles of their walking shoes spewing dust and gravel. Unlike Donald, I'd discovered that being deprived of food in France was the ultimate torture. So far, I had only slim pickings to share with the readers of *Travelux*. No doubt arriving in a red convertible, delayed only by a leisurely lunch at a four-star country auberge, would have been a more appropriate entrance. I walked over to the convertible. Even parked it seemed to be generating rpms. Its grille flashed a chrome grin that really rubbed it in, letting me know that the only thing about the car I could afford was the fantasy. Was the driver the typical reader of *Travelux* or the person that the reader wanted to be? And what about the motorcycle, which was a Ducati with enough ccs to power a fleet of compact cars, the perfect vehicle for the easy rider of the life of ease? A writer needed to know his audience. But then, I remembered, I don't know the members of the Curiosi either and so far they seemed to be pleased. By the time I returned, Claude had finished loading the cart. Only a handful of the passengers remained. The rest apparently had the same idea as Donald and Lavinia and had gone ahead to the hotel, or maybe they couldn't wait to go shopping for postcards and souvenirs. Whatever the reason, included among the missing was the man in the black leather jacket. Although my stomach was growling in a language that needed no translation, I decided to stay with Claude. I figured the unknown Curiosi I was supposed to meet might be expecting me to arrive with him.

***

From where I stood on the bridge, above the middle arch that spanned the gorge, there was an unobstructed view of the town. It was almost indistinguishable from the stone wall that surrounded it. At the far end of the town, the land rose suddenly to a rocky promontory, where a fortress loomed over the red tile roofs of the town. Although the walls of the fortress appeared on the verge of collapse, the octagonal tower inside them boldly jutted into the cloudless sky. The fortified town, Claude told those of us walking with him, had withstood a siege by the French crusaders for six months before it surrendered. "Hundreds of Cathars and the knights who defended them had been thrown from this very bridge along with a number of ordinary citizens who were judged to be collaborators." Below the bridge the river threaded its way between the rocks and gravel shoals. The ripples sparkled in the sunlight and, in the distance, two men stood in the current whipping their fly rods back and forth. Now that's something that might appeal to the *Travelux* reader, a place to use all sorts of expensive fishing gear. I make a mental note to find out how good the fishing was, although I doubted it was as important to them as how good the fishermen looked in their outfits.

"Just around the bend in the river, beyond where those fishermen are, is the confluence of the Cesse river you see here and the Tarn that flows through a canyon on the other side. The town is surrounded on three sides by the two gorges and rivers." Claude's arm swept across the skyline before stopping at the tower. "And on the fourth side is the fortress. The only way in is by this bridge. Unfortunately, it is also the only way out. Even though the crusaders could not get in, the defenders could not escape. As we say, their fate was sealed."

"What's this?" a middle-aged woman wearing jeans and a burgundy windbreaker asked holding up a wooden cross.

"Where did you find that?" Claude demanded, his voice breaking from that of the jocular tour guide.

"It was leaning against the stone railing," she answered, de-fensively. "Does it mean a car ran off the bridge?"

Claude snatched the cross from her, "Just a joke. Nothing has gone off the bridge...until now," he said, flinging the cross. We all watched as it spun in a slow, corkscrew dive into the foaming water. It bobbed to the surface and was carried by the current past the fishermen, fouling one of their lines. As one of them cut his line to free it, the other one raised his right arm at us, slapping his bicep with his left hand in a gesture that needed no translation. I wondered what he would have done if he had been able to read the inscription on the sign, which I was able to see just before Claude grabbed it from the startled woman, 'We have not forgotten – MAL.'

***

"You seem surprised to see me." I could only nod since my mouth was full of ham and cheese, and my lips crusted with bread crumbs. Liv continued. "Ah, now I understand. Leonard didn't tell you that I was the person you were supposed to meet. I thought it odd that you didn't say anything and that you refused my offer to give you some of my breakfast on the train. I thought it was because you suspected someone might be observing us when, in fact, you were suspicious of me."

I swallowed. "You're right that he didn't tell me who, exactly, I'd be working with or even a description but that's not why I refused your offer of breakfast. I thought I'd be eating lunch as soon as we arrived in Montpellier. If I'd known I'd have had to wait this long to eat, I would have accepted."

She sat in the chair opposite me. We were the only customers in the restaurant. It was more of a bar than a restaurant, a dark place with low, thick beams and an entrance a couple of steps below street level. Getting the bartender to take my lunch order hadn't been easy. Lunch was over, he told me. All I wanted was a sandwich and some pommes frites, I told him and offered to pay more than the price listed on the bar menu. That seemed to work. That, and the realization that he could keep the entire amount and tell his boss the sandwiches had to been thrown out as stale leftovers. I ordered a beer, a Kronenbourg, as well.

Now, as Liv sat opposite me, the bartender seemed energized and scurried over to ask what the mademoiselle would like to eat. No? "Then surely something to drink?" He asked in a voice that seemed on the verge of begging. She shook her head no. His shoulders, which had been brought up to square, slumped back to their previous position and his smile collapsed as well. He looked at me as if I had something to do with his rejection, then retreated to the bar.

"I didn't see you on the bus."

"That's because I didn't take the bus. I took another form of transportation although I left my bag with Claude to take on the bus since I didn't have room for luggage. After I registered at the hotel I waited in my room for you to contact me but when I didn't hear from you I called your room. However, the operator said that you had just stopped at the front desk and asked if there was a place where you could eat."

"I think I should have asked for a place where they wanted my business."

"Oh, him?" she said, not bothering to look in the direction of the bartender who was contemplating a glass of beer he'd just poured for himself. "He probably thinks that people attending a symposium can't be big tippers."

"What symposium?"

"Le Symposium des Cathars that begins tomorrow morning. Didn't Leonard tell you about that either?"

"Tell me? He gave me a train ticket to Montpellier and the name Claude Tremblay and that's all." I took another bite from my ham sandwich.

"Leonard told me to meet you at the hotel but there we were sitting across from each other on the train. It couldn't be a coincidence, I thought. But you really didn't know who I was?"

"Not a clue. I looked at you that way because you reminded me of someone. A Swedish girl I once knew."

She picked up another pomme frite. "When?"

"When what? I'm still working on where we are."

"We are in Montsaf, which means safe mountain in Occitan," she replied matter of factly. "Now when did you know this Swedish girl? Also, where and why, that is, why do I remind you of her?"

Her eyes fastened on me intently, and I found myself involuntarily backing away, the legs of my chair scraping against the stone floor. "Well," I answered after realizing what was happening and halting my retreat, "for one thing, she had the same color hair." Minus the purple, I thought to myself. "It wasn't as short but hair was longer then. Then being when I was in high school. She was an exchange student from Sweden."

"Perhaps she was my mother?" she said letting me know that I was old enough to be her father.

"I doubt it. Her name was Ingrid Lindstrom."

"Lindstrom is my mother's maiden name, which is quite common in Sweden, but her first name is Anna. Sorry."

She sounded sincere enough that I felt like I should apologize as well. "Sorry for what?"

Her face brightened. "I have an aunt named Ingrid, though. She's my mother's older sister."

"I suppose it could have been her. Who knows?" I felt even more ancient.

"If you can describe this Ingrid you knew, maybe I can determine if she is my aunt. For example, what did she look like besides having long hair?"

Just look in a mirror is what I wanted to say. "As I said, you remind me of her. Other than that..." I shook my head, "It was a long time ago."

***

As we walked from the restaurant toward the square, the sun dipped behind the jagged roofline. It was cooler in the shadows and Liv pulled on the sweater that had been draped over her shoulders. Racks filled with postcards stood like sentinels outside the open shop doors. Next to one of them was a poster for a Cathar diorama inside. The photos on it depicted lifelike figures being tossed off the bridge and others being burned at the stake. As if to mitigate the violence, one photo showed a group on their knees praying, although there was no way of knowing if they were Catholic or Cathar. It sure didn't depict a safe mountain for the Cathars, I thought.

"I never get used to the way they cater to the tourists," Liv observed. "It seems like a heresy."

"You've been here before?"

"This is my second time." She stopped in front of a display of belts and purses. "You are surprised that someone who could be your niece if you had married your high school sweetheart would spend so much time in a place like this?" She asked, her fingers playing with the hanging belts.

"I don't remember saying anything about her being my sweetheart."

"If it was my aunt then you would regret that you were not sweethearts."

Before I could think of how, or whether, to respond she unhooked one of the belts. "You know Languedoc means the language of Occitan and it was the language of the troubadours."

"Does that have anything to do with the book you were reading by W.S. Merwin on the train?"

"In *The Mays of Ventadorn*, Merwin writes about Bernart de Ventadorn, one of the most famous troubadours. Even though the songs he and the other troubadours sang were called lays, they were about a courtly love that wasn't physical, not what someone today thinks when they hear the word lay." She held the belt in front of my eyes so that I could see an embossed platoon of knights on horseback riding across the tanned leather. "Can you see the small cross on their backs? They are supposed to be Knights Templar. This belt looks strong enough to support one of their broadswords. The knights were here as well as the troubadours, but unlike the troubadours they took a vow of celibacy. Cathars believed in celibacy as well." She said, snapping the belt with a crack. The sound was amplified in the narrow street. A head popped out from the door of the shop – a startled look on a man's face. Liv told him that she was just testing the leather. To his disappointment instead of buying it she replaced it on the rack.

Resuming our walk, I asked her, "Is there something special about this place or the symposium that has to do with troubadours?"

"Because the Cathars and the troubadours came from the same place at the same time, it is hard to study one without learning about the other as well."

"Study? Then you're doing this for school?"

She laughed. "My parents would love for that to be the reason, but it has more to do with the musical group I'm in."

It was the first thing she said that didn't surprise me. "What kind of musical group? A rock band?"

"It's not a rock band?"

"Jazz?"

"Not that, either."

"Folk?"

"Please stop," she pleaded. "I don't like categories. They're oppressive. Just because a CD comes in a box doesn't mean the artist who created the music must also be in one."

"It's hard to find a CD now, in or outside of a box. Everything is streaming."

"We still record on CDs," she laughed. "We're into anachronism. Of course, recording on vinyl would be even better."

"What the name of your group?"

"JAM."

"Jam? Sounds like a rock group to me. You know, like in Pearl Jam?"

She gave me a blank stare.

"They recorded on vinyl."

"JAM stands for Jongleurs du Âge Moyen."

"Jugglers of the Middle Ages?"

She laughed and jabbed me in the arm with her right hand. "No, jongleur is another name for troubadour. Although troubadours also wrote their songs while jongleurs just sang. It can be confusing. We also write our own songs, by the way. Sometimes even the experts can't tell the difference."

"How do you know?"

"Because I am an expert." Instead of another jab to my arm she threw her hip into me for a brief but distracting moment.

"Are troubadours going to be part of the symposium?" I asked as we approached the town square.

"In a way, because the topic is a chanson that has been discovered. They say it could lift some of the mystery surrounding the Cathars and the Albigensian Crusades. The symposium will be the first opportunity for others to examine it and discuss its meaning."

"So, the whole point of this symposium is to bring together experts to discuss a song that was sung about a thousand years ago? Now, that's a real golden oldie."

She closed her eyes, her violet painted lids making it hard to ignore that she was pretending to take a nap. "You make it sound quite boring."

"I just wonder how I'm supposed to juice it up for the readers of *Travelux*."

"*Travelux*?"

"That's the name of the magazine I'm writing an article for. It's my cover story. If it makes the cover I guess you could call it a cover-cover story. Anyway, its readers are a pretty exclusive group, both in terms of wealth and the way they like to think of themselves."

"Your readers are the kind of people they would hope to attract to the symposium. There is so much competition for tourists that the sponsors decided to come up with something that would attract the more intellectual tourist, at least the wealthy tourist who wants to believe the reason they are rich is because they are smarter than everyone else."

"You're right, that sounds like a reader of *Travelux*."

By now we had entered the town square. On our right was a Romanesque church and on the far side, facing the church, was the Hôtel Hospitalier. An arcade of two-story buildings with shops and a restaurant on the ground floor was on the left side of the square. On the opposite side was the Musée de Cathar. It reminded me of a Roman temple. Over its entrance was a banner announcing the symposium. In the middle of the square was a fountain and some benches ringed by trees, the only trees that I'd seen inside the village walls. Several children were playing with small inflatable toys in the water of the fountain's basin while their mothers sat in the shade on one of the benches. Lavinia and Donald, the couple from the bus, were ascending the steps to the museum entrance. The wind rustled the yellow leaves of the trees sending a half dozen sailing into the bright, crisp afternoon. A woman and a man came out of the museum and greeted Lavinia and Donald. The man appeared to be introducing them to the woman.

I nudged Liv, "Those two sat behind me on the bus. We need to come up with something if they or someone else asks us how we know each other. Maybe we can just say we bumped into each other?" Wanting to be around Liv probably wouldn't need any explaining on the part of most men. It would be seen as just another middle-aged man chasing his Lolita. But why would she want to hang out with me? That never made sense in Nabokov's book either.

"Leonard said that we are to tell everyone that I am helping you with research for your story. That way we are under the same covers, so to speak."

I had to agree that it wouldn't hurt that my research assistant was also young and beautiful – at least for the male readers if I included a photo of her. Since any professional photographer *Travelux* was sending wouldn't be here until after we were long gone, they would have to use mine if they wanted her picture in the article. It would be pretty easy for them to edit out the diamond in her nose and the purple in her hair.

"I might need to explain why you weren't on the bus with me if you are here to help me with the story?"

"Don't you remember?" she asked.

"What?"

"You don't remember that I asked you to come with me but you refused."

"And why would I do that?"

"You didn't want to be my passenger."

"I don't understand. No one's going to believe that I wouldn't want to share a car with you."

She smiled at me and replied, "A car, yes, but I think they will all agree that you didn't want to be my passenger on the Ducati motorcycle that I rented."

"That was you at the stoplight? I didn't recognize you with the helmet and the leather suit on. I thought you were a guy."

"I suppose that means it was a good cover."

***

"Monsieur Scriviner," the man announced as he presented me with a key. Based on the officious tone of his voice one would have thought it was the key to the city rather than my room. "I hope you are happy with your room." He was an older, heavier version of the young clerk who checked me in earlier.

"No complaints so far."

"Complaints?" he recoiled as if I'd dropped a mouse on the counter. "Please, please if there is the slightest, the smallest, the tiniest thing that concerns you, bring it to my personal attention." He held out his hand. "I am Maurice Beauchambre, the proprietor. My son, Charles, was supposed to inform me as soon as you arrived but he forgot. He was checking everyone in at once and there was no one to assist him, but still, I told him it is no excuse. Not for a first-class hotel. We are honored that *Travelux* chose our establishment for your stay." And what were the alternative accommodations, I thought of asking as I shook his hand. And how did he know I was with *Travelux*?

"And is this young lady with you?" Monsieur Beauchambre asked looking at Liv, who I had forgotten was standing beside me.

"This is Liv..." I stammered since I didn't know her last name.

"Lindstrom," Liv said, giving me a playful nudge with her elbow. "I'm Monsieur Scriviner's research assistant. I was hired by *Travelux* to work with him on his article and we just met."

"Ah, what a delight," he said shaking her hand. "Charles told me that a young woman had checked in. Obviously, what I said to the monsieur is equally true for the mademoiselle. Do not hesitate to come to me directly if you have the slightest problem." Or, even if you don't have a problem in the case of Liv, I thought, judging from the look in his eye.

"I hope it doesn't bother you about using Lindstrom for my cover name," She said. "I use it as my stage name instead of my real one, Bjornstjerna."

"I certainly won't have any trouble remembering it."

As we were leaving the lobby I noticed the man in the black leather jacket sitting in one of the lobby's chairs. He was reading the same newspaper that he had on the bus. I was about to ask Liv if she had noticed him when the woman who had been talking to Lavinia and Donald on the museum steps approached us, remarkably fast for someone in high heels, I thought. Her low cut black dress allowed for maximum display of both her figure and the diamond necklace that matched her chandelier size earrings. I seemed to need no introduction as she held out her hand and announced that she was Madame Margarite, the director of Montsaf's visitor's bureau and coordinator for the symposium. After she ushered us to a table in the small combination lounge and breakfast room next to the lobby, she pulled from her large handbag a glossy folder with pictures of the fortress on its cover. "This is the official press packet," she said. "We are particularly honored that an exclusive magazine such as *Travelux* has decided to write about our town and the exciting discovery of the lost Chanson des Cathars."

"Song of the Cathars," Liv said. "I didn't realize it had a name."

Madame Diderot looked at Liv, as if she had just noticed her and would rather not. "This is my research assistant, Liv Lindstrom," I said.

The woman answered with a strained smile. "Chanson des Cathars is not its real name but one must call it something."

"*Travelux* is always looking for a spiritual aura in the places it features," I said trying to convey the appropriate enthusiasm. "And I understand the Cathars had a lot of that."

Madame Diderot smiled at me, "Yes, we are particularly proud of our spiritual aura." Leaning toward me she tapped the folder on my lap, "In addition to information on our town, you will find in the folder background on the symposium and the participants. You are invited to the cocktail reception that begins at 6 p.m. in the Musée de Cathar. We have some very special guests including Declan Fox, the famous author, and Monsignor Vacluse, who is the Pope's special representative, as well as a distinguished scholar. I'm sure you will want to interview all of them. Do you have any questions?"

"Not at the moment."

"No?" She seemed a bit disappointed in my answer. "Please call on me if you do."

"Wait, I do have one question."

Her face brightened.

"When some of the bus passengers were walking across the bridge one of the group found a cross with the words, 'We have not forgotten – MAL' written on it. Our bus driver threw it off the bridge. Who are MAL?"

Madame Diderot's face suddenly lost its soft flaccidity as her muscles strained. "MAL is the Movement for Albigensian Liberation, although it should stand for malcontents. It's a small fringe group that likes to pull pranks like that. They're really quite harmless."

***

"You are early," Madame Diderot said as she greeted Liv and me. "I mean that you are early in comparison to those who have not yet arrived." She looked at the slender watch on her left wrist and smiled, "In fact, you are exactly on time."

Judging from the nearly empty room we seemed to be about the only guests who were. There were several waiters standing around while a bartender polished a glass behind the portable bar. Madame Diderot nodded at one of the waiters who lifted a tray with glasses of wine and walked over to us. We each took a glass of wine. I gave mine a sniff, then a sip, and an approving nod. "I'm so glad you like it," she said. "It is only recently that the world is beginning to discover how extraordinary our wines are."

"I thought Languedoc only produced table wines, the vin ordinaire?" Liv said.

Madame Diderot's plump lips contracted into a thin red line. "Ordinaire? I'm afraid that Languedoc has not been given the attention that we deserve. It was not until 1985 that our wines received their own appellation, Coteaux du Languedoc. Because of our marketing and publicity effort, something I must admit in all modesty to have been part of, we are no longer France's best kept secret."

"That must mean that the location of the Holy Grail is their best kept secret," Liv whispered as Madame Diderot motioned for us to follow her toward several people who had just entered the room from a hallway leading into the exhibition area.

"Professor Le Forge is the director of the museum," Madame Diderot said introducing us. "He is also a professor at the university in Montpellier and volunteers his time for our museum," she added. I recognized him as the man who greeted Lavinia and Donald at the top of the stairs.

"Please call me René," he answered cheerfully. "As for volunteering, given the museum's lack of funds, it was the first requirement for the job. In fact, it may have been the only requirement."

"You would not expect a renowned scholar to be so humorous, would you?" Madame said with a forced smile.

I wouldn't have suspected him to be a renowned scholar, period. Although he couldn't have been more than five and half feet tall, his shoulders seemed almost as broad and his button-busting chest made me think of someone who worked with his arms as much as his head. He pumped my arm with a hand that confirmed that impression. The museum's finances might not be robust but the director certainly was.

Madame Diderot continued, "Although the Musée has not been as financially sound as we would like, we are very optimistic that with our great discovery that is about to change, aren't we Professor?" Before René could respond, Madame Diderot turned to Donald and Lavinia, who had been standing next to the professor. "And we are also very fortunate to have Madame and Monsieur Pierce-Hadden, who are both professors from Oxford in England."

"We've already met," Donald replied. "We were fellow passengers on the bus.

"Yes, of course. You would have come in the same bus. Monsieur Tremblay is quite entertaining as well as informative, isn't he?" Madame Diderot said.

"Very entertaining," Lavinia answered, her left hand pressing on Donald's right arm. In response Donald's mouth opened and closed without saying anything. He turned to Liv and said, "I don't recall seeing you on the bus."

"And Donald would not have missed you," Lavinia added dryly. "He's a very keen observer."

"Liv used alternative transportation," I answered for Liv.

"I'm sorry I missed Monsieur Tremblay's entertaining commentary," Liv said.

"Perhaps, Professor," Madame Diderot turned to René, "you and your colleagues could provide some background for Monsieur Scriviner for the exclusive article that he is writing for *Travelux* magazine. You must excuse me while I attend to my duties and greet some of our guests."

Before I could respond, Liv asked them, "For example, what do you believe the Cathars would think about a cocktail party such as this?"

"They wouldn't have had anything to do with it," Donald gave an emphatic answer before René could say anything. "After all, their name comes from the Greek word 'katharoi,' which means pure ones. Since God must be perfectly good, the Cathars, his followers, must live a life of purity and virtue. That would be hard to reconcile with a commercial festival and parties like this. They believed the material world had to be the creation of the evil one – Satan or Lucifer or whatever name you want to give the poor Devil. On the other hand, since the dualism of the Cathars can be traced back to the Christian Gnostics of the first century, and 'gnosis' means knowledge in Greek, they would have been great supporters of your museum, René. After all, your museum is about increasing knowledge. It's a pity the Catholic Church didn't share their views."

Lavinia turned to me and Liv, and in a cheerful voice that contrasted with the seriousness of the subject, said, "I think Donald paints a much too severe picture of the Cathars. They were quite a joyful group, as a matter of fact. As to Donald's comment about the Catholic Church, it is true that since the

Cathars believed, as did the Gnostics, that one could experience God directly and that there was no need for intermediaries, this undermined the Catholic Church. As a consequence, the Church branded it a heresy and did all they could to suppress it, as they did with the Manichaeans of the 2nd and 3rd centuries and, later, the Bogomils in the 10th."

"Bogomil," I repeated the name. "It sounds more like an automobile than a spiritual movement."

"What I find almost as strange as the name," Donald said, ignoring my joke, "is that the French would accept a belief system that came from the east, Macedonia and Bulgaria by way of Constantinople. I mean, with all due respect, René, the French are the original 'if it's not invented here' culture, especially when it comes to philosophy."

"But you forget, Donald, that Languedoc was not part of France at that time," René said. "We, and as a native of the area I feel I can use the first person, even had our own Occitan language."

"And a beautiful language it was from what I hear," Lavinia said with a smile, "even more beautiful than French. Perhaps it reflected a culture that was more open as well?"

Before René could answer, Donald interrupted, "What I find ironic is that some of the crusaders who invaded Constantinople in order to convert the Bogomils to Catholicism, instead ended up being converted by them."

"To understand why it was such a threat to the Catholic Church, as Donald asserts," René said, his voice shifting from cheerful to professorial, "you must have a little more history. These Bogomils believed that this evil being, the Devil, fell from heaven. However, he was able to seduce a number of the souls of angels, and took them with him to his fallen state. He then created the material world where he entombed the souls. These angelic souls were trapped inside the matter that he'd created. It was this belief that the Cathars originally held, and it was only later that they came to believe that this being wasn't a fallen angel from heaven but, in fact, another god. An evil god who was coeternal and independent from the good, spiritual God, who remained in heaven, separated from the material world. That was what really caused the problem, because up until then their belief wasn't that inconsistent with the Catholic belief in the fall of man."

"Nicetas," Donald intoned, his voice rolling over René's. "That was the name of the Greek who persuaded the Cathars to change to the more absolute dualism from the more moderate form. Given all of the troubles that resulted, it reminds me of the saying, 'Beware of Greeks bearing gifts,' even if the gifts are spiritual."

That wasn't nice of Nicetas, I was about to say, but fortunately Rene saved me. "If it were only about the spirit, Donald, the Catholic Church would not have been so concerned. It was the fact that the Cathars had established four dioceses with their own bishops that really concerned the pope. These were facts on the ground, as one might say. They were a direct threat to the power of the Catholic hierarchy, and couldn't be ignored."

"But René, it wasn't just the establishment of the dioceses was it?" Lavinia said, then preceded to answer her own question. "Wasn't it also because the Cathar priests, who they called Perfecti, included women? What could be more threatening to the Catholic Church than women in positions of power?"

After waiting to see if Donald was going to jump in again, René responded, "You're quite right, Lavinia. The Perfectae, which was the name they gave the women, were a threat although they were relatively few in number. For that matter, there weren't many male Perfects either. Most of the Cathars were the Credentes, who were believers but not ready to fully commit themselves."

"Commitment is an understatement, René," Donald said. "The Perfecti lived a pure, anti-material, ascetic life. They refused to eat meat, eggs, or cheese and they fasted regularly – sometimes for as long as forty days." He paused and looked at his glass of wine. "That's what I was getting at when I said they wouldn't be seen at a party like this."

"You make them sound so boring, Donald," Lavinia said, not hiding her irritation.

"It's true that the Perfecti were living the pious life," René said, continuing to address those of us who were a captive if not captivated audience, "The contrast between the corruption of the Catholic Church and the puritanical behavior of the Cathars wasn't lost on the laity, and they began to actively sympathize with the Cathars. There was also the Cathar rejection of all of the sacraments, including the Eucharist. The

Consolamentum, the initiation ceremony the Credentes went through to become a Perfecti, wasn't taken lightly either, given the ascetic life that the Perfecti were expected to live. Most of the Credentes waited until they were on their deathbed, because they weren't sure they'd be able to live the life of a Perfecti. A deathbed conversion, you might say."

"However," Donald said, "the Credentes did go through the Convenientia in which they promised to receive the Consolamentum on their deathbed, if not sooner."

"That meant if you died prematurely," Lavinia added for our benefit, "your soul would need to start over in another body, which was very inconvenientia."

"It was even more inconvenient for the Catholic Church, as you know full well, Lavinia," Donald answered without even a smile. "After all, they were making money by selling indulgences that bought your soul's way into Heaven. You could even get your dead relatives out of Purgatory and into Heaven if you paid enough. It was like buying an eternal life insurance policy. No wonder they were threatened by the Cathars who didn't believe you could purchase salvation and that's why they were so ruthless in their persecution of them."

"You can't blame the persecution of the Cathars entirely on the Catholic Church," René said. "After all, it was the age of the feudal system and the feudal lords depended on the established Catholic Church for their legitimacy. Because of that, the Cathars were a threat to the established order, and were seen by many of the feudal lords as revolutionaries."

"As far as I can see the Church is still run like a feudal system," Donald said. "There is the pope as the king, then the cardinals and bishops are the lords with the dioceses as their fiefdoms."

"And the priests are the knights in shining surplices," Lavinia said. "Of course, everyone else is a peasant. It isn't just the Catholic Church since our own Church of England did away with the pope and made the king, himself, the head of the Church."

"In any case," René said, "the Cathars were proponents of a post-feudal system, one that was far more advanced. That is one of the reasons why they found such a receptive audience here, because Languedoc did not have as strong a feudal system as most other parts of Europe, including France. There was no king here. The most powerful person was Raymond VI of Toulouse. Although he was supposedly a Catholic, he protected the Cathars against the efforts of the Catholic Church to suppress them."

"He even had the pope's representative, his legate, Peter of Castelnau, killed," Donald said. "Castelnau was trying to stop the conversion of Catholics into Cathars. Unfortunately, he was more successful as a martyr since his death became the rallying cry for the pope, the crusaders, and the inquisitors."

"It was never actually proven, Donald," Lavinia said, "that the Count was responsible for the murder of Castelnau. There are those who think it was a false accusation and that the death of Castelnau was a convenient excuse to justify the Crusade and Inquisition."

"I must confess that I find myself agreeing with my wife," Donald sighed. "His death was the beginning of the end for the Cathars as well as an independent Languedoc. With the Pope's blessing, crusaders were recruited from all over Europe just as if they were going off to fight the infidels in the Holy Land. They were even offered indulgences if they joined the Albigensian Crusade."

"It wasn't just the indulgences that were offered," René added. "They were also promised land and property, the spoils of war. Languedoc, primarily because of its weak feudal system, had become quite wealthy from business and commerce. However, this weak feudal system that created a strong economy made it difficult to field a large and effective army as was the case where the feudal system was stronger. The fact that the Cathars tended to be pacifists didn't help either. As a result, the Count of Toulouse and the other lords of Languedoc depended on hired mercenaries. Near the end they were no match for the cohesive and committed army of crusaders led by Simon de Montfort and were quickly defeated. The Cathars would have been totally destroyed then and there if it hadn't been for the Pope's intervention. He didn't want to set a precedent by disinheriting Raymond's son. Such an action would have undermined the very feudal system that they were trying to defend. Instead, he issued a decree that Raymond VI's land would remain in trust for his son, Raymond VII. It turned out to be a big mistake because the son and father got together against the

Pope and the crusaders and, in the process, Simon de Montfort was killed."

"That was in 1218," Donald said, for our benefit, or at least for mine, since judging from Liv's expression, none of it seemed new to her. Good thing she's my research assistant so she can explain it all to me. The fact that I was secretly recording the conversation with a digital recorder in my pocket didn't mean I understood what was being said.

"Unfortunately, his death brought in the French monarchy," René said, picking up where Donald left off. "It was Louis IX, Saint Louis, who finally subdued and then annexed Languedoc to France with the Treaty of Paris in 1229. That was the plan all along, of course. The French rulers were just looking for an excuse to take over. Even then they didn't eliminate all of the Cathars. It took a combined effort of the inquisition and Saint Louis' army to finally defeat them. The Cathar fortresses were besieged and conquered one by one, including Montsaf. You could say, Mr. Scriviner, that Montsaf was a Cathar version of your American Alamo."

I tried to imagine a Cathar Davy Crockett as Donald asked René, "Does this chanson you've found have anything to do with who really killed Castelnau?"

"You know I can't answer that until tomorrow," René answered.

"That's right, we must have the suspense before we have scholarship," Donald sighed.

"Speaking of Peter of Castelnau," Lavinia said. "Isn't that Monsignor Vacluse with Madame Diderot? And, odd as it seems, I believe that is Declan Fox standing next to him."

Madame Diderot was talking to a stocky man with a tan that stretched over his sagging jowls. Brown, gray-tinged hair swept over his ears and back collar. He stood solidly, legs spread apart, bracing himself against the crowd that was now swirling around the room. The other man was much thinner, with short black hair that didn't come close to touching his Roman collar, the only white in his otherwise black on black wardrobe. He turned and scanned the room through silver-framed glasses, as if he were looking for someone in particular.

"I believe it is," Donald said. "I recognize Fox's face from the back cover of his books, which is the only page of his work that any serious scholar would ever read. The clerical collar seems to be a pretty good identification for the good father."

"And that blond woman next to Fox and the Monsignor?" René asked.

"She was the passenger in the red car sports car Fox was driving," Donald said.

"She might be his wife," Lavinia said.

"He's divorced," René said.

"Maybe she's his research assistant," I offered, giving Liv a sidelong look.

"Why don't we find out?" Liv asked.

As we approached, we could hear Vacluse's voice, which was as hard-edged as his facial expression. "The way that the

Crusades and the Inquisition have been misrepresented it is no wonder that people think the Crusades were done without any provocation and that the inquisitors were all demented sadists. But after 9/11 we can look at them with a new frame of reference. One cannot wait until one is invaded, you must take preemptory action. And it is not just action against an external enemy, but also against the moral weakness within that undermines our values and beliefs and makes it easy to be conquered or cowed."

"Let me get this straight, Padre," Fox said, not making any effort to hide his incredulity. "You're claiming that the Crusades and the Inquisition, in which thousands of people were burned at the stake or stoned to death, not to mention the thousands more who died while being tortured, was a war on terrorism?"

"I'm not saying the Cathars were terrorists, but remember that they started it by killing Peter of Castelnau. Instead of using reason to debate their beliefs they resorted to treachery. Why? Because their beliefs couldn't stand up to the light of day. In fact, their belief system was quite dangerous. It not only led many simple people to eternal damnation, but just look at how Hitler used it as a justification for Aryan supremacy and Nazism."

"Castelnau lost every debate he had with the Cathars," Fox countered. "Instead of winning people away from the Cathars, because of his ineptness he was one of their best recruiters. Whose interest did it serve to have him murdered? And equating the Cathars with the Nazis is baloney. That was the work of Otto Rahn." Cutting off any attempt by Vacluse to get a word in, Fox turned to us and, sensing an audience, he switched from Back Bay swagger to Brahmin Harvard lecturer. "For the rest of you who've been listening to our little debate, let me fill you in on Rahn. He was a German Nazi who spent 1931 and 1932 exploring Languedoc, researching the Cathars, the Knights Templar, and the Holy Grail. When he returned to Germany he wrote a book about his theories in which he reinterpreted the two major stories of the Holy Grail. The first one was *Le Conte del Graal*, about the knight Perceval's search for the Holy Grail written by Chrétien de Troyes and the second, *Parzival*, which was about the same knight but written by Wolfram von Eschenbach. Both were written between the late 12th and early 13th centuries. Wolfram claimed his was based on an earlier work by a Provençal poet named Kyot or Guiot although no one has been able to find the original. In any case, Rahn decided that these poems were really about the Cathars and the Albigensian crusade. He claimed that the Templars were also secretly Cathars and they brought the Holy Grail back from the Holy Land to Languedoc and that was the treasure kept at Montségur. According to Rahn, it was the Grail that was smuggled out of Montségur by four Cathars and hidden in caves. All of this Rahn claimed to have discovered by deciphering a sort of code that was imbedded in the poems about the Grail that I mentioned before. He wasn't the only one who thought that, by the way. Von Eschenbach, for example, placed the location of the Grail castle in the Pyrenees, and even Richard Wagner included that idea in the opera *Parsifal.*"

"You have left out that you agree with Rahn that there is a code," Vacluse said, arching his right eyebrow.

"Padre, Padre," Fox answered, shaking his head. "Just because I agree that there is something like a code doesn't mean I believe that Rahn figured it out, and it certainly doesn't mean that I share his belief that it justified the Nazis – that they were the forces of light fighting the forces of darkness."

"The forces of darkness being anyone who wasn't an Aryan fascist, which would include Jews and, as you are obviously aware, Roman Catholics," Vacluse retorted.

"Didn't Heinrich Himmler, Hitler's head of the SS, order Rahn to return to Languedoc to search for the treasure?" Madame Diderot asked.

"We know that Himmler sent him back here, but he was unsuccessful," Fox answered. "Himmler wasn't happy to say the least. Rahn resigned from the SS and committed suicide in 1939. Some people believe he faked his suicide, assumed a new identity and continued on his quest for the Grail."

"Perhaps someone should make a movie about Nazis who came here and found the Grail," Madame suggested.

"They already did; it's called *Raiders of the Lost Ark,*" Fox snapped.

Noticing me and Liv, particularly Liv, Fox introduced himself. The blond woman standing next to him quickly introduced herself as his personal assistant, Michelle Tavernier.

After the introductions, Madame Diderot resumed her questioning, "Do you believe this troubadour song that's been discovered contains some sort of code that you have been able to decipher? Is that what you will tell us tomorrow?"

"I'm afraid you will have to wait until tomorrow to find out, Madame."

"Breaking the secret code!" Madame Diderot clapped her hands as if she had been transported to public relations heaven. She turned to me, "Aren't you glad you're here, Monsieur Scriviner to get the scoop, as you journalists say, on the Cathar code?"

Fox protested, "Anything I say is off the record."

"Of course," Madame Diderot, replied, pressing her right index finger to her lips and turning to me. "It's for background only, Monsieur Scriviner. We certainly do not want anything to get out before we have all the press here. It's only fair."

"Remember, Madame, that there are other experts here as well," Vacluse said. "They may have a different interpretation than Monsieur Fox. One interpretation is that the chanson might be evidence that the Cathars were not as holy as they claim and that they were not innocent victims of an evil inquisition."

Madame Diderot put her right hand on Vacluse's wrist as if celibacy was no obstacle to her seductive abilities. "Monsignor, I am sorry if I gave you that impression. It certainly is not what I intended to convey."

Vacluse moved his arm away letting her hand suspended in mid-air. "And what did you wish to convey, Madame?"

"Come on, Padre, cut the Grand Inquisitor crap," Fox bellowed waving his wine glass. "Give her a break. She's only trying to do her job, which is to get some good press. God knows, the Vatican could use some, right now. Look at your pope, for God's sake."

Vacluse stiffened, "Really, I don't need to be lectured to by you. And quit referring to me as 'Padre' and insulting the Holy Father. The fact remains that the Cathars and their sympathizers started everything with the murder of Castelnau. Despite what you think, Fox, you have no proof that it was anything other than a cruel and murderous act, an act that brought into the open their true and evil nature. One could even say it was intended to provoke a violent confrontation. Now, I'm afraid that I must excuse myself. I have agreed to assist with Mass tonight." He looked at Fox, "I will tell you this, Monsieur Fox, it is not all about getting oneself in the press. Public relations might be the first thing on your mind, but it isn't for serious scholars."

As Madame Diderot walked Vacluse to the door, Fox emptied his glass of wine and said, "If not having a sense of humor made someone a great scholar, Vacluse would have a Nobel Prize. Imagine the Grand Inquisitor being awarded the Nobel Prize."

Madame Diderot returned and with a forced smile told us that the Monsignor wasn't as upset as it appeared and that he really did have to leave.

"I'm afraid we must leave as well, Declan," the blond woman said. "Remember the phone call?"

Fox looked at his Rolex, "Yes, Michelle, you are right." Turning to us he explained that he was expecting an important phone call from Hollywood about a documentary they want him to do. He tried to persuade them to pick a more reasonable hour but with the time difference, that would be asking them to get up before noon and it is Hollywood, after all.

"A documentary movie," Madame Diderot gushed. "I do hope that the discovery of the chanson will be in it."

"That's a bit premature, Madame," Fox replied.

After they left, Liv announced that we also needed to get back to the hotel. Madame Diderot looked at her slender, diamond studded watch and announced she had many things to do as well before tomorrow morning and asked if she could walk back with us.

***

On our way back to the hotel we came across Fox and Michelle, both of whom appeared shaken by something that had just happened. Standing next to them was the man in the black leather jacket.

"What happened?" Madame Diderot asked with alarm.

"Michelle and I were returning to the hotel when we were attacked by two men. They came from that street over there," Fox stammered, pointing to a narrow side street that was even darker than where we stood. "At first I thought they wanted an autograph but when I saw they were wearing ski masks, I decided it was something different they were after. When they grabbed Michelle it was pretty clear they weren't fans. I was about to free her when this gentleman arrived and they made a run for it. I would have gone after the bastards except I didn't want to put Michelle in harm's way." As Fox explained, Michelle glared at him, a far cry from the adoring look a damsel in distress would give her knight in shining armor.

"They must be from Marseille," Madame Diderot declared emphatically. "We don't have criminals who would perpetrate such a despicable act. A pickpocket or two, perhaps, but thugs who would accost someone like this, never! I'm sure that they are well on their way back to Marseille by now." Having firmly closed the case and just as firmly closed the discussion she took Michelle and Fox by their arms and led them away.

"Why would two professionals from Marseille come all this way to mug someone?" I asked the man in the black leather jacket.

"The answer is simple," he replied. "They didn't come from Marseille and they weren't professionals, at least not professional criminals."

"What makes you say that?"

"First, they wore those silly masks, and second, they stupidly thought he would give them what they wanted if they threatened his personal assistant. That's a mistake an amateur would make."

"I don't understand. If Fox didn't care about Michelle then why was he trying to free her when you came along?"

"That's what he would lead you to believe, but he was heading in the opposite direction from her and the assailants when I arrived.

"I'm not surprised," Liv said. "Fox is a jerk."

"But what do you think they were after?" I asked.

"This." He handed us a piece of paper. They dropped it when they ran off. The words printed in English on it were large enough to be read in the light of the full moon. It read, 'You must give us the copy of the codebook or you will never see your lady friend again.'

"But why hold her hostage when they could just go with Fox to the hotel and get the code themselves?" I asked.

"They may not have been professional crooks but they weren't so stupid as to think they could just walk into the hotel, stroll past the front desk wearing those ski masks and hustle Fox to his room without raising suspicion."

"Okay, that makes sense. But why did they write a note when they could have just told him what they wanted?"

He dropped the spent cigarette onto the stone and ground the embers with his shoe. "I don't think it was because they were trying to disguise a Marseille accent, as the Madame would probably suggest. My guess is that they didn't trust their English enough to believe he would understand them, and they assumed Fox didn't know French."

"Who do you think they are?" I asked.

The man shrugged. "Some people who believe the chanson is really a message in code and they think Fox has a codebook that can make sense of it, just as their note says."

"Should we tell the police?"

"No, we don't want them involved," the man replied firmly.

"And why should we do what you say?"

"Because we are all working together," Liv said, matter-of-factly.

"We are?"

"My name is Chêne," the man said as he held his hand out.

"And I thought you were a bad guy," I said as we shook hands.

Liv looked at Chêne, as a smile played across her lips, "Maybe he is."

***

Chêne tapped a cigarette against the back of his left hand in the dim light of Liv's hotel room. "Smoking is now forbidden in hotel rooms in France," Liv told him as she plopped onto the bed. The light from the lamp on the table next to the bed covered Liv and the bed and not much else in the room. "Besides, you have all of the outdoors to smoke in, so can't you allow me my tiny space?"

"Of course." He carefully placed the cigarette back in the pack.

"Thank you for respecting my rights," Liv said.

"As a Frenchman I deeply respect the rights of those who are constantly under threat from authoritarianism, terrorism, and religious fanaticism," he continued, covering all of the -isms. "For example, people believe that religious fanaticism and violence in the name of God is something new, but we have been living with it for centuries in France."

"As far back as the Inquisition and the Albigensian Crusade," Liv said.

"What's a thousand years when you're dealing with God and the Devil," Chêne replied, shrugging his shoulders.

"I have to say after listening to everyone talk about the Albigensian Crusade at the reception, I still don't understand why this Cathar chanson that's been discovered is so important."

"Then your research assistant should explain it to you," Chêne said, nodding at Liv.

Liv's face lit up, "Fox was right in that a lot of what we know about the Cathars and the Albigensian Crusade and even Occitania is from the troubadours, who wrote and performed in Languedoc. Most people think they were just singers in tights with mandolins, but they had a big influence on the politics of the time. Take Bernart de Ventadorn, the troubadour that Merwin wrote about. He was a major influence on Eleanor of Aquitaine. When Eleanor married Henry II of England, Bernart went with her to Henry's court and helped tutor their son who grew up to become King Richard the Lionhearted. Bernart had a real impact on Richard, who became somewhat of a troubadour himself, something that I'm sure didn't endear him to his father, who would have thought it was for sissies. However, when Richard became king, he turned into quite a warrior, which would have made his father proud. He was known as the crusader king because he led a crusade to drive the so-called infidels from the Holy Land, and also, incidentally, to find the Holy Grail. After Henry imprisoned Eleanor in what could only be called a display of uncourtly love, Bernart escaped and finally ended up in the court of none other than Raymond V of Toulouse. This was the very same Raymond who was planning to attack King Richard as he returned from the crusade. Raymond wanted revenge on Richard for all the pillaging by his crusaders while they marched through the duke's lands on their way to the Holy Land. Someone warned Richard, who, incidentally, was being guarded by the Knights Templar, and he took a detour to the east. Unfortunately, he was captured by the Austrians and kept a captive for a number of years."

I recalled Robin Hood and his merry men fighting the sheriff of Nottingham while they waited for King Richard to be freed and get rid of his evil brother Prince John. "At the reception, René said that Raymond helped the Cathars."

"That was Raymond VI, his son, and it was his grandson, Raymond VII, who was finally defeated by the French with the help of the Inquisition in the Albigensian Crusade."

"Seven was not a lucky number when it came to Raymonds," Chêne said.

Liv stretched toward the nightstand and retrieved a book. Scooting to the edge of the bed, she dangled her bare feet over the edge and paged quickly through the book. Then in a quick movement worthy of a gymnast she jumped up. For a few moments she swayed unsteadily on the mattress, her arms were stretched out, the right hand held the book. Finally, she stopped swaying and began singing. It wasn't the voice I'd expected. Instead of the one note shouting of the lead singer in a rock band there's a beautiful, rich soprano. I didn't understand a word of what she sang.

"It's in Occitan," she said when she had finished. "The translation is, 'Deceitful Rome, your greed leads you astray / You shear too much off your flock / May the Holy Spirit who took human form / Hear my prayer / And smash your beak!'" She stopped singing and looked at us. "That wasn't exactly what you expected, is it? A protest song rather than something romantic?"

"It depends on your idea of romance," Chêne answered. "It's been my experience that some people like the rough side."

Liv laughed, "You sound like someone who's smashed a few beaks."

***

Chêne and I both left Liv's room at the same time. Although the shadow on Chêne's face was way past five o'clock, he told me he still had some work to do. He agreed to let me accompany him, and skipping the elevator we took the stairs. On the ground floor we exited into the lobby and walked past the night clerk, who didn't look up from the magazine spread out on the front desk. The night air was cooler and there was a breeze that rustled the leaves in the square across from the hotel. In the center of the square Chêne stopped and lit a cigarette then pointed the pack of cigarettes at me.

"No thanks."

"So, you really don't smoke?" he sounded disappointed. As the end of his cigarette flared we walked toward the church on the far side of the square. Just before we entered the church he threw the half-smoked cigarette to the ground and, without breaking stride, squashed it with his right shoe. I'm not sure why he bothered, since the church was filled with lit votive candles and incense smoke. Electric lights offered only a feeble boost to the sputtering candles and we quickly slipped into the darkness behind the columns of the right aisle. We stopped just before the transept, where the sanctuary stretched out in both directions in the form of a cross. In front of the high altar, Monsignor Vacluse was mumbling a benediction as half a dozen congregants rose from their knees and crossed themselves. After Vacluse blessed each of them they turned and walked away. Chêne whispered for me to follow him and walked over to Vacluse.

"We'd like a word rather than a blessing," Chêne said and then told him about the mugging of Fox and his mistress.

"It is most distressing that there would be hooligans even here in such a peaceful community," Vacluse replied. "Why would they want to do such a thing?"

"Because he claims that he has a codebook that can decipher the chanson. Either they want to decode it themselves or they want to make sure no one else does, or both. I'm thinking both."

"Terrible," Vacluse said, shaking his head. "These people who accosted Monsieur Fox must be terrorists."

"Perhaps they were working for the Inquisition. Isn't that who you work for?"

"What? Why would you even say such a thing?" he asked, his hand flat on his chest as if he'd actually been wounded by what Chêne had said. "Everyone knows that the Inquisition is no longer part of the Church. Now, if you will excuse me, I must leave you. I am staying at the rectory and they are expecting me."

"Do you think he was lying about being a member of the Inquisition?" I asked Chêne after Vacluse left us.

"No, but only because he didn't deny he was a member. He only said it wasn't part of the Church."

We were interrupted by the sound of scuffling and a cry for help. Chêne dashed to the main aisle and turned sharply toward the rear of the sanctuary, knocking over several chairs. I followed him, tripping over one of the chairs. By the time I picked myself up and joined him he was helping Monsignor Vacluse to his feet. The Monsignor wobbled for a minute before finding his balance.

"What happened?" I asked, breathless from running the obstacle course.

"There were two of them hiding behind the column there. When they heard you coming they let me go and ran. I never thought that anyone would be so sacrilegious as to attack a priest inside the church," Vacluse answered as he brushed the dust off his cassock. "They said they wanted to show me what it was like to be tortured the way the Cathars were so it must have been that terrorist group, MAL."

***

There were only a handful of empty seats left when Liv and I entered the museum the next morning. The marble floor of the room where the reception had been held the night before was now covered with folding chairs. Five chairs were at the front of the room next to a lectern. To the left of the lectern, at the end of a central aisle, was an overhead projector facing a screen. "We have reserved the seats in the front row that you requested for you and your assistant," Madame Diderot said in a chirpy voice.

"I didn't ask for front row seats," I said to Liv.

"But a writer with *Travelux* shouldn't be relegated to the back," Liv answered with a Cheshire Cat smile. "I was happy that Madame Diderot agreed with me when I pointed this out to her yesterday."

We followed Madame Diderot down the aisle and took our seats in the front row. I was tempted to ask her if there was any word on the thugs from Marseille. After a few minutes, René walked to the lectern. There was a thumping sound, followed by a screech. "Sorry," he said, yanking his hand away from the microphone as if he'd touched a hot stove. "I was just checking to see if it was on." René welcomed everyone to the symposium, explaining that this was an historic moment. He described the purpose of the symposium as the unveiling of an historic document that was recently discovered.

"The document, as you all know, is a chanson, or poem, written by an unknown troubadour in the early 13th century. It is written in Occitan and is an account of the Albigensian Crusades. To discuss the meaning of the document, we have assembled an illustrious group of leading scholars."

On cue, the Pierce-Haydens, Fox, and Monsignor Vacluse appeared from a side door and lined up beside René. After being introduced, they sat down in the chairs facing us next to the lectern. "We will now show the document for the first time in public. No one on our expert panel has seen it until now. I will be using the original so that you all know that it is authentic." René picked up the briefcase that he had placed next to the lectern, unlocked it, and carefully pulled out what I could see, thanks to our vantage point near the projector, was a sheet of parchment-like paper sealed in plastic. He held it up so everyone could see. Then he took it over to the panel of experts and let each of them look at it briefly before he placed it on the flat glass of the projector and asked that the lights be dimmed. Instead of dim, the room suddenly went black. Since there were no windows in the room and the doors were shut everything went completely black. "Merde," René cursed then shouted, "Turn on the lights quickly, something is happening!" As he spoke there was the sound of footsteps, chairs being shoved aside, a side door opening and then slamming shut. When the lights came back on René stood beside the projector empty-handed.

***

"How did he get away?" Madame Diderot asked. We were standing near the open doors in the back of the hall.

"You have some reason to believe it was just one person?" Chêne asked.

"You think it was more than one?"

"I am open to the possibility."

"Well, of course, I agree it is possible."

"I agree that it must have been more than one person involved," Vacluse said. "One person to turn off the lights while their accomplice grabbed the document out of Professor Le Forge's hands. Then they both ran out the door."

"No, not necessarily," Chêne replied. "The one who grabbed the document could have remained here. In fact, both of them might have remained in the room, with one of them opening the door to make it look like they had escaped."

"Why would they do that?" Vacluse asked.

"Because they knew that most of the people in the room would run outside chasing the person who had escaped with the document. All that the real thief or thieves would have had to do was to infiltrate that group."

"Whatever happened, they're gone now along with the chanson," Donald said.

"I suppose they stole it for a ransom?" Madame Diderot sighed.

"Where will we get the money for a ransom?" Rene answered. "If we had money we wouldn't have had to hold this event in the first place."

"How much do you think these thieves would want?" Madame Diderot asked.

"Because I am the only person who has had a chance to examine it in detail I can only say that it is priceless." He looked at Madame Diderot, "As you know full well a decision was made that we should not let anyone else look at it until we unveiled it at this symposium in order maximize the publicity."

"Can you at least tell us what was written?" Lavinia asked. "When you showed it to us we only had a chance to see that the parchment appeared genuine and that it was written in Occitan."

"You should not divulge anything at this point, Professor," Chêne interrupted. "Like any investigation, it is better that the criminal does not know what we know. And there are likely to be a lot of people who claim they have it and want money for its return. The easiest way to determine who might be speaking the truth is if they can tell us something about it that only you know."

"You sound just like the police," Fox said.

"Maybe because I am a policeman," Chêne said, showing them his police identification.

Madame Diderot broke the stunned silence, "But certainly, you can trust us, Inspector."

"Why should he?" Fox, who had remained uncharacteristically silent, replied. "After all, one of us might be involved with the theft."

"Why would one of us want to steal it and then sell it back for ransom?" Donald asked.

"Perhaps the thieves aren't interested in ransoming it," Fox said. "If the chanson contained proof as to who really killed the papal legate, Castelnau, and started the Albigensian Crusade, then it would be in the interest of those who have something to lose by such a discovery to make sure it never comes to light," he turned to Vacluse, "Don't you agree Monsignor?"

"Not if you are accusing me of being involved in this crime," Vacluse replied, then asked, "What about this terrorist group MAL? Perhaps the chanson proves that the Count and the Cathars were murderers rather than the innocent martyrs they claim they are? Why, someone attacked me last night in the church after Mass and if it weren't for Inspector Chêne and Monsieur Scriviner I might be dead." He stopped then smiled grimly at Fox. "Perhaps you are involved because you knew that this theory of yours about a code would be exposed as a lie."

Fox's face flushed with anger, "Are you accusing me of being a liar and a thief who would steal the chanson in order not to be proven wrong? It's far more likely that those were your men who accosted Michelle and me and tried to steal the codebook so that it couldn't be decoded. When that didn't work because of Inspector Chêne's intervention you then stole the chanson yourself as a desperate attempt to cover up the Church's involvement."

"Gentlemen," Lavinia interrupted, sounding like a teacher breaking up an argument between two unruly schoolboys, "remember that René has examined the chanson." She turned to him, "René, without providing any details as the Inspector has warned against, can you at least tell us if it says anything that implicates the Inquisition or is written in code so that we can settle this argument?"

Everyone looked at René. "I'm afraid I must follow the Inspector's orders and say nothing at all on the subject. However, if either of you two are right in your accusations I am afraid that the chances of getting the chanson back are quite remote even if we had money for a ransom."

***

"Do you agree with the others that there's not much hope in recovering the stolen chanson?" I asked Chêne after we had returned to the hotel where we gathered in Liv's room.

"I believe it can be found, but it will require some of my best detective work."

"Of course," Liv said, folding her legs under her on the bed, "Chêne is on the case."

"Who are the suspects?" I asked.

"I have already narrowed it down to one suspect," he replied.

Surprised by his fast work I asked, "When will you make an arrest?"

"I have them cornered, you might say, and I don't think they will resist."

"Nor do I," Liv added.

"So, you admit that you are the perpetrator of this terrible crime," Chêne said, to Liv, sternly.

"I'm afraid I have no choice," she answered with another of her Cheshire Cat smiles. "I confess that I took the document."

"But how?" I asked, completely bewildered.

"When the lights went out, all I had to do was reach over and grab it."

"But where did you hide it?"

"In here," Liv unbuttoned the front of her loose blouse and pulled out the letter size, clear plastic envelope with the Chanson inside.

"The case is solved," Chêne announced while Liv buttoned up her blouse.

"But how did you know?" I asked, then quickly added, "But of course, you were in on it as well. It was you who turned out the lights. But why?"

"Are you asking out of personal curiosity?"

"No, for the Curiosi – for the record."

"In that case, I suppose we must answer or Leonard will be very upset with us," Liv said.

Chêne replied, "You have noticed that there is a great deal of interest in what the chanson says about the murder of Castelnau, an unsolved murder."

"Unsolved? It's eight hundred years old."

"Still, it is unsolved. And there is no statute of limitations when it comes to a murder such as this."

"You mean you stole it in order to pursue a murder case?"

"Stole? I would say that we confiscated evidence. The problem is that this is a very sensitive case. You probably noticed this from the emotions that have been displayed and the assaults on both Monsieur Fox and Monsignor Vacluse. What if the Inquisition, the Catholic Church itself, is involved, as Monsieur Fox seems to think? Or perhaps it is this group called MAL as Monsignor Vacluse claims? It is one of those cases that could lead to more harm than good if it is not handled very carefully. After all, the entire claim that France has on this region, indeed the entire south of France, might be cast into doubt if this chanson says that it was not the Count of Toulouse or the Cathars who were behind the murder."

"What about René? Remember that he examined it," I pointed out. "Won't he disclose what he read when he examined the chanson?"

"I think not."

"Why?"

"Because Leonard would be very upset with him," Liv said. "After all, it was René who asked us to help him. As soon as he examined the Chanson des Cathars, he knew it would be nothing but trouble if it was made public. It would create so much controversy there would be no chance for serious scholarship. Unfortunately, withholding it from the public was not his decision to make. As you yourself know, Madame Diderot and the people she represents care only about publicity, not about scholarship. He had to come up with a way to keep it from the public. René will lead the team of scholars that the Curiosi have assembled who will translate and decode it, if there is a code."

"And after that is done?"

She smiled at Chêne who smiled back. "That will be a decision René and the Curiosi will have to make."

"Can you read it to us?"

"I am not supposed to read it to anyone. We will transport it safely to a place where it can be examined by René and his team of experts." Her face brightened, "But since I am a troubadour I will sing it, in Occitan, of course."

***

Although I didn't understand a word, Liv sang beautifully and I caught myself humming it the next morning while taking a shower. I wanted to tell her, but when I was checking out, Charles informed me, in a voice tinged with disappointment, that she had left an hour before. "I hope that you were pleased with your stay and that you will convey to the readers of *Travelux* that we strive for perfection."

"I assume you don't mean perfection the way the Cathars did?" I asked, arching my right eyebrow.

"How do you mean?" Charles asked, his voice registering more than a little anxiety.

"From what I understand they considered luxury as a barrier to perfection," I said, then quickly reassured him, "a view of perfection that the readers of *Travelux* don't share, by the way."

***

I walked alone across the bridge feeling my own disappointment at not having a chance to say goodbye to Liv. It looked like the same fly fishermen as the day before were casting their lines in the river below. One had reeled a fish in and was removing it from the hook. Instead of keeping it he gently placed it in the water and let it swim away. I wondered if over the past couple of days I hadn't been subjected to a human version of catch and release.

When I got to the parking area, Liv's Ducati was gone. At the bus, Claude greeted me like a long-lost friend. He told me I had made it just in time and that everyone else was already aboard. I apologized and added, "At least you won't have to provide any narration on the trip back since we already saw everything on the way here."

He shrugged his broad shoulders and answered, "You may be surprised at how different things can look when you are traveling the opposite direction."

Really? I thought as I climbed up the steps into the bus. Chêne was in the same window seat he'd occupied on the trip up. He had a newspaper in his lap. It was open to the sports page. I was about to pass him when he looked at me and patted the empty seat.

Claude greeted everyone and settled into the driver's seat. Then, after closing the door, he put the bus in gear and we pulled out. I waited for Chêne to initiate the conversation but he was looking out the window. Maybe since he'd been reading his newspaper on the way up he wanted to see the scenery on this way down. I pulled out my notebook and was writing when the air brakes went off and the bus came to sudden halt. A long black van filled the front window. It was parked sideways across the road, blocking all but a small opening near the edge where the road dropped off into a ravine. A couple of men with black ski masks hiding their faces and brandishing handguns approached the bus. After knocking on the door of the bus, Claude opened it and they stepped inside and stood at the front. One of them pointed his pistol at Claude and the other one aimed his at us.

"Pardon the inconvenience," one of them said. "We are looking for someone."

"And who exactly are you?" Donald piped up from behind us.

The man shifted the barrel of his gun in Donald's direction. "We are with MAL, so you should take us seriously."

"You heard the man, Donald," Lavinia said with alarm.

The man walked down the aisle while the second remained at the front with his pistol still pointed at Claude. When he got to us he stopped.

"Where is your friend?"

"Friend?" Chêne answered, looking up from the newspaper.

"The mademoiselle, you know?"

"What mademoiselle?" Chêne folded the paper and put it on his lap.

"Don't play games with me. We saw you together, both of you." He waved the gun barrel at us.

"Oh, her. She left earlier," Chêne answered matter-of-factly.

"She had alternative transportation," I added.

"We have been here for more than two hours and no one has come by."

"Maybe she went the other direction," Chêne offered.

"We also have people stationed on the road going north."

"But why do you want to find her?" Chêne asked.

"Because she has it."

"It?"

"The chanson," the man replied. "Do you think we are so stupid we couldn't figure it out?"

"Then you can figure out where she is."

"If she isn't here maybe you or someone else on the bus has it?" He turned and announced to all of us, "Everyone must come outside so we can search you and your baggage."

Before we could respond there was the full-throated roar of a motorcycle. We looked out the window next to Chêne where a motorcycle, its helmeted rider clad in black leather, had stopped. A gloved hand flipped up the tinted visor of the helmet and Liv's face appeared with a broad smile. Before the man could aim his gun at her she quickly pulled the visor down and the motorcycle shot forward past the bus and through the narrow gap between the edge of the road and the van. The two men cursed and ran outside, rushed to the van and clambered inside. They started the van and put it in reverse so they could point it down the road and give chase to Liv. At the same time Chêne pushed past me and ran to the front of the bus where he said something to Claude. Claude quickly put the bus in gear and it lurched forward ramming the rear bumper of the van before the van's driver could shift out of reverse and into a forward gear. Our bus continued to push it off the road until it rolled over the edge and into the ravine. Claude applied the air brakes, opened the door, and he and Chêne walked over and looked down into the ravine. A minute later they returned, closed the door and Claude put the bus in gear and we started back down the road.

Chêne returned to his seat next to me.

"Shouldn't we call an ambulance?" Lavinia shouted.

Claude moved the microphone into position and answered. "Mobile phones don't work at this particular spot. No doubt that is one of the reasons why they selected it as a place to waylay our bus. However, the ravine is not as steep as it is in other places and the van rolled down into a vineyard. We observed the two men getting out so they apparently are not injured. However, since they are armed and presumed dangerous I don't think it wise to stay here. Instead, we should proceed until we get out of this dead zone and I can call the local police."

"You should get a medal for saving us," Donald yelled. This was followed by applause.

"I was merely doing my duty," Claude answered, although he took a bow despite the claim of modesty. "After all, I am responsible for my passengers."

"Just like the captain of a ship," Lavinia piped up.

"Fortunately, I didn't have to go down with the bus," Claude laughed then started the bus.

"Did you know Liv was using a motorcycle as her alternate form of transportation?" I asked Chêne as he pulled out the newspaper that he'd placed in the sleeve of the seatback in front of him.

"Of course. You can see what would have happened if she had been on the bus with us."

"Yes," I whispered. "But what I don't understand is why Liv didn't turn her bike around when she saw what was happening and then pulled up her helmet visor so they could see her face? It was like she wanted to save us but the worst thing that would have happened is that they would have searched us and let us go. Instead, she risked being caught and them finding you know what."

Chêne opened the folded newspaper on his lap. Rather than the sports stories that I expected to see there was the envelope with the Chanson de les Cathars inside. He quickly turned the page, hiding the envelope behind photos of brawny soccer stars and scantily clad women. "From what I understand from René, the Cathars were dualists who believed there were two primary forces in conflict with each other," he whispered, "and since this is also what sports fans believe, I think that hiding the Chanson inside the sports page is appropriate, n'est-ce pas?"

"Perfecti."

5

PROJECTION POINT

Venice, Italy - October 1992

After landing at Marco Polo Airport I took the ferry, and the boat was already plowing through the blue green waters toward Venice by the time I entered the cabin. There was plenty of space on the benches, so I picked a spot on the port side behind a German couple who were seated across the aisle from their two young sons. The only other passenger was a hefty American who sat directly behind the boys. He had a map of Venice spread out on his lap and held it in place with his left hand while his right hand gripped a worn leather briefcase resting next to him. I had been to Venice several times, but each time was like the first time and I still didn't know my way around.

I took a deep breath of the salty sea air blowing in through the window that one of the boys had opened. As we approached the Island of the Dead, a half dozen pallbearers were hoisting a coffin from a flower-laden gondola. The two boys fought to see who could get the best view of the coffin. Death was only a rumor for them. The older and bigger one finally shoved his kid brother away from the window, so he could get a better view. As the child skidded across the seat and was about to bounce onto the floor his father grabbed him like he was fielding a line drive and handed him to the mother. Then the father pried the older boy loose from the window. Spray shot through the open window and plastered the American. His face dripping, he leaned forward, across the empty space and closed the window. The map on his lap slid to the floor. I picked it up and handed it to him.

"Thanks," he said. "I figure this map will come in mighty handy. From what I've heard you can get lost in Venice quicker than a penny and I'm pretty much a penny pincher." He spoke with an accent that reminded me of cowboys and he pointed a thick finger toward the bow of the boat where Venice floated on the horizon. "By golly, that's like seeing the front range of the Rocky Mountains from the Great Plains."

I'd only seen the Rockies from the window of a plane flying over them on the way to California. They didn't seem real looking down at them from thirty thousand feet. Neither did Venice from a boat at sea level.

***

It was a small hotel, but, unlike the one in Sarajevo, where I'd recently spent a lot longer than I'd intended, the Hotel Alto hadn't been whittled down by war. When I checked in, the desk clerk informed me that the bill had been taken care of and gave me a note from Signor Bassantino. After taking an elevator slightly larger than a coffin to my room, I tossed my bag on the bed and opted for the stairs down to the wine bar next to the hotel's restaurant. The wine bar was small and windowless with a barrel ceiling of thick stone and a damp coolness that was probably good for the wine. It reminded me of the cellar in the Sarajevo hotel. That one didn't have booze or food but since it was also the bomb shelter, it was standing room only whenever I was there as opposed to here where I was the only customer inside. I took my glass of wine and went outside into the sunlight.

"Signor Flynn?"

I looked at the dapper man in the white linen suit sitting at one of the half dozen small marble-top tables outside the entrance to the wine bar.

"Signor Bassantino?" I asked as I approached.

He stood and replied, "Sì, but please call me Ugo."

"Dante."

"Such a magnificent name. I wish my parents had been as literary-minded when they named me."

I took the seat beside him, where I could sit with my back to the wall and see the canal. On the other side of the canal a wooden rowboat was tied to an iron ring set into a brick wall.

Cut into the wall above the ring was a heavy wooden door and on either side of the door there were two windows. Above the windows were two more floors, each with five windows. The door was closed and all of the windows were shuttered. Everything seemed secure so I looked at Ugo who had raised his glass in a toast.

"I was named after my maternal grandfather, who immigrated to America from Italy. He was the literary one," I said, leaving out that when I was growing up the other kids teased me about the name so I went by Dan instead. It wasn't until college when I read Dante's *Inferno* in freshman English that I realized the name was actually cool.

"Let me be the first to welcome you back to your ancestral home."

"I've lived in Italy for fifteen years."

"Of course, I know that. You live in Rome so that is why we have not met before even though you have worked for us several times. What I meant is welcome back from your recent trip to Yugoslavia."

"The former Yugoslavia," I corrected him politely.

"Ah, yes, the country of Yugoslavia no longer exists."

"Some people say it existed more as a Frankenstein's monster stitched together by Marshall Tito than as a nation."

Ugo gave a sympathetic frown, "In any case, I imagine it was not a pleasant experience for you."

"At least I got out." I sipped the wine. It was a Brunello. My first glass of good wine since I'd left Italy two months ago to cover a war that I thought would be over in two weeks. "By the way, thanks for arranging to get me out. I know you, the Curiosi, have some pull but how you were able to get me a ride in one of the military convoys that made it out of Sarajevo..."

He held up his hands as if it were nothing, "We did not want you to miss your assignment for us. It was not as if you could call for a taxi or hitchhike."

I looked at the calm waters of the canal only a few meters away. One of the shutters opened on the top floor. It was the middle window. A man wearing a crisp white shirt leaned on the sill with a cigarette in his right hand watching a young woman in a tight black skirt and long black hair who walked toward us on our side of the canal. Although she was wearing stiletto heels she managed to miss the cracks in the stone without looking. Trailing her by a couple of meters was a black gondola, its gondolier stirring his pole in the thick water.

"Speaking of hitching, the first time I was in Yugoslavia, or what was then called Yugoslavia, I was hitchhiking with a girl from California I'd met at a youth hostel in Vienna. The deal between us was that she would stand by the side of the road and get us the rides and I would protect her from the driver. It was strictly utilitarian on her part. She needed to get to Dubrovnik where she was going to meet up with some guy she knew who had a yacht, and they and some friends were going to sail down to the Greek islands."

"Sounds very romantic," Ugo said.

"It probably was, but I wasn't invited for that part. In any case, it meant that I had to sit in the front seat while she sat in the back, out of the reach of the driver's frisky fingers. Of course, the guys who picked us up weren't interested in me so they spent more time looking at the blond in the back seat instead of the road in front of us as we're going down the Dalmatian coast on narrow two-lane roads with nothing but curves and rocky cliffs. Still, that first time hitching into Yugoslavia wasn't as scary as the ride I took out of there in that military convoy."

Ugo nodded his head and we sat there in silence as still as the water in the canal. I took another sip of wine and looked at the woman in the stiletto heels as she turned and stepped onto the bridge over the canal. She was walking slowly, her hips swayed and her dark hair rustled in the breeze. The man in the window leaned over the sill, cocking his right elbow, this time aiming his cigarette at her. I reminded myself this wasn't Sarajevo. The woman looked up at him and then down at the gondola and began to lose her balance. She grabbed the railing and steadied herself. Once back on her heels she released her grip and continued across the bridge, the trailing fingers of her left hand stroking the iron railing just as the high prow of the gondola approached. The gondolier looked to the left as the woman reached the far side then quickly ducked his head just as the gondola entered the darkness under the bridge. The man in the window flicked his cigarette into the canal where the gondola had been and closed the shutters.

"Buongiorno," a voice boomed, surprising me. Red Brunello spilled out of my glass onto the white marble tabletop before I steadied my hand. I looked up at a man in his early twenties with a tanned, relaxed face an easy smile and an expensive pair of sunglasses.

"Niccolò," Ugo answered, "this is Signor Dante Flynn."

Niccolò slid into the empty chair next to me and shook my hand, "It is a great pleasure to meet you Signor Flynn."

"Just call me Dante."

"A good name."

"So I've been told."

"Niccolò is going to take you to the meeting with the people whose case you'll be writing about," Ugo explained then said goodbye and walked off.

***

"You had no problem finding your hotel?" Niccolò asked me as we began walking to wherever the meeting Ugo had mentioned was going to take place.

"I took one of the boats from the airport to San Marco where I caught a water taxi. I've been to Venice before but I can't say where we are exactly other than we're not that far from the Grand Canal."

He gave me a smile that looked as comfortable on him as his sunglasses. "You are correct, but, of course, everything in Venice is not far from the Grand Canal."

"I guess not since it cuts Venice in half."

"More or less, but neither side feels they get the lesser half. However, the Grand Canal curves like a snake so that at any particular point it is not easy for someone who is not familiar with Venice to know exactly where they are relative to the Grand Canal."

"So which direction is it from here?"

He looked both ways then pointed to the right, past the arched bridge in the direction the gondola had taken. "It is that direction."

"For a second there I thought you didn't know where we were."

He laughed and stood up. "I had to think because since we are on an island, it can be reached by going in the opposite direction, as well." He pivoted and pointed the other way. "You see if you go that direction when you reach the water, which is the Giudecca Canal, then you can go in either direction and eventually you will arrive back at the Grand Canal. If you know that then you will never be lost in Venice, at least not forever." He paused as if he wanted to give me time for this to sink in, and then asked me if I liked the hotel.

I told him that I did. "This part of Venice, wherever it is, seems very quiet. In fact, just before you arrived I was thinking how peaceful it was."

"You want peace?"

"I just came from Sarajevo so a little bit of peace goes a long way."

"Then you are in the right place, because this fondamenta is especially peaceful."

"Fondamenta? I thought a street that runs next to a canal is called riva?"

He shook his head slowly and answered, "It is a common mistake. However, a riva is a street that runs along a much larger canal than this or the lagoon."

"What do they call a street that isn't next to a canal?"

"A calle, or a calletta if it is a narrow calle, unless it is lined with shops, in which case it is a ruga or a main street, which is a salizada, or if it is a covered passage, it would be called a sotoportego. Then there is the ramo, which is a street that ends at a canal and, of course, there is the rio terà, or river of earth, which is the name for a canal that has been drained and filled in so that you can now walk on it. For those who give up trying to understand which is which, they are all called a riva derci."

After I finished laughing at his joke, another thing I hadn't done much of recently, he added, "Speaking of rio terà, my favorite name is the one called Rio Terà dei Pensieri, 'Filled In Canal of Thoughts.'"

"Does that mean it's a canal that is filled with thoughts or a canal where all thought has been covered up?"

"Perhaps both. Although we Venetians never cover up our thoughts completely, we disguise them very well. Of course, most of our canals are filled with water. In fact, Venice has 177 of them and their total length is more than 45 kilometers. The Grand Canal alone is 3 kilometers long. It is 90 meters at its widest and 3 meters at its narrowest where it flows under the Rialto Bridge. Coincidentally, the average width of all of the canals is only 3 meters." As he spoke I noticed that his torso hardly moved as he walked, as if he was in a gondola gliding along beside me while I bounced up and down on the riva's uneven stones.

"The Rialto," he continued, "was named after the Rivo Alto because in the beginning the Lagoon that surrounds us was all mud and the Rivo Alto was one of three rivers that ran through it. We Venetians kept building on this mud until we constructed an island, which is Venice. At that point the Rivo Alto was no longer a river so it became the Grand Canal. Now it flows only with the tide." He stopped and looked at me again to see if any of these facts had sunk in.

"In other words, Venice was created out of mud like Adam in the Bible."

He put his hand on my shoulder and smiled, "Ah, that is very good. I will use that in the future when I give a tour, with your permission, of course."

"If anyone asks just tell them you got it from a source who wishes to remain anonymous."

After walking for a short while more, Niccolò pointed across the canal. There were several black gondolas nestled on a stone ramp in front of a two-story wooden structure with wide double doors that made it look like a barn. "You see that building over there? It is a squero, a boatyard where they build and repair gondolas. Although gondolas are very strong with eight different woods, they must be scraped and tarred once a month or they will rot and then you are in big trouble. We could use metal or fiberglass or some other synthetic material, but then they would not be true gondolas. Gondolas have changed very little in the thousand years since they were introduced to Venice."

"Where did they come from originally?"

"From Turkey, just like the body of our patron saint, San Marco. At one time there were as many as ten thousand gondolas but now there are only a few hundred so we must take care of those we still have. It is very sad that there are so few. Most of the gondoliers come from families who have passed the trade down from generation to generation but the young people today, they only want to go fast. It is very sad because if it continues we will not have enough for the Traghetto."

"Isn't that the name for the gondolas that are used as ferries?"

"No, those are traghetti. The Traghetto is the guild that every gondolier must join. Although each gondola is privately owned, the Traghetto protects the rights of the gondoliers as well as the tradition." He added solemnly, "Every gondolier is like a brother."

"Are women gondoliers like sisters?"

"We don't have any women gondoliers," he laughed heartily. "Perhaps it is because we treat our sisters much better than we do our brothers."

As we crossed the canal on a humpbacked bridge, my shoes slipped on stones worn icy smooth from the glacial rub of centuries of soles. An elderly man who was unmistakably American walked from the other direction up the incline, gripping the wrought iron handrail with one hand and clutching a map with the other. He stopped, rested heavily against the railing, and waved at us with the unfolded map. Niccolò switched from Italian to near perfect English as he asked if he could be of assistance.

The man thrust the map at Niccolò, "How does anyone find their way around this place?"

Niccolò took the map and spread it out on the railing of the bridge and politely asked the man, "Where is it that you wish to go?"

"A place called the Academy. My wife and the rest of the tour are there already. They took a boat but I wanted a break. It's mostly women, you know. Anyway, I figured I could walk it with no problem since I play golf everyday back in Boca Raton, – that's in Florida, in the USA – but this map is about as helpful as a plate of spaghetti. In fact, it looks like a plate of spaghetti."

Niccolò listened patiently before responding, "The place you are looking for is the Accademia, where many of the works of our most famous artists are on exhibit."

"Another damned museum. I was hoping it might be your naval academy, this being Venice. I was in the US Navy, myself."

"I am afraid Venice no longer has its own navy, Signor. But the good news for you is that there is a very nice bar opposite the entrance that overlooks the Grand Canal where you can look at the boats as they go by. You see it is right here," Niccolò pointed to a spot on the map. "It is not far."

The man bent down and looked at the map, "You say that's close, huh? But where exactly am I right now?" He looked around, gripping the rail of the bridge as he straightened himself.

Niccolò traced a line with his finger on the map as he answered, "You are right here on this bridge. Now, first, you must continue across this bridge and then you turn right at the first street and you continue on that street until you come to a little square where there is a restaurant and then you turn left. You must go on that street until you cross another canal and then you turn left and follow the canal for a short distance until you reach the Accademia. You see, it is very simple."

"Simple? Maybe to someone who's done it a million times," the man said. "Anyway, you say there's a bar next to it where I can have a beer while looking at boats instead of art?"

"Absolutely, the bar you cannot miss."

"Thanks, I mean grazie," the man said as he made his way down the opposite side of the bridge, holding the map in front of him and still gripping the railing with the other.

***

A few minutes later we turned our back on the canal we had been following. In front of us was a passageway between two palazzos. "Now, this is a calle," he announced. "As I told you earlier, a calletta would be much narrower and also it would be darker. In fact, there is one named 'Alley of the Blind' because it is so dark you must use your hands instead of your eyes to guide yourself and there is another one that is only a meter wide." He held his hands apart, adjusting the distance until he was satisfied that it approximated a meter, which didn't seem much narrower than the one we were about to enter. "You cannot allow yourself to get fat or you will soon find yourself stuck in one of them."

"They must call it the Venetian diet," I said as I followed him into the calle whose walls seemed on the verge of collapse. A few minutes later when the calle opened onto a broad sunlit plaza, I suddenly felt exposed and had to fight the urge to duck back into the safety of the trench we'd just left.

"This is one of my favorite campi," Niccolò told me, "because of the trees, which are very rare in Venice."

I just stared as he spoke until everything came safely into focus: the trees next to the fountain in the center, the buildings with the shuttered windows and weathered stucco and benign cracks with brick peeking through, and the cafés that spread out along the edges of the campo with people sitting and reading or talking and sipping wine or espresso while others walked across the broad, sun-bleached stones, through the filigree shadow net cast by the trees before disappearing into one of the passages.

"Is something wrong?" Niccolò finally asked.

"Not a thing," I answered. "It's just that the trees and all the calli opening off the campo reminded me of the passage in Dante's *Inferno* where he wrote of waking up in the middle of his life in a dark woods and not knowing which path to take to get out."

Niccolò sighed, "Yes, I can see what you mean. Fortunately, Dante had no trouble finding his way out of Venice after he completed his diplomatic mission here."

"As I recall he died of malaria shortly afterwards," I answered with a slightly forced laugh as I stepped gingerly into the campo.

As we approached the trees a small dog ran toward me barking, followed by an elderly woman dressed in black who yanked on his leash snapping the dog back onto his hind legs. The dog turned to look at her and then resumed his attack, dragging the frail woman. Niccolò had already disappeared into one of the calli on the far side so I took off in a fast trot in the same direction with the dog yapping behind me. When I got to the entrance to the calle it was deserted. I continued at a jog for several meters when suddenly I was grabbed and pulled through a cleft in the wall.

"Dante did not escape death but this Dante," Niccolò poked my shoulder, "has escaped from the little dog from hell."

I followed him through the dark tunnel until we came out into the daylight. Directly in front of us was a canal with a gondola moored to an iron ring in the fondamenta. The fondamenta followed the canal for only a few meters before it reached a dead end at a bridge.

"This must be a ramo since it rams into the end of the canal," I said.

Ignoring my wisecrack, Niccolò replied, "You are correct that this is a ramo. It empties into the Grand Canal just beyond that opening," he pointed to the slot in the stone and stucco walls beyond the arched bridge that ended at the massive door of a palazzo.

"So we use the gondola to get to the Grand Canal?"

"No, our destination is the Scuola di San Dismas, that palazzo on the other side of this bridge."

"Saint Dismas? Isn't he the patron saint of thieves?"

"You are correct. He was the good thief who was hung on the cross next to Jesus. Although the Bible doesn't give his name, the Greek word for dying is dysme. Not that I can personally verify that since the only words in Greek I know I picked up while on holiday on Mykonos and none of them have to do with dying. However, it does not really matter because the Scuola is not named for San Dismas because he was a thief, but because he is also the patron saint of antiquaries. The Scuola was established as a confraternity for antiquarians. It is a truly secret organization even for a confraternity, and isn't on any maps nor is there a sign outside that identifies it."

By now we had crossed the bridge and were at the massive door, which had a large black metal knocker shaped like a raven. Niccolò rapped the beak against the door several times then we waited a minute or so before it slowly swung open. Standing in the doorway was a man with thick hair in the same shade of gray as his bushy eyebrows. He wore a dark blue suit whose coat was unbuttoned, having lost its struggle to contain his barrel chest and broad shoulders.

"This is my grandfather, Emilio. He will take you to meet the dottore," Niccolò said, and immediately sat down at a small desk with a black rotary telephone on it.

***

Emilio ushered me through a door with a brass plate on it that said 'Map Room' in Italian. "Buongiorno, Signor Dante Flynn." A slim, balding man with a black goatee trimmed to a dagger point greeted me as soon as I entered the room, "I am Dottore Federico Presti and this is Signor Harold Bunch, who also just arrived in Venice."

The man standing next to him grabbed my hand and pumped it enthusiastically, "Why, we already know each other, Fred. Just call me Harry, by the way," he said to Federico. "We both took the same slow boat to Venice from the airport. I must admit I was tempted to take one of those speedboat taxis they've got here instead."

"You mean the motoscafi," Federico replied.

"Whatever you fellows call them. They remind me of the speedboat that the Hardy Boys had," Harry said as he sat down in a straight back chair, which looked too frail to support him.

"The hearty boys?" Federico asked.

"The Hardy Boys," I answered, emphasizing the 'd', then sat down carefully in one of the other antique chairs. "They were two teenagers who were amateur detectives and they had a motorboat, a sports car, and motorcycles."

"I don't remember the motorcycles," Harry said. "I just remember the speedboat in the *Clue In The Embers.* That was my favorite book as a kid because it had a map of buried treasure. If you don't mind me being nosy but how did a kid who read the Hardy Boys end up with a name like Dante?"

"Dante was my grandfather's name on my mom's side. My mom's family immigrated to the States from Italy when she was a kid. After my parents were married they lived in the same house as my grandparents and didn't move out even after they had me and my sister. We spoke Italian around the house, except my dad who was Irish as you probably figured out from my last name. To make a long story short, my dad still had the Hardy Boys books that he'd read when he was a kid, and I read them all."

"You know, maybe we are like the Hardy Boys on this assignment, aren't we?" Harry said.

"I don't think Signora Evesham, who you will be meeting later, would want to be referred to as a hardy boy," Federico said.

Harry laughed. "She can be Nancy Drew. She was a girl detective who had her own series of books, so she didn't have to share the leading role with a sibling."

Federico gave us a look that told us he wanted to change the subject to something more serious than teenage detectives. Instead of joining us in one of the chairs he walked over to the massive oak library table that faced us. Resting on one end of the table was a globe and on the other a bust of a noble Roman that was missing its left ear. Next to the bust was a black telephone similar to the one on Emilio's desk. Against the walls were mahogany bookcases that rose to the ceiling as well as framed maps and paintings with gods and goddesses, nymphs and satyrs cavorting in the woods or dancing among Roman and Greek ruins. There were other statues and busts of Romans and Greeks scattered around the room and, like the bust on the table, many were missing some piece of their anatomy.

"Some digs, huh?" Harry observed looking around, with a 'by golly' smile. "The room that they put me in is just a tad smaller than this one. Good thing it doesn't have a painting on the ceiling like the one up there." I followed his eyes to the painting on the ceiling. It depicted a group of men dressed in Renaissance garb seated in several tiers of concentric circles looking down on us. "Because, to tell you the truth, there's no way I'd be able to sleep with those guys watching me."

"Those guys, as you call them, were all leading members of the Scuola in the middle of the 16th century," Federico said, his explanation just short of admonishment. "The man sitting in the top row with the red hat painted it."

"Don't they make you nervous looking down at you like that?"

"Not really."

"Do they ever give advice?" Harry asked.

Federico decided to ignore the question and told us that before we met Signora Evesham he wanted to give us some historical background concerning geography and cartography.

"I think it will be helpful since our investigation involves those subjects."

"Let her rip, Fred," Harry said, settling into his chair as if it was a recliner. "You're the Dottore."

"Thank you, Harold," Federico answered, clearly not feeling comfortable calling him Harry. "Although Dottore is an honorific that is used in Italy and doesn't necessarily mean one has a doctoral degree, although I have a PhD in geography."

"That makes you a doctor, Dottore," Harry said, twirling the toe of one of his cowboy boots. "And in geography of all things. By golly, I am impressed. All I know about maps is what I learned in the Boy Scouts."

Federico gave a quick look up at the old men staring down from above then began his lecture. "Geography as a discipline evolved from astronomy."

Harry immediately interrupted him, "I would have thought it would have been the other way around."

"Then you would be wrong," Federico replied with a slight smile. "Mapping the stars enabled man to map the world, allowing him to determine where he was at any particular time by plotting it relative to the heavens. The earliest practitioners of geography that we know of were the Greeks, but only because they left a written record. The Greek philosopher Pythagoras deduced the earth was round and Aristarchus claimed the earth rotated almost 2000 years before Copernicus. In the 1st century Strabo wrote a book called *Geography* in which he estimated the earth's circumference to be 18,000 miles. That turned out to come up 7,000 miles short but it was a good estimate given that most people had not ventured beyond the Mediterranean. Then Claudius Ptolemy came along in the 2nd century and wrote his eighth book, *Geographia*, the only atlas of the world to survive for the next thousand years. Nothing is known about Ptolemy except that he knew his math and astronomy and his way around a library. Whether he was an original thinker or passing on what he'd heard from others we will never know, but *Geographia* separated the earth from the heavens and gave us geography and cartography."

"Sounds like it's some sort of spiritual activity the way you put it, Fred," Harry said, reverently.

"I wouldn't say spiritual, Harold. This is science after all." Federico walked over to the globe on the table where he paused to look at it as if it were a crystal ball and pointed to the top and then the bottom. "Now, Ptolemy was the one who proposed that all maps have north on the top and south on the bottom. No doubt he proposed this because most of the known world at that time was north of the equator. He also gave us what was called the orthographic projection in which the round earth can be converted to a map on a flat surface." He took the globe in his hands then put it back. Then with a flourish he picked up a map that had been lying unseen on the table and held it up for us to see like a magician who had conjured something out of thin air. "You see he subdivided the surface into parallels running east and west that form latitudes and meridians that run north and south to form longitude, each with the 360 degrees of a circle.

With this you could begin to know where you were, or where anything was on earth, if you knew your position in the heavens using stars and sun. Another innovation of his were scales so that the map of the world can be subdivided into areas that can be mapped in more detail and still fit into the larger map and, finally, he gave us a method of illustrating features on a map, what are called hachures."

Federico put down the map and, in a solemn voice, recounted how the Dark Ages arrived and brought back the flat world. Latitude and longitude were replaced by images of devils and dragons and all sorts of fantastic beasts and serpents. He illustrated this period by walking over to one of the framed maps on the walls and pointing at a square world surrounded by water with a border of grotesque creatures in menacing poses. In one corner was the biblical land of the evil tribes Gob and Magog, he told us, and in the upper right-hand corner was Paradise. In between was the fictitious Christian realm of the Prester John. "Although some adventurers claimed to have reached Paradise, Pope Innocent IV's special emissary to Prester John never returned."

"I know that I sure as heck wouldn't want to return from Paradise." Harry's laugh as he said this was accompanied by the rattle of the chair he was sitting in.

There was a flush of fear on Federico's face as if he was afraid that the antique chair would collapse under the torque generated by Harry's belly laugh. After biting his lip, he continued, using the map to illustrate as he talked. "As you see, here in the center was Jerusalem. It was always at the center of the maps of this period and, as more and more of the world was discovered, primarily to the east, Jerusalem moved east as well. Incidentally, all maps begin from a single point. It's called the projection point. It is the central point on the map and it is chosen because of its singular importance to those who draw the map. As you can imagine, the one thing common to all maps throughout history is that the projection point has moved depending on when and where the map was drawn and who drew it. That was why most of the maps from this period that were drawn by Christians put Jerusalem at the center. And there it was to remain even as the world expanded to take in newly discovered lands that were not Christian."

"I bet the people in those other lands weren't too happy to find out that their own center of the world had been shoved out to the boondocks," Harry said. "Must be why so many people ended up fighting over who got to draw the map."

"Quite right, Harold, but unless you were lucky enough to go on a pilgrimage to the Holy Land or you went there as a crusader, a map with Jerusalem in the center or anywhere for that matter, had very little utility. In fact, since most people never ventured farther than a few miles from where they lived their entire life they hardly needed a map to go to the village or the castle. Besides, most were illiterate so none of these types of maps were of any use to them. However, even for such people there was a type of map they could use and, indeed, wanted to use." He pulled a book from one of the shelves and opened it and passed it to Harry.

"Looks more like an x-ray of someone's intestines than a map," Harry said then handed it on to me.

Federico seemed pleased that he had succeeded in baffling Harry. "This is a photograph of the labyrinth in Chartres Cathedral in France. It is one of only three such labyrinths that still survive from the Middle Ages and it is constructed from stone that has been laid in the floor of the nave. You can see that the loops end with a circular stone at the center. If a person crawled on their knees through the labyrinth until they arrive at the central stone they were entitled to the same forgiveness of their sins as if they had actually made it to the Holy Land."

Harry shook his head in awe, "You mean this is some weird sort of labyrinth map that people followed on their knees?"

"Granted, it isn't a map of the physical geography, but of the spiritual geography," Federico answered. "And for those who wished to travel farther than a labyrinth could take them, there were shrines with the relics of various saints and martyrs. Since these were much closer than the Holy Land, they served as substitute destinations for pilgrimages. The maps of the Dark Ages were filled with such sites." Federico walked to another one of the maps on the walls and pointed to several spots on it, then returned and stood behind an empty chair, gripping it as he continued. "But let me resume the story of maps, which is, after all, my area of specialization rather than religion and church history. Sometime in the 13th century the *Geographia* was discovered in Vatopedi monastery of Mount Athos by a monk, Maximus Planudes, and thus geography as a science, and maps that were more science than religion, were reintroduced. It was in this same approximate time period, the 13th century, that Venice's very own Marco Polo made his famous travels. Two centuries later Christopher Columbus from nearby Genoa also relied on Ptolemy's maps when he set out for India. They were maps that the King of Spain had stolen. Of course, if the Spanish monarchy or Columbus had used a map that indicated the true circumference of the earth in which each degree equaled 70 miles rather than 50, they probably never would have set sail since there would be no advantage to such a long sea voyage to the far east. Even at his death Columbus insisted he'd found the old India rather than a new world. He also thought he'd discovered paradise at the mouth of the Orinoco River in Columbia, a country which was named after him."

Federico stopped and looked at Harry, who was yawning. "Am I boring you?"

"Don't take the yawn personally, Fred," Harry replied, "I'm still on Colorado time. I have to say that what you've been telling us sure makes me respect my dog-eared Rand McNally road atlas a heck of a lot more."

Federico closed his eyes for a moment and then sat down in the chair that he had been standing behind. Harry didn't notice since he was busy hoisting onto his lap the briefcase that I had seen him carrying on the boat from the airport. "Guess it's my turn, huh?" He said twiddling with a combination lock until the latches popped open. He pulled out a package wrapped in heavy brown paper and returned the briefcase to the floor. He unwrapped the paper revealing a small red book. "This here little red book isn't a copy of one of Chairman Mao's in case you're wondering." He handed me the book. The title read *Baedeker's Northern Italy*. "It was published in 1913. The fourteenth edition it says, in English, that is. Baedeker was a German publisher and there were four German editions before the first English one. Guess the German tourists were here first." He said with a wink, "You think their children behaved any better back then?"

The book was compact and could fit in a person's pocket although it would have been a tight fit because of its thickness. I opened it from the back where a fragile looking map was folded. You could tell that it had once been glued to the binding so that it could be unfolded without being detached. I decided not to tamper with the map and after looking at the book gingerly I passed it to Federico.

"It's just a couple pages shy of 700 and not one of them is missing. I checked the numbers on each page," Harry announced with more than a little pride. "The maps in the Baedeker guides were glued into the binding so that you could unfold them without them falling out and getting lost. Sort of reminds me of the accordion I used to play as a kid. Hated it, by the way, but my mom loved Lawrence Welk. Anyway, I guess the map of Venice lost its sticking power because it was just folded and stuck between the pages. The type is really small, which just goes to show how much they packed into each page, and that's only for their book on Northern Italy. I'll tell you, they don't publish travel books like this anymore, and I know old books like Fred knows old maps. Of course, we don't travel like they did back then, either, what with their ocean liners, steamer trunks and grand tours."

"And you found this in a town in Colorado called Pueblo?" Federico said, unable to hide his incredulity.

"Yes siree, Bob. Bob is just an expression by the way, Fred. It was discovered in a building right across from their old train station, which has been restored, although we still can't get any trains to stop there. To get back to the story though, some fellas were renovating what was once the Santa Fe Trail Hotel into one of those boutique hotels, the kind with jacuzzis and stuff like that. I guess they figured even folks visiting Pueblo get tired of motels. They came across a couple of trunks of old books and called me up since I own *Bunch of Books* bookstore in Picketwire, a town east of Pueblo. We have a lot of used books and some are even rare, although that's not the same as rarely used," he laughed. "Some folks like to call used books pre-read but I figure either they've been read or they haven't. As you can expect, anything that's been sitting in a trunk for god knows how long, well, it's going to be considered used even though it's in pretty darn good shape considering. The air's pretty dry on the prairie of southeast Colorado since there's not much in the way of rain. Anyway, I paid them about twenty bucks for the kit and caboodle. When I got back to Picketwire and sorted them out, I found this one."

"It's not exactly the place you'd think a travel book on Italy would end up," I said, dryly.

"Dante, you'd be surprised what ended up in that part of Colorado back then. There were people from all over the world looking for gold and silver up in the mountains in places like Cripple Creek. And in Pueblo there was Colorado Fuel and Iron, which was the biggest steel mill west of the Mississippi, owned by the king of the robber barons, John D. Rockefeller. CF&I is where they made all the steel for the railroads they were building out west. Lots of money and lots of folks from all over the world came there looking for their fortune, or at least a living. And then there were folks who were just passing through on the train. Pueblo was a big stop on the Acheson, Topeka and Santa Fe Railway. Anyway, the fellow who the book belonged to might have been out there looking for the Wild West or on his way to the gold mines or going out to California to see the stars – if they had Hollywood stars then."

"Perhaps he was setting out in the other direction on his way to Europe and Italy," Federico suggested.

"You know, Fred, I hadn't thought of that. In any case he seems to have left it at the hotel. When I looked at the inside cover and saw the previous owner's name, I realized that this was the very book that Hilary Evesham had asked us Curiosi members in the US about. Being in used books, I always take a special interest when a fellow Curiosi is looking for a particular book – not that I've ever had one they were looking for until now. So, to make a long story short, I got ahold of Hilary and she asked me if I could join her and Fred here in Venice ASAP and to bring the book with me. The next thing you know, here I am." He yawned again. "Well, part of me is and the other part is sleeping back in Colorado."

As if on cue the black phone on the table rang. Federico, who had been stroking his goatee, picked it up. He listened for a minute, nodding his head several times before he said, "I understand. We will meet you there. Ciao." He put the receiver back into the cradle and turned back to us. "That was Signora Evesham. She wishes to meet us at the Piazza San Marco."

"She must have heard me talking about her," Harry chuckled.

***

The Piazza San Marco was filled with pigeons. Those that weren't strutting around pecking at the ankles of tourists in hopes of a handout were swirling overhead casting a whirlpool of shadows. Their fluttering wings accompanied the Mozart being played by the string quartet seated at the front of the café where we were seated while Harry sipped on a coke and I nursed a glass of San Pellegrino. Federico, who had quickly downed an espresso, was giving us another lecture, this one on the Basilica di San Marco, as we waited for Hilary Evesham to make her appearance.

Federico told us that, "The bones of San Marco were stolen in 829 from Alexandria, Egypt by Venetians. According to the legend, the thieves concealed them in a barrel of pork. Since Egypt was and is a Muslim country, and Islam considers the pig an unclean animal, it was the perfect hiding place. There was quite a market for stolen religious relics in the Middle Ages, and as late as the 15th century, members of the Scuola di San Rocco stole from Montpellier, France, the relics of San Rocco, the patron saint of victims of the plague. In the 9th century, Venice, being a wealthy place, was in the market for relics, and the only bones of a saint they had acquired were those of San Teodoro who was a minor saint compared to San Marco. San Marco was one of the twelve apostles and even wrote a Gospel, while Theodore, well, God only knows what he did. So, they absconded with the bones of San Marco and sailed off to Venice. While carrying the remains to the Doge's Palace for temporary storage, the container they were in – one assumes the relics had been extracted from the pork – suddenly became so heavy the carriers had to put it down and were unable to pick it up again. The doge decided that this was a sign from God that he should build a basilica at that very place rather than placing the bones in the Cathedral. It seems that the very first miracle in Venice attributed to the apostle's bones was to build a basilica next to the Doge's Palace. Not long afterwards Venice was awarded a bishopric by the Pope." Federico paused and raised his right index finger to signal the waiter for another expresso, and then with a slight smile concluded, "And that is how the relics of San Marco put Venice on the map, so to speak."

"Sounds just like us Americans when we build a stadium to lure a pro football team, and a domed stadium, at that." Harry said as he pointed his coke bottle at the onion towers of the Basilica of San Marco.

"I imagine it didn't hurt the doge's image and power to have the basilica with relics of San Marco built next to his palace," I said.

"In fact, they built it twice. The second time after the first basilica burnt down in 976," Federico replied. "Unfortunately, that was when the body of San Marco was lost. They rebuilt the basilica but without the body. The legend was that the bones were hidden and the location known only by the doge and a senior priest but then the location had been forgotten some-how. Miraculously, just before the basilica was about to reopen in 1094 without San Marco the entire population of Venice, led by the Doge Vitale Faliero, fasted and prayed, and a column of the south transept of the Church suddenly opened revealing the bones. Just in time since our rival city, Bari, in the south of Italy had acquired the body of San Nicola, who most people know as Santa Claus."

"Sounds like Venice was the one that was saved in the nick of time," Harry chuckled.

"Speaking of the nick of time, I'm terribly sorry for being so late," a woman's voice intruded.

We turned in unison to see a woman standing behind the empty chair between Federico and Harry.

"You must be Hilary," Harry exclaimed as he half rose from his seat. "Fred here was just giving us a little lecture on old Saint Mark."

Hilary Evesham pushed her sunglasses over her forehead into her thick auburn hair. "Harold, it is so nice to meet you in person. I must say you look just as I envisioned you when we spoke on the phone."

"Nice to meet you, as well. I have to admit that my imagination isn't as good as yours and I couldn't find of a photo of you anywhere so it's great to see you."

"I'm afraid a photograph would blow my cover," Hilary laughed and then turned to me, "and you must be Dante Flynn? As one writer to another, let me say how happy I am that you agreed to observe and chronicle our investigation, although you will probably find this quite boring compared to what you have been writing about."

"If you mean boring as in no bombs, then that's fine with me," I replied as I stood, shook her hand and then offered her the empty chair next to me. "From what Harry has said you must have written a number of books?"

Federico replied before Hilary could, "Signora Evesham is the author of the 'visiting again for the first time' books. Her most recent one, not coincidentally, happens to be *Visiting Venice Again for the First Time*."

"You don't need to preface my name with Signora, Federico," Hilary said then turned to me. "But of course, you wouldn't know my real name, Dante. I use the pen name E. Hilary. It would make it very difficult to write the type of books I write if people recognized me."

"So that's what you meant by not wanting to blow your cover," I said. "I've read your books and wondered what the E. stood for."

"Some readers seem to think it's for Edmund as in Sir Edmund Hilary," Hilary replied, "but as you can see, I am definitely not a sir, and the closest I've come to climbing Mount Everest was to spend several nights in Katmandu. However, I have managed to climb the campanile over there instead of taking the elevator," she nodded at the tower that loomed over the piazza, "although I won't claim to be the first to reach its summit."

"Doggone, I never figured that something that old would have an elevator," Harry whistled.

Federico said, "That is because this is not the original campanile, Harold, but a second one built after the first one collapsed on July 14, 1902."

"Did they find any bones in its ruins like they did with the basilica?"

"If you mean the bones of someone who was struck down when it collapsed, fortunately no, but they did discover that the Marangona, the most famous bell in the campanile, was completely undamaged, which many Venetians believe was an even a greater miracle than that no one was killed."

"The real miracle, Federico, is that anything remains standing at all in Venice given that the entire city is built on mud," Hilary said. "But while we're on the subject of miracles, I consider Harry's discovery of the long lost Baedeker to qualify. Did you bring it with you?"

"I sure as heck did," Harry passed the red volume to her.

"Yes, yes, this is truly it, Harry," Hilary said as she held up the inside page. "You can see William Bancroft's signature is still here. It's faint but unmistakable. If he'd only known..."

Interrupting, Federico snapped, "Yes, Hilary, we already know that the book belonged to Bancroft."

"I'm sorry if I was a bit carried away. But to actually hold the book in my hand is to finally have some proof when up until now it's only been a theory."

"I wouldn't go so far as calling it proof, Hilary," Federico said. "If that is all the proof that was needed then we wouldn't have to undertake this investigation."

"Evidence then," she said as she eagerly paged through the book, "that my theory might be right. Even, more than just evidence, this is the key that unlocks all the rest."

"I'll grant you that it is evidence, Hilary. Although whether it unlocks anything remains to be seen. But tell me, why did you ask us to meet you here? Isn't the Scuola a more private place for an examination of scientific evidence?"

Hilary set down the book, "I was thinking about Harry. This is such a nice sunny day and sunshine is the best thing for jet lag. You know, it helps reset the biological clock to local time. Also, I thought meeting in the Piazza San Marco would be appropriate since the tours that were described in Bancroft's Baedeker begin right here in this very plaza. What better place to begin than where William Bancroft began?" Without waiting for a reply, she picked up the book again, pulled out a map of Venice that was tucked inside and gingerly placed it on the table.

"It wasn't me that unstuck that map," Harry explained. "I didn't touch it at all since I figured you'd want everything as undisturbed as possible. It was already unglued when I found the book. Probably the glue dried out."

"You needn't worry, Harry. I fully expected it to be detached. In fact, I would have been quite surprised if it was still bound to the book. It would be much more likely that Bancroft would have detached it instead of it becoming unglued on its own, in order to use it for his purpose, although it has retained a crispness that makes me feel as if I'm opening it for the first time." She unfolded the map and then bent over to examine it. Pulling back, she smiled broadly and turned it around on the table so that we could all get a view. "Tell me what you see."

"A map of Venice?" Harry volunteered.

"Yes, Harry, but what else do you see?"

"I see colors, the water, the canals, the lagoon, and all of that. They're colored pink, or maybe salmon would be a closer color."

"Do you see anything else? For example, do you notice any-thing about the printing?"

"It's black, some of it is pretty itty bitty and," he pointed at the serpentine Grand Canal with a stubby finger, "there are a lot of pizza places."

"Those aren't pizza places. That's the abbreviation for piaz-za," Federico said, impatiently, pointing at one of the markings. "See, this is the Piazza San Marco, which is where we are right now."

"You must be right because I don't see any pizza parlors," Harry laughed and rubbed his stomach. "Not that I need any."

"Now, Harry, could you turn the map over and tell me what you see on its backside?" Hilary asked.

"Somebody has written a whole bunch of numbers. They're pretty faint."

"Let me see," Federico said taking the book from Harry. "These look like compass readings and the times that they were taken."

"Correct," Hilary said. "Bancroft's hobby was wayfinding, which is similar to orienteering," Hilary said. "He liked nothing better than to use his compass to find his way around. Bancroft took his compass and a pocket watch with him when he was in the gondola with his guide, and these are the readings that he took every time they changed direction and the time notations as how much time had elapsed between readings. Taken togeth-er, these would have allowed him to calculate their position."

"If Bancroft was just keeping track of his location on the back of the map as a way to entertain himself through wayfinding, how does that help you prove your theory?" Federico asked.

"Because Bancroft wasn't entertaining himself by wayfinding," Hilary replied, calmly. "It was the only way he could know where he was because his guide, who was a gondolier named Rudolfo – Bancroft doesn't tell us his surname – made him travel in an enclosed gondola with curtains over the windows."

"Like the kind they use as hearses," Harry nodded. "We passed by one of those docked on that cemetery island when we were coming over on the boat from the airport."

"Similar, I imagine. In any case, Bancroft wouldn't notice any canal or street names or other landmarks as they traveled through the canals. Second, when he finally arrived at the destination, Rudolfo blindfolded him and the blindfold wasn't removed until they were inside the building. By making these notations he would be able to retrace the entire route and find the place again."

"And that's where he found this old map," Harry said with a nod, "the one you mentioned when you sent out that request to the members of the Curiosi for help."

"Tell me, Hilary," Federico asked, "how did you come to know this was what Bancroft was doing when he marked up this map and what, exactly, is this ancient map he claims to have found?"

"Bancroft kept a journal of his Venetian trip, and in his journal he wrote that he had come across a map used by Venetians since at least the 11th century and that it was the map that the Venetian fleet used to sail to the Holy Land during the First Crusade following a route through the Adriatic and Mediterranean. It was this map that enabled them to monopolize the trade routes in the Adriatic and Mediterranean Seas. That supremacy lasted until the Portuguese discovered an alternate route that went around the Horn of Africa. Bancroft wrote in his journal that he had marked its location on the back of the map in his Baedeker guidebook. I stumbled onto the journal he kept during his stay in Venice at the Royal Society for Wayfinders. It was among the papers that were donated by his estate after he vanished in 1914 while on an expedition to the Rocky Mountains in Colorado. Since the Baedeker wasn't with the rest of his papers I thought he might have taken it with him to Colorado and left it somewhere. I put out a request to antiquarian book sellers and collectors in Colorado asking them if they had come across it and, as luck would have it, Harold saw my request."

"How do we know that the map is still here?" Federico asked, hardly hiding his skepticism. "Maybe Bancroft went back the next day without his minders and stole it."

"Because he wrote in his journal that he was able to find and mark its location on the back of the map in his Baedeker. The next day he left Venice for England and we know he didn't return to Venice before his trip to America. Although he doesn't note it in his journal, I think the most probable reason as to why he didn't try and retrieve the map is that he knew he was being watched by Rudolfo and the others who were guarding the map. No doubt he planned on returning after his trip to America, when enough time had elapsed so that he could sneak into Venice without being detected, retrace the route he had written down in his Baedeker, and find the map."

"It reminds me of Jim finding the pirate's treasure map in Robert Louis Stevenson's *Treasure Island*," Harry said. "I've got one of the early editions, by the way."

"Except that in this case the treasure is the map," I added.

"A map to a buried map," Harry chuckled.

"Very well, you might be right," Federico conceded, then asked Hilary. "But did Bancroft describe the map in any way such as its dimensions or the condition it was in so that at least we would have some idea as to what we are looking for?"

"Unfortunately, he didn't write down any description in his journal. Perhaps he was afraid that if he wrote down those details someone might get their hands on what he wrote and be able to find the map before he returned from America. That might also be the reason why he took the Baedeker with him rather than leaving it in England along with the journal of his trip."

"Sure, explains why he'd have a Baedeker guidebook for Northern Italy with him on a trip to the American West," Harry observed with a sage expression. "It was like tearing a treasure map in two and taking one half with him. Just what a pirate would do."

Visibly annoyed by the talk of pirate maps, Federico asked Hilary, "Might I ask why you were interested in Bancroft and his papers in the first place?"

"Excellent question, Federico. I became a member of the Royal Society so I could have access to their archives whenever I'm writing one of my books. As you know, I try to make my reader look at a place from a fresh perspective, so that even though they have visited there before, even multiple times, they will see it the next time as if they had never been there at all. The archives of the Royal Society are filled with the papers of explorers so what would be a better place to get a first impression from a unique, some would say eccentric, perspective. It was while I was researching my own book on Venice that I stumbled on Bancroft's papers and the journal. Now," Hilary said, "I propose that we begin our search for the map tomorrow morning here in the Piazza San Marco at the Café Florian."

"But why wait until tomorrow morning?" Harry asked. "I mean, what you just told us has me bright-eyed and bushy-tailed, and I feel like a bull rider in the chute ready to take his ride."

Federico looked at Harry, "You're in Venice not in some rodeo, Harry, and the only thing we ride is a boat and while they might sway they certainly don't buck."

Hilary smiled as Harry settled back into his chair. "In answer to your question, Harold, the reason we need to begin tomorrow rather than immediately is because Bancroft set out from this very Café on his journey with Rudolfo at 10 AM in the morning and I believe we need to follow his timetable since he noted the time when he took each of his compass readings.”

“Well, I suppose after all these years the map can stay buried another day.”

“Now that we’ve settled that,” Hilary said, “I want to invite all of you to join me for dinner at the restaurant in the hotel where Dante and I are staying. It has an excellent reputation.”

***

“I still don’t get why these old maps are such a big secret if there’s no treasure attached,” Harry said toward the end of dinner.

Apparently taking that as a cue to launch into another lecture, Federico explained that it wasn’t a simple task. “Maps were carefully guarded secrets because they gave the owner an advantage over their enemies and competitors. It allowed them to go places that were only imagined, to travel beyond the horizon, to sneak up on their enemies and arrive at places before their competitors did. So important were these sea charts and maps that the Spanish kept their extensive collection in a strongbox with two locks, each of which required two keys and each key was held by a different person.”

“Think of maps back then as being like the code for computer software today,” Hilary added, patting Harry’s right hand.

“Good analogy, Hilary,” Federico said, then resumed in his professorial voice, “As I was saying, in 1508 they created a master chart called the *Padrón Real* which they also kept under lock and key. Unfortunately for the Spanish, a Venetian cartographer employed by the Spanish named Sebastian Cabot managed to get his hands on the chart and offered to sell what was called the secret of the straits – meaning the straits of Magellan – to both Venice and England. By the way, Cabot also claimed to possess the secret for longitude, but said that it was such a divine secret that he could not divulge it to any mortal. Of course, the Venetian and English maps were also kept in very safe places. In the case of Venetian maps, only the doge and a few other trusted persons knew where the maps were kept."

"What museum did they put them in after they found them?" Harry asked.

"I'm afraid they never found them," Federico sighed, throwing up his hands. "You see, just like the bones of San Marco, they forgot where they hid them. Unlike the case of San Marco, however, they have not miraculously reappeared. That is why my life's work has been engaged in the reconstruction of as many of these ancient maps as possible. In all modesty, I must say that with only a few fragments of those that have survived, plus archeological and other historical data, I believe I have managed to come very close to what many of these maps looked like. I have even published some of my research this past year."

"*An Atlas of the Lost Maps of the Ancient Mariners*," Hilary interrupted. "The International Association of Ancient Cartography has called the maps in your book the closest thing to the originals we will ever have."

"Why, thank you, Hilary," Federico said.

"But if we find the real map that Bancroft said he found, then we will have an original, won't we?" Harry said, stifling a yawn. "And that beats a copy no matter how good it is, at least in my book."

"But that is only if this story of Bancroft's is true and, even if it is, we still need to find this map that apparently even he was not able to get his hands on," Federico sputtered in protest.

"Perhaps it doesn't exist or that we can't find it if it does," Hilary sighed. "But as you noted, miracles have been known to happen in Venice."

A sudden breeze rustled the flowers in the window box next to our table and beyond it in the canal a gondola was gliding to a stop. The gondolier looked familiar, and as he stepped off the gondola I recognized him as Niccolò even though he had changed into the traditional gondolier's uniform of tight shirt with horizontal bands of black and white and black pants.

"I called the Scuola and asked Niccolò to bring the gondola," Federico said, happy to change the subject. "Niccolò is also our gondolier. He succeeded his grandfather, Emilio, who took over from his own father. Being the Scuola's gondoliers has been passed down from father to son for centuries."

"Is there a reason they skipped over Niccolò's father?" I asked.

"I'm afraid his father was a plumber. I must say, Emilio seemed very disappointed in his son's choice of profession and that the family line of succession with the Scuola might end with him, but now that his grandson has become our gondolier his family honor has been saved and he couldn't be prouder. It also made it easier for him to retire. Although, as you have noticed, he didn't remain retired long because after only a week he asked us if he could be the doorkeeper at the Scuola as a way to keep occupied. I do think, though, that he might be taking advantage of us."

"In what way?"

Federico leaned over the table and lowered his voice, "For many years, even before I joined the Scuola, we have allowed him to use the Scuola as a place where he and some of his fellow gondoliers could meet. Although it is highly irregular to allow outsiders to meet at the Scuola, it was something that the members viewed as harmless. After all, the gondoliers were Emilio's friends and all growing older, so it would end soon enough. But, instead of growing older and smaller, younger gondoliers joined the group and they could be meeting indefinitely. I fear that Emilio is taking advantage of our generosity. I have already suggested to the Council that we ask Emilio to find another place for their social club. In fact, I told them that I thought Emilio should be asked to retire completely because, to be perfectly honest, we hardly need a doorkeeper anymore with all of the digital technology available today. Every time I hear that antiquated telephone ring it makes me cringe."

"I'm sorry to hear that," Hilary said. "I find Emilio and your present system to be quite charming. The latest technology isn't always the best."

"The fact that we study antiquities doesn't mean we must use them ourselves," Federico answered dismissively then he turned and nudged Harry who had dozed off. "Harold, our boat has arrived and we need to board."

Harry, who had dozed off, opened his eyes, "Is it one of those Hardy Boys taxi boats?"

"No, Harry," Hilary said. "This is a real gondola."

Harry rubbed his eyes and leaned over the table to look out the window, "Well, I'll be. Seems sort of a waste to just have only guys in it." He shot Hilary a look and then broke into a grin.

We watched as Federico boarded the gondola first and then Harry climbed aboard with an assist from Niccolò. The gondola dipped from the added weight and then bobbed until Harry finally settled into one of the plush red seats. With a push of Niccolò's foot the gondola slid forward. Casually Niccolò stepped onto the stern and with a circular sweep of the long oar the boat glided away leaving only the moon-washed fronts of the buildings on the opposite side of the canal filling the frame of the window.

"Sounded like Harry was inviting you along for a ride in the gondola," I said.

Hilary turned from the window and looked directly at me. "Perhaps, but Saint Dismas isn't a very inviting destination as far as I'm concerned."

"We don't have a gondola at our disposal but we could go for a walk," I suggested.

***

"What direction?" Hilary asked after she came back from her room with a black shawl around her shoulders.

"I've been here several times but I'll be just as lost no matter what direction we take," I replied. "You wrote a guidebook on Venice so you must know your way around."

"We'll see," she said. After looking in both directions along the canal Hilary turned right and started walking with me beside her. Just past the hotel we turned right again onto a calle. After a short walk we came to another canal. Its surface was covered with a smooth crust of moonlight. "I believe that this canal is called the Rio Pietro," she said. "It certainly looks like a river of stone in this light, although it's filled with water so we shouldn't try walking on it."

"It's actually a relief to know that the most dangerous thing you can step on is water," I answered as we crossed a bridge and then walked along the left side of the canal.

"I forgot that you were just in Yugoslavia or the former Yugoslavia or whatever they call it now."

"A lot of people call it hell and leave it at that. In fact, a lot of them would leave if they could."

"I can only imagine how dangerous it was covering the war."

"It might be better to say the war covered me just like it covered everyone and everything else. The fog of war over there is so thick it's impossible to see the way out."

We had come to the end of the riva, forcing us to stop. The canal continued on into the darkness. It was another dead end ramo. The only alternative was to turn left and after we walked down a narrow street that was almost pitch black we came out onto another canal and turned left again and continued until we came to another bridge. We stopped in the middle and looked at the canal. I asked her how she got the idea for her books and why she didn't want people to know that she was the author. "Most writers are trying to figure out how to get noticed and here you are, the writer of a popular series of books and no one knows who you are."

"It's partly because I don't consider myself to be the author." She pulled the shawl up to her ears and told me how she had grown up in a small Cotswold village where her father had been the vicar. She managed to study hard and escape the picture postcard when she went to Oxford. That's where she met Edward and managed to fall completely in love. He was a couple of years older than she was and was the second son of one of those old families who managed to make some new money so they didn't have to turn their manor house into a tourist attraction. Edward was more interested in seeing the world than making money, and after he graduated he traveled around the world, writing her from all the places that she would have wanted to visit. Not having a trust fund, Hilary applied herself to her studies and when she graduated got a job at Marsdale Press, a small publishing company in London. Whenever Edward passed through on his way to some other foreign place he would stay with her, but never invited her to come with him when he resumed his traveling.

She waited five years while he was off to Asia, Africa, North and South America, the South Pacific, the Orient. By then she was an editor and she told him she didn't want to continue to be treated as a lay-by on a motor route. His response was to ask her to marry him, which she did. After a one week honeymoon in Cornwall they went to Plymouth where, to her surprise, he had a sailboat all fitted out. She thought for a minute that it was part of the honeymoon and that they were finally going to travel together. Only it turned out to be a solo voyage across the Atlantic that he was going to take. "He told me he was getting tired of the traveling and wanted to settle down when he got back," she said. "His boat disappeared somewhere in the North Atlantic."

She stopped and looked at me, as if she wanted to show me that she wasn't crying. I didn't know what to say and was relieved when she said, "It turned out that Edward left me more than the memory of him sailing off into the sunset. He also left a trunk with all of the journals he had been keeping of his travels. I decided to use them as the source for a book. Since there was so much material I used only the first three journals. After a year of editing and writing I was able to create a manuscript that I thought could be published. Of course, every publisher I sent it to rejected it. They said that there would be no way to verify Edward's account since he was dead, which meant that they couldn't publish it as a work of nonfiction and that is an obvious prerequisite for a travel book.

"I was quite depressed. The top editor at Marsdale Press, noticed and asked to look at it. He thought it was very engaging and suggested that the solution to verifying the accuracy of Edward's account was to have it be my account as well. He pointed out that I had already contributed quite a bit through my editing and writing and now all I had to do was visit the same places. I submitted a proposal to Marsdale and they accepted it even though they had never published a travel book. They also gave me an advance to cover my expenses as I visited the places that Edward had written about. The result was a book that was based on Edward's journals and my own account of seeing these places for the first time. The first book was a great success and even though I've written five books since I've still only visited half of the places Edward wrote about."

"It sounds like you have your future pretty well mapped out?"

"Yes, but it's a bit too mapped out and I was starting to feel constrained by Edward. It was as if his ghost was my tour guide. That's why a year ago when I was invited to join the Curiosi, an organization I didn't know existed, I jumped at the chance. This case has nothing to do with Edward."

We kept walking in silence until we reached a canal from which all the water had been drained. I told Hilary that Niccolò had mentioned a filled in canal of thoughts.

"I suppose if there were pennies buried with each of them it would add up to quite a fortune," she replied.

***

I woke up in the middle of a bad dream. I was inside a half-destroyed building trying to hide from a sniper, the sniper's bullets striking closer as he zeroed in on me. When I opened my eyes, there was only sunlight shooting through the window. I lay there until the sweat turned cold.

Breakfast was in the restaurant where we had dinner the night before. The waiter told me that Hilary had already eaten. There was still plenty of time so I took my place at the same table we had occupied the night before and had coffee, then cereal and toast and a poached egg, and then more coffee. I looked through the newspapers and found the wire service story by my replacement in Sarajevo. The war continued without me.

When I arrived at the Café Florian in Piazza San Marco, Harry and Federico were already there. Harry was dressed in wrinkled khakis and a polo shirt that barely covered his belly while Federico wore a crisp white linen suit. They were sipping coffee just like any other odd couple.

"You just missed the darndest thing," Harry said. "There was a couple sitting right there." He pointed to the table next to us. "The lady asked the waiter after they paid the bill if she could take his picture but that she wanted him to keep his mouth closed. As she took it I asked her husband why she wanted the waiter to keep his mouth shut. He said that she's taken up painting and she takes pictures of people that she'd like to paint later, but she asks all of them to keep their mouths shut because she has trouble painting teeth. Isn't that a hoot? Of course, people who saw her paintings probably would think it was because they had bad teeth or maybe that it was some kind of symbolism or something."

"Ready everyone?" Hilary announced her arrival like someone who had already been up for several hours doing something more stimulating than drinking coffee.

Federico peered at her over round sunglasses that had slipped down the bridge of his nose. "I've been thinking, Hilary, if we knew who this Rudolfo person was who guided Bancroft we might be able to find this map, or at least determine if there was indeed a map, without going to all of this trouble."

"Unfortunately, Federico, Bancroft didn't give Rudolfo's last name. He just wrote that he was a gondolier. Oh, he did write that this Rudolfo claimed to be a member of the Dalmatian Brotherhood of Saint George, which as you know was a confraternity named after the famous slayer of dragons."

"This Rudolfo person couldn't be a member of the Dalmatian Brotherhood of Saint George," Federico interrupted, "because it no longer existed at the time of Bancroft's trip."

"Well if its members were all dragon slayers," Harry drawled, "I could see why it's no longer in business since there don't seem to be any dragons around."

"The members of the Dalmatian Brotherhood had nothing to do with slaying dragons," Federico said. "They were Schiavoni, who are Slavic people from the Dalmatian coast, which is the eastern coast of the Adriatic where Croatia, Bosnia, and Serbia are today. They were notorious for their pirates who harassed Venice until we conquered them. After that they were a source of cheap labor. Although they were very accomplished seaman, they were only allowed to be boatmen, who were the lowest members of the crews because no Venetian wanted such a menial job. In the 15th century they were also permitted to form their own minor scuola to provide assistance to their more unfortunate compatriots. However, as I just said, this Rudolfo couldn't have been a member because the confraternity was disbanded by Napoleon after he captured Venice along with all of the other confraternities. That was long before your Mr. Bancroft."

"What about Saint Dismas?" Harry needled him. "I mean if your Saint Dismas managed to sneak past Napoleon then why not some others like the Dalmatian Brotherhood. Of course, they'd be secret societies, which is why we don't know they exist."

Hilary cut them off, "I hate to end this discussion of secret brotherhoods and dragons, but we really do need to shove off. Is Niccolò ready?"

"Niccolò?" I asked.

"Yeah," Harry answered, "Nick is going to be our own personal gondolier. He brought us over here and was a pretty good skipper, I have to say."

"He also took you home last night."

"He did indeed, but I was pretty zonked out so I wouldn't have noticed anything, even if we'd hit an iceberg. Well, I guess I would have noticed if I had ended up in the water, especially since I can't swim."

"I'm absolutely certain we won't be encountering any icebergs today," Federico proclaimed as he got up from his chair.

As we walked toward the Grand Canal, Hilary told us that she would read out the compass readings at the proper intervals of elapsed time just exactly as they had been transcribed by Bancroft, "using this pocket watch," she said, dangling a silver watch on a chain. "It is the same type Bancroft used. Federico will tell us which direction we should turn and will also trace the route we take on this photocopy I just made from the map in Bancroft's Baedeker."

With that we set off past the campanile to where the piazza ended at the Grand Canal. As Niccolò steadied the black gondola we boarded with Hilary and Federico in the front and Harry and me in the rear. Hilary looked at the pocket watch and told Niccolò to shove off at exactly 10 a.m. in the direction of the first compass reading. After a few hundred yards, Hilary, who had been counting off the time, gave another reading. Federico told Niccolò to turn into the Rio di San Moise. For several hours we glided through a maze of canals, under arching bridges and passageways between buildings that were so narrow that I could almost touch both sides of them at once. With only narrow slots of blue sky overhead I soon lost all sense of direction.

***

"So, where the heck are we now?" Harry asked. "We've sure covered a lot of ground although I'm not sure how far we've come as the crow flies, or make that a pigeon, this being Venice."

"It may only be a coincidence, but the building over there is the Scuola di San Giorgio degli Schiavoni," Federico said putting down his pen after marking the spot on the map. "This is the building that the Dalmatian Brotherhood built in the 16th century for their scuola. It has several very good paintings by Carpaccio."

"Hey, isn't the Dalmatian Brotherhood the group that Rudy the gondolier claimed to be a member of even though it didn't exist?" Harry asked.

Federico sighed, "Yes. But if this is where the map is kept he certainly took Bancroft on the most indirect route one could ever imagine. We are only a few minutes from where we started if we'd walked here or taken the most direct route using the canals."

"Still, we wouldn't have known that this was the place without taking the route Bancroft wrote down," Hilary said. "Clearly, Rudolfo was leading Bancroft in a very roundabout way so that when he arrived here he would be completely lost.

If Bancroft had known it was this close he would have been able to narrow his search considerably."

"If Rudy had only known that Bancroft was a tricky little cuss and taking compass readings so that he could find his way back," Harry said, "sort of like Hansel and Gretel with the breadcrumbs."

"But if the map were here in the scuola wouldn't someone else have found it as well?" Federico snapped in response. "And if it was hidden, as it must have been, what was he proposing to do, demolish the building looking for it? This is Venice, not Treasure Island. We must stick to the facts. No one would ever let us dig up an architectural and artistic treasure of Venice based on this story about some supposedly lost map."

"Bancroft was no fool, Federico," Hilary replied. "He would know you can't just take a hammer and pick axe and begin excavating. He knew where it was located from what he said in his journal so it must be somewhere inside the scuola that was easily accessible and also a spot that he knew he would remember without having to write it down in his journal. All that was necessary was to retrace the route he'd recorded."

"Well, enough jawing about it. As long as we've come this far let's have a little look see," Harry said as he stepped from the gondola. "Heck, at least I can get a look at George and the dragon he killed."

***

"Can't say I saw anything in there that would help us find the map," Harry said as we left the scuola two hours later. "I liked those pictures of George, though, particularly the one of him showing the dead dragon to all those lords and ladies. Sort of reminded me of how I felt after I shot my first prairie dog when I was a little kid. Wanted everyone to see it, mangy critter that it was."

"Are you satisfied, Hilary, that there is no map, at least in this location?" Federico said.

"I was positive that Bancroft actually knew where the map was and that if we retraced this route so would we," Hilary replied, unable to hide her disappointment.

We returned to the Piazza San Marco using the most direct route, which took less than ten minutes. After Niccolò tethered the gondola in a spot next to a flotilla of other gondolas, Federico held up the photocopy of the map and pointed at the black line he had marked on the photocopy. "Here's the route we took going to the scuola. You can see why it took so much longer than this direct route."

"Seems like a pretty roundabout way to go in a circle," Harry replied as he looked at it. "I know that Bancroft got a kick out of it because of his wayfinding or orienteering or whatever they call it, but to me it's more like one of those labyrinths Fred was telling us about."

"Labyrinths?" Hilary asked. "I would say it's more like a maze. Unlike a labyrinth that is one continuous path a maze has numerous paths that branch out and lead to dead ends rather than the center, which is the ultimate goal. You can't get lost in a labyrinth, but it's easy in a maze unless you know the right path."

"Speaking of right paths, could we find one to a place to eat?" Harry asked. "I can't do much thinking on an empty stomach and this seems to be a situation that's going to require some real thinking."

"I suggest we disembark and have some lunch," Federico said. "I know just the place and we won't get lost finding it."

As we began to climb out of the bobbing gondola Hilary said, "I don't really have much of an appetite so if you don't mind I'll meet you back at San Dismas."

"Certainly," Federico said magnanimously. "It is no problem at all." He turned to Niccolò and instructed him to take Hilary to San Dismas and then return to pick us up after our lunch.

***

A couple of hours later we arrived back at San Dismas. Instead of Emilio, another man opened the door. Federico exchanged some words in Italian with him and then turned to us to explain, "This is Giovanni. He said that Hilary asked Emilio to show her to the map room and they have not returned. I can't imagine what use Emilio could be to her with the maps. We should go there straight away so that I can help her find whatever she is looking for."

"What does this look like?" Hilary asked as soon as we entered the map room. She pointed at a thin sheet of paper on which was drawn a long, irregular loop from the top left hand corner to the bottom right hand. All of us looked at it intently after she placed it on the table in the center of the map room.

"I give up, what are we supposed to be looking at?" Harry said.

"It appears to be something that was traced. It does look familiar though," Federico said. "But really, Hilary, what is the point and why did you ask Emilio to help you when he knows nothing about maps?"

Instead of answering Federico, Hilary turned to Emilio, "Emilio, could I have the book please?" Emilio immediately placed a book on the table that he had been holding. "I hope you don't mind but I went through some of the books in the library until I found this. I believe you'll recognize it."

Federico looked at the book, "Of course, I do, it is *An Atlas of the Lost Maps of the Ancient Mariners* that I wrote."

"Yes, you did. In fact, you mentioned it last night at dinner." Hilary opened the book and placed the thin sheet of tracing paper next to the map that was printed on the page and then slid it over the map. The traced lines fit almost exactly over the route marked on the map.

"Almost a perfect match," Federico said. "The scale is slightly different, of course."

"But you see, this map not only shows the Adriatic and the Mediterranean but it also has an ancient sailing route to Palestine."

"Yes, I know," Federico answered. "After all, I created the map. It is the most accurate reconstruction there is of the map that once existed but has been lost. This point at the top left quarter of the paper is Venice and the point in the bottom right hand quarter where the loop turns back is Jerusalem. Do you mean to tell me you've been up here making tracings of this map? Why on earth would you waste your time doing such a thing?"

"It isn't a waste of time, Federico, because the tracing isn't of this map. It's a tracing of the route we followed today, the one you drew on this photocopy of Bancroft's Baedeker." Hilary said sliding the photocopy onto the table and underneath the sheet with the traced lines.

"Well, I'll be a son of a gun!" Harry exclaimed.

Federico looked intently at the tracing and then the photocopy and, finally, the map in the book. "As improbable as it sounds the resemblance can't be coincidental. The only difference I can see is that the projection point is reversed. When you overlay this route onto the map I reconstructed, then the Piazza San Marco is on the Dalmatian coast rather than in Venice and the Scuola di San Giorgio is where the Holy Land is supposed to be. Still, the lines of the map match almost exactly. But I don't understand how the route that Rudolfo took Bancroft on could be the same as the original that I reconstructed."

"A map that allowed the Venetians to sail along the coast of the Adriatic and Mediterranean all the way to the Holy Land and back," Hilary added.

"That means Rudy and his friends must have had the original map after all," Harry said.

"But how would this Rudolfo and his companions get their hands on this map?" Federico asked in exasperation. "It just doesn't make sense. And yet I myself have to admit that here is the map and that is a fact that cannot be disputed. Still, I doubt we will ever know how a mere gondolier ended up in possession of such a great secret. After all, we know nothing about this Rudolfo except his first name, that he was a gondolier, and that he claimed to be a member of an organization that no longer existed."

"Perhaps Emilio could enlighten you," Hilary said. "After all he was the one who helped me,"

A surprised Federico answered. "Emilio?"

"Yes, Emilio," Hilary replied. "Our conversation about labyrinths and mazes made me think – it seemed like a wild idea, mind you – but it seemed to me that perhaps the canals Bancroft and we traveled were similar to a maze. Then I remembered you telling us about the atlas you had written which reconstructed a number of ancient maps that have been lost, so when I returned I asked Emilio if he could take me to the map room. When I looked through your book I found that the photocopy seemed to resemble this particular map, and as I began tracing it, Emilio suddenly seemed quite agitated. When I asked why, he finally told me that this very route was one he knew as the voyage of pilgrimage."

"Voyage of pilgrimage? I have never heard of such a thing." Federico turned to Emilio and asked in Italian, "Is this true, you know this route?"

Emilio nodded as he answered. "Sì, Dottore. That was what we call it. It is a big secret so I was very surprised that the Signora knew about it."

"It seems to be a fantastic statement for you to make, Emilio," Federico exclaimed. "How would you know such a secret?"

Hilary held up her hands, "Not so fantastic. You said yourself, Federico, that the Slavs, the people from the Dalmatian coast, were excellent sailors but that the Venetians allowed them to serve only as deckhands and boatmen, jobs that were considered too menial for a citizen of Venice. Wouldn't those menial jobs include that of a gondolier?"

"Yes, of course, but..."

"Rudolfo could have been a Slav," Hilary said. "After all, he claimed that he was a member of the Dalmatian Brotherhood. They worked on the boats that sailed the route to the Holy Land, and even though they weren't allowed to be captains or navigators or given access to the maps, they must have memorized the route, possibly with different members memorizing different sections. Then they recreated the map on the canal system of Venice."

"But if they were never allowed to have their own ships, what use would it be for them to have such a map?" Federico asked.

"Not useful in the same way that it was for the Venetians," Hilary answered, "but even more valuable to them was that they could use it as a way to go on pilgrimages to the Holy Land. For centuries they must have taken this route using the canals of Venice for their pilgrimage in a way similar to those who used the labyrinths in the great cathedrals, and no one suspected what they were doing. Remember that San Marco represents the Dalmatian coast on the map so their pilgrimage could start from their homeland and end in Jerusalem, which is represented by the scuola. That's exactly the route that Rudolfo took Bancroft on. He showed him the map."

Emilio nodded. "That was why we call it the voyage of pilgrimage. It has been handed down to us as a route drawn by San Giorgio himself. The others will be disappointed to learn that it is only a map made by Venetians and not by God."

"What do you mean the others?" Federico asked.

"The members of my club that the Scuola di San Dismas allows to meet here."

"But how would this club of yours know about this map?"

"Dottore, I cannot tell you. Please do not ask me to reveal anymore."

"Let me offer a possible explanation on behalf of Emilio," Hilary said. "Perhaps, just perhaps, the Dalmatian Brotherhood did not cease to exist as was thought and continues to meet in secret. Perhaps Emilio's club, whose members are gondoliers, is the Brotherhood."

"Is this true, Emilio?" Federico demanded.

"As I already said, I prefer not to say anything, Dottore," Emilio answered, lowering his head.

"I think that's as much of a yes as you can expect, Federico," Hilary said. "After all, the Dalmatian Brotherhood is a secret confraternity just like Saint Dismas."

As soon as the exchange with Emilio had been translated into English for Harry, he turned to Federico and gave him a hearty clap on the back. "Well, son of a gun, Fred. While you were working overtime reconstructing this map of yours it turned out it was right at your own front door all along."

"Just think, Federico," Hilary added. "If you hadn't kept Emilio on and allowed his group of gondoliers to meet here, this map would have never been discovered."

Federico looked up at the 16th-century painting on the ceiling as if he were searching for a sign from the former leaders of Saint Dismas who looked down on us. Turning to Emilio, Federico smiled and said, "I believe I can speak on behalf of the members of the Scuola when I tell you how much we appreciate your continued service to San Dismas and we look forward to continuing to host the meetings of your group."

DARK MATTER

Venice, Italy - October 1992

I woke in a shroud of sweat. I hadn't escaped Sarajevo after all. There was a ringing in my ears. Maybe from the blast, but how could I still hear if I were dead? Had I been buried alive in a Balkan mass grave? I opened my eyes and rolled out of bed onto the floor and reached up and grabbed the ringing phone off the nightstand.

"I'm sorry if I woke you." It was Ugo.

"I'm the one who should apologize since I forgot to ask for a wake-up call."

"Then I am your wake-up call." He sounded cheerful like he'd had nothing but sweet dreams.

"From the dead," I muttered in English as I held the phone in my hand, the cord stretched as far as it would go. I looked at the outline of my body tangled in the sheets and added. "It's an expression. I'll be down in five minutes."

It took ten minutes, and when I entered the hotel's restaurant, Ugo was sitting at one of the tables reading a newspaper. Before he folded it I saw that the war in the former Yugoslavia was still headline news even if I wasn't there. He had already ordered coffee so I poured some for myself and took one of the warm rolls from the plate.

"I read your case report. It is very good, as I knew it would be. We have deposited your fee into your bank account as we agreed."

"Thanks," I mumbled, dribbling some breadcrumbs.

"And what are your plans now?"

"I don't have any for the next couple of weeks. Some R and R."

"You will return to Rome for this R and R?"

"Rome and rest don't exactly go together so I was thinking I'd spend a week here in Venice. It's nice and quiet.

He smiled in relief, "I agree, Venice is much more restful than Rome." He poured some more coffee into his cup. "Since you are planning on spending a week here I wonder if you would consider taking on another little case. You see the person who was supposed to work on it has had to cancel at the last minute. We cannot postpone the case because it is very time sensitive. If you agree to do this, we will pay for the rest of your stay in Venice in addition to your fee and regular expenses."

"Why not," I smiled.

His face relaxed into a smile, "I had hoped you would say yes." He removed an envelope from the breast pocket of his jacket and handed it to me. "This envelope has the instructions as well as an advance."

"What would you have done if I'd said no?" I asked taking the envelope.

He sighed and began spreading butter on a piece of bread. "Fortunately, I do not have to find out. Your assignment will not start until 2:00 p.m. so you have some free time today to have some R and R, as you say. Perhaps a gondola ride?"

"As you saw in my report, I already had a ride. No, I was thinking of going to an art museum."

"Excellent. Art is one of the best ways to restore oneself and there is so much art to see in Venice. It is filled with masterpieces. There are the Tintorettos in the Scuola di San Rocco or the masterpieces in the Accademia, and then there are the churches where ...," he waved the bread knife as if it were a conductor's baton.

"So much of that art is filled with dead people and even if they're martyrs and saints who are all having a great time in the afterlife I don't think I'm quite up for it," I replied. "I was thinking that something more modern and abstract might be better."

"Then there is always the Guggenheim. I don't believe there is a single work of art there with a dead saint or martyr."

"That's exactly what I was thinking."

***

A grocer's boat was moored to the Fondamenta Bragadin on the Rio de San Vio. The grocer stretched his right arm over the gunwale with a head of lettuce in his hand. He reminded me of the gravedigger in Hamlet holding the skull of poor Yorick. An elderly woman on the Fondamenta looked it over carefully and then nodded her approval. After she shuffled off dragging her shopping bag, I bought an apple, put it in my pocket and continued on to the Guggenheim.

After spending a couple of hours in the galleries, I walked out into the Guggenheim's courtyard. I sat down on a bench and took out my apple and looked at it. It was large and shiny and fresh and I couldn't help thinking that for some of the people in Sarajevo, it would be a lot more important than anything displayed at the Guggenheim. It looked like it was from a still life painting of a bowl of fruit. A dead apple instead of a saint. I took a bite.

"You'd be surprised how many people spend more time staring at the place where Peggy Guggenheim's dogs are buried than they do looking at the art hanging on the walls inside. It's not like they can really see anything and even if they could there would be nothing but dust anyway."

Looking at the young man reminded me of a Bosnian I'd seen in Sarajevo, although that young man had a bullet hole in the middle of his broad unlined forehead. The flat Midwest American-accented English in which he'd made his observation and the name Brad Swenson engraved on the nametag pinned to the breast pocket of his blazer told me he was a lucky Lutheran from Minnesota.

"I hope it's not considered an act of disrespect to eat my apple here?"

"I don't think this is exactly holy ground," he answered with a white-toothed smile. "Besides, I'm only a student intern not a guard."

"What do you study?"

"Art history. Yeah, there are actually people who study art history in college and don't just sleep through the slides. A lot of my friends would love to be here. I don't necessarily mean here at the Guggenheim but in Venice, or even Italy, or to be honest, anywhere but where they are, which is in Minnesota."

"I thought you might be from Minnesota."

"My college is in Minnesota but I grew up in North Dakota."

"Not much in the way of canals in North Dakota."

"Not much in the way of art either. So being here is like a pig rolling in s...," he suddenly stopped and seemed paralyzed as his white face turned red.

"Slime?" I offered.

"Yeah, slime. A pig rolling in slimy mud," he smiled with relief.

"So, tell me, Brad, what history is there to study in a museum of modern art? Doesn't modern mean the present?"

"Good question." I could tell any question on art, no matter how silly, was a good question as far as Brad was concerned. He furrowed his brow as if it required some heavy thinking. "My answer would be that even the most recent works of art can only be appreciated fully when you know their historical context. I mean that when they claim to represent a break with the past, you need to understand the past that they are supposedly breaking with in order to understand them. Besides, the modern art that Peggy Guggenheim collected is almost a hundred years old now."

"So, what kind of art comes after modern other than the future?"

"Postmodern. There was a group that called themselves futurists but they were more of a political rather than an art movement like postmodernism."

I took another bite of my apple before responding, "It sounds confusing. After all, wouldn't something that comes after modern be in the future and that would mean it doesn't exist yet? All you would be able to show would be a blank wall and who would want to look at that?"

He looked over at the ground where the dead dogs were buried as if there might be some wisdom or a witty retort he could scoop from the dirt. I felt like sharing my apple with him but there wasn't much left but the core and there couldn't be much knowledge in that. "Guggenheim and her dogs don't exist, at least not anymore, and that doesn't stop people from coming here and looking at nothing. The story is that when they were burying her last dog just before she died they uncovered the skull of one of her other dogs. We don't mention that in our guided tours, of course. It would freak people out."

***

I've heard stories about tourists who refuse to get off at the Santa Lucia railway station because they think there's another station farther down the line but if the train went any further they'd be swimming in the Grand Canal. However, it looked like everyone on this train knew exactly where they were going and how to get there as they walked past me without a bit of hesitation. I had written the name of the person I was supposed to meet in large letters on a sheet of paper that I held to my chest. Since the instructions didn't say if she was a signora or signorina I just printed Gloria Hernandez.

"Signor Flynn?"

I didn't expect an attractive woman dressed in a trim black skirt with a white blouse. Her black hair that brushed her shoulders had just a hint of gray, which meant she was old enough to have it and not worried enough about her age to hide it.

"Sì..." I drew out the first syllable not knowing if it was Signora or Signorina, hoping she would cut in before I had to make a choice as to her current marital status.

"Sister." I could see she was amused at my reaction to the word. She added, "I guess Ugo didn't tell you I'm a nun. In any case, you can just call me Gloria since, as you can see by the absence of a habit, I don't wear my religious vocation."

"And you can drop the Signor and call me Dante," I answered.

"After the poet?"

"Once removed. My grandfather's name was Dante. He and my grandmother were both Italian. My father's side was Irish American. I get my Italian language skills from my mom's side of the family and my appreciation for a good story from my dad's."

"Sounds like you inherited the best of both cultures. I'm Spanish on both sides, which gives me both a tragic sense of life and a love of fiestas."

I took the handle of her suitcase without asking but she didn't object. "It has a bent wheel, which makes it want to veer to the left," she warned me as we walked down the platform. After passing through the lobby of the station and through the front doors, we descended the dozen steps to the broad fondamenta. Gloria stopped and took a deep breath as if she was taking in the smells as well as the view. As she inhaled she turned in a 360-degree arc out over the Grand Canal and around back toward the station. A breeze pushed her skirt above her knees. She didn't seem to notice and just kept looking at the station. Smooth white stone sliced the cloudless sky until it ran into the ancient church that was its neighbor.

"Santa Lucia is like a time machine," she declared after she completed her circle. "You leave the train in the present, walk through the station and come out into the past. Just look at Santa Maria degli Scalzi there," she pointed at the church with its Corinthian columns holding up a triangular roof that reminded me of a Roman temple except for the angels perched on top. "It looks like it's been there forever."

"Didn't Mussolini build the station?"

"Yes. He tore down a church named after Santa Lucia, and then gave the train station her name. No doubt, he thought it appropriate given how many people he and the Fascists sent to eternity in train cars," she waved her hand in a vague direction beyond the church. "The old Jewish Ghetto isn't far from here. Over there on the other side of the Cannaregio canal."

Unlike the subway trains that run under Manhattan through black tunnels and stations as bleak as a Hopper painting, the vaporetto we boarded zigzagged up the Grand Canal on a technicolor tour. Gloria pointed at a church, "That church there, with the dome and the tower behind it, is San Geremia. That's where the relics of Santa Lucia were moved when they built the railway station.

"Is she the patron saint of railway stations?"

Gloria laughed. "No, Santa Lucia is the patron saint of the blind because she plucked out her eyes in response to the advances of a powerful man. He couldn't take his eyes off of her so she took hers out. Instead of getting the message that she didn't appreciate that type of adoration, he was so upset that he had her tortured and killed. As if driving her blind wasn't enough."

"If that had been enough for him we would have one less saint."

"And one less abused woman. She could be the patron saint for abused women as a matter of fact. Probably more important for Venice is that Santa Lucia is also the patron saint of artists. You know, in the Middle Ages the test for whether the relic of a saint was authentic was whether it could perform miracles."

"If creating great artwork is a miracle, then based on the number of such works in Venice it would seem the relics in the churches are legitimate," I replied, the soles of my feet vibrating as the boat shifted into reverse. Sister Gloria gripped my arm when the boat bumped into the dock. "And how do they authenticate relics today?"

"The same way they authenticate art, by relying on experts and documentation," she replied.

A hoard of embarking passengers pushed us toward the railing and reminded me that this was Venice's version of the rush hour. "You sound like an expert," I said.

"I know something about religious artifacts including relics."

Suddenly a spray of water from a motoscafo that had pulled astern pelted the side of the vaporetto. Two men in trench coats and wraparound sunglasses, one tall and thin and the other short and stocky, stood in the front on either side of the helmsman. They reminded me of the Blues Brothers. Instead of passing us they dropped back, bouncing across our wake as we slid under the Rialto Bridge.

"We should get off at this stop," Gloria said. I found the handle to her suitcase and lifted it off as we docked. As soon as the gate was pulled back we shoved our way through the crowd and out onto the fondamenta. Gloria turned left and walked up the steps onto the bridge. I followed her, as we crossed the bridge between its rows of shops to the other side. There we wended our way through the stalls of the fish market followed by souvenir kiosks before making a sharp left hand turn into a narrow passageway partly hidden by a vendor's cart overflowing with T-shirts.

Feeling bombarded by color and smell, and slightly shell-shocked, I bumped into Gloria, who had stopped abruptly and was looking at a sheet of paper. She whispered that according to the directions the place we were going was on the next street. She put the paper back in her purse and we continued through the dark alley until we came out into a relatively uncluttered and deserted calle where we turned right.

Gloria stopped in front of one of the shops and, after looking back to make sure she hadn't lost me, she opened the door. A bell on top of the door jangled as we entered. Masks with painted faces and empty eyes looked down on us from the walls and ceiling. Some were laughing, some crying, a few looked demented, and others seductive. There were also some whose expressions were hard to decipher. A young woman came out from behind the counter. Gloria asked if she had a mask of Pinocchio. The woman nodded and motioned for us to follow her. We entered a room with a paint-spattered, wooden table in the center on which several unfinished masks rested. Two of them looked like skulls but the third was pink with full red lips and black arched eyebrows. A man sitting on a stool next to the table, put down the paint brush in his right hand, wiped his hands on a rag, and walked over to us.

"Giuseppe Sarni," he announced tilting his face up so that he could see us through his glasses that had slid to the tip of his nose. Pinned to his shirt was a small mask that looked, appropriately, like a demented happy face. "I see that you were able to find us."

"Yes, we got off the vaporetto at the Rialto rather than San Silvestro, which would have been more direct, and took the circuitous route in your directions."

"Did you notice anyone following you?" he asked, motioning for us to sit on the stools next to the worktable.

Gloria sat down before she answered. "There was a motoscafo trailing behind the vaporetto with two men in it. In their trench coats and dark glasses they didn't look like typical tourists. If they were following us we seem to have lost them once we got off the vaporetto and took the route you gave me."

Giuseppe pushed his glasses up the bridge of his nose, "One can never be too careful."

"Now that we're here...," Gloria said.

"Ah, yes, of course," Giuseppe said, then opened a drawer in the counter next to him and pulled out a large envelope. He placed it on the table, slipped out a photo, turned it around, and slid it toward Gloria, "Do you recognize this?"

She looked at it and quickly responded. "That is easy. It's the *Traslazione del corpo di San Marco,* depicting when they brought the relic to Venice. It is in San Marco and is the most famous mosaic in Venice, and there are a lot of mosaics in Venice, as everyone knows."

His face lit up like the Lido on a summer night, "That means you recognize it. Of course, why am I surprised since I have heard so much about you, Sister Hernandez."

"You can call me Gloria."

"As you know, Gloria, the mosaic illustrates the discovery on June 25, 1094 of the relics that were thought to have been lost in the great fire that destroyed much of San Marco. They were miraculously found hidden in a pillar of the church when the new San Marco was completed."

Gloria put down the photo, "To be clear, the mosaic isn't entirely accurate since the Doge who is depicted isn't the one who found the relics. In fact, there is even some doubt as to the authenticity of the relics."

"I see that you are already quite knowledgeable on the subject."

"I would hope so," Gloria answered, "since the reason I am here is because of my expertise in lost religious artifacts."

"As you correctly pointed out, the Doge in the picture is the one who commissioned the mosaic, Reniero Zeno, who held the office from 1253-1268, rather than Doge Vitale Faliero who actually made the discovery."

"If pictures can lie, why not mosaics," I said.

"Yes, yes, of course," Giuseppe nodded and proceeded to tell us that after the original San Marco burned down in 976, the relics of San Marco were saved by the Doge at that time, Domenico Selvo, in his role as their protector, who had them stored in a supposedly safe place. Unfortunately, he died before the restoration of San Marco was completed and they couldn't find the 'safe place' where he hid them. This put his successor, Doge Faliero, in a bind because San Marco was built to be a giant reliquary for the remains of the saint. Venice's claim to a special relationship with God because of San Marco would allow them to assert their independence, including from the Pope, who claimed the right to rule not only the spiritual world but the temporal as well, and controlled a large swath of Italy from Rome to the Adriatic. If Doge Faliero didn't come up with the relics, his credibility and that of the ruling families and all of Venice would have been undermined. Giuseppe tapped a spot on the photograph. "But after praying and fasting, the relics miraculously appeared in a pillar of the church. Quite a timely miracle, huh?" He picked up another photo from the envelope and passed it to Gloria, "Now look at this."

Gloria examined the photograph, "This one shows only a portion of the mosaic. The part that depicts the doge." Gloria placed it next to the first picture and looked at both of them, "Wait, I am wrong, because the face of the Doge is different in this photograph."

"You are correct. The Doge in this picture is none other than Doge Francesco Foscari!"

Gloria looked at him with surprise, "But that would be impossible. Foscari wasn't elected Doge until 1423, almost two centuries after the mosaic and four centuries after the relics were found."

"Yes, but what if the suspicions as to the authenticity of the relics that you mentioned earlier were true, and Faliero hadn't really found the relics of San Marco after all and that there are two mosaics, the one in San Marco and another one that shows Foscari finding the relics."

"But why?" I asked.

"Because whoever found the true relics would increase his power immensely," Gloria replied. "Given Foscari's reputation he certainly would have been the one to exploit the situation."

"You are correct," Giuseppe said. "As you know the other powerful families of the nobili tried to limit the power of the Doge as much as possible to that of a symbolic ruler, like the present Queen of England. Does anyone think that the dear lady has any real power when she can't even control her children? Foscari, however, used the symbolism to increase his power when he became doge. For example, he commissioned the triumphal arch in the Doge's Palace and the person carved into the stone kneeling before San Marco was none other than himself. And he isn't kneeling as a loyal subject, but as someone about to be crowned the king. He was quite good at self-promotion, not unlike other leaders we have had."

"Mussolini, for one," Gloria answered.

Giuseppe nodded gravely, "Although there are others, even today, who are tempted to do such things. However, unlike Mussolini, Foscari was an older man when he was elected. It was a form of term limits. With Italy's parliamentary system no government lasts more than a year, so we no longer need to worry about such things. In addition, unlike Mussolini, the doges were democratically elected."

"Democracy for wealthy men, you mean. If you were a woman or didn't have money, it was a dictatorship."

"That was unfortunately true for women, but not for men," Giuseppe replied. "Until the 13th century all of the male residents of Venice could vote even if they were poor. It was only later, after the disappearance of San Marco, that the right to vote was restricted to the wealthiest 2500 families. They were the ones designated as the nobili, and their names were entered into what was called *Libro d'Oro*, the Golden Book. Once a family's name was entered into the *Libro d'Oro* they could not be removed even if they lost their wealth. They formed the Great Council. Even those members of the lower class, the cittadini, who acquired wealth that matched or surpassed that of some of the nobili, did not get their names into the Golden Book.

"It remained that way until Napoleon defeated Venice and took over control of the city. The real importance of the nobili was that they were all equal with each having one vote, including the doge. This meant that the doge's power was more symbolic and his executive power was restricted. As a further check on his power, after the Doge died, his family was held responsible for whatever indiscretions he might have committed, especially those that favored his family. It was this concern that the Doge would enrich his family that was really behind the practice of electing only old men. They wouldn't have that much time to hand out favors to their families, nor were they as likely to be influenced by sexual favors. It was the same problem the Church faced. Remember that celibacy was mandated only in the 12th century and only then because of the fear that the families of certain clergy were acquiring too much property and power."

Gloria looked at me and explained, "A problem with family values, particularly the families of a cardinal or pope. Although, the celibacy rule didn't stop the Borgias or the Medicis."

"You are right, Sister Gloria," Giuseppe answered.

"You can call me Gloria, Giuseppe."

Giuseppe acknowledged the request with a nod and then responded, "Yes, Gloria. The big problem was with the popes at that time. They wanted to take over everything so that their families would prosper while the other rich families wanted to prevent it. In the case of the families of Venice's *Libro d'Oro*, they wanted to prevent the doge's family from taking over. In fact, the Council of Ten, which unfortunately has become known as a sort of Venetian gestapo, was created in the 14th century in order to keep watch on the nobili, including the doge. Their mission was to make sure that the Doge and individual members of the nobili didn't abuse their position and power. They were to protect the nobili from each other, and the people from the nobili. It was organized after a member of the nobili, Bajamonte Tiepolo, tried to take over and become a dictator. The revolt ended when an old woman dropped a large stone on his head."

"An all too rare example of a woman casting the deciding vote," Gloria observed drily. "But if the relics weren't found by Faliero, what happened and how did Foscari get involved?"

"Ah, yes," Giuseppe rested his elbows on the table and we both did the same as if the ears on the papier-mâché masks were real and couldn't be trusted with what they might hear. "It seems that Faliero pretended to find the relics in order to save himself. The Council of Ten had uncovered the truth and had been searching for the relics. Of course, it was top secret, because it was in no one's interest that the truth should come out. Foscari led the Council of Ten before being elected Doge in 1423 so of course he knew about the situation and the search for the relics. He also knew the weaknesses of the other members of the Council of Ten quite well and when he became Doge he must have bribed or blackmailed the council member who was leading the search. As a result, when the relics were located, Foscari was able to have them removed and hidden in another place so that when the other members of the council searched the hiding place they found nothing and assumed they had made a mistake. He then had the other mosaic made that showed him finding the relics in the new hiding place."

"And Foscari hid the mosaic he had made until he was ready for the switch," Gloria said, nodding her head.

"Fortunately, his plot was uncovered by the other members of the Council of Ten before he could make the switch and that was the real reason why he was deposed in 1457. Foscari refused to divulge the place where he had hidden the relics or that he'd commissioned another mosaic that would show their location. The relics were never found and the Council of Ten was forced to continue their search. All of this was kept completely secret."

"That means the Venetians have been lying about the relics of San Marco being in the Church for more than half a millennium."

Giuseppe seemed hurt by the assertion, "The Venetian people were not lying since one can only lie if one knows the truth and only the Doge and the Council of Ten knew the truth. Besides there was a piece of his body that did not disappear."

"A piece of the body?" I asked.

Giuseppe closed his right hand then unfolded each finger one at a time until they were all displayed. "The right hand was chopped off after the body arrived from Alexandria. This was after they unpacked it from the pork in which it was concealed. You know that after they stole the body, they hid the mummified body in a barrel of pork brine because they knew no Muslim would want to be anywhere near pork. The reason it was the right hand was because they wanted to give the hand that wrote the Gospel to the Pope as a peace offering. They assumed San Marco was right-handed. After they lost the body, Doge Faliero kept the hand and put it in the reliquary under the high altar along with the body of a pauper and gave the Pope the hand of the pauper, instead."

"Pardon the pun," I said, "but didn't that leave the Pope empty-handed?"

Giuseppe shrugged, "But it seemed better at the time to lie to the Pope than to the people. Unfortunately, once the truth is discovered they will demand that we give them not only the real hand and head, but the entire body," Giuseppe wriggled the fingers of both of his hands. "But we are now very close to finding the true relics. If we can look at the entire mosaic that Foscari made and then hid, not just this section that is in this photograph, we will be able to see where the relics are hidden and return them to where they rightfully belong, in the Basilica."

"How did you get this photograph if the mosaic he hid has never been found?" Gloria asked.

"It was in a collection of photographs of buildings in Venice that were taken almost a century ago. There is nothing on it that says which building, unfortunately, and, as you know, most of the buildings in Venice are old. However, we believe we have found the location."

"When you asked me to come and help, you said it was urgent that I come immediately. I don't understand the urgency if it is still a secret and you are close to finding the relics and putting everything right."

"You know about COPR?"

"Most certainly," Gloria replied, "I know about the Catholic Office for the Preservation of Relics. After all it is the official Church agency responsible for investigating stolen or missing relics. COPR reports directly to the Vatican and, although they deny it, they are suspected of engaging in clandestine operations."

"In that case you will understand the significance of COPR's director, Father Pietro Lupurelli, being in Venice. It is our belief that he knows that the relics of San Marco may not be in the Basilica. A week ago the Vatican requested from the Patriarch of Venice, which is the title for the Archbishop, permission to do some tests on the relics. The story they gave was that it is part of a new initiative to determine the condition of the holiest of relics so that any preservation measures that are required can be instituted. Of course, the Patriarch of Venice, not knowing the truth about San Marco nor the Vatican's real motives, has granted permission and the testing will be done a week from now. "

"You think Father Lupurelli is behind this?" Gloria asked.

"Why else would he come to Venice as a member of the team that is going to inspect the relics? I believe he has already done carbon testing on the hand that was given the Vatican and has concluded that it isn't old enough to have belonged to San Marco. Once he sees the relics, he will not only find the real hand but will discover that the rest of the relics are not old enough to be those of San Marco. The Vatican will tell the Patriarch of Venice the truth and demand the real hand and tell him that the rest is a fake. It will be a catastrophe for San Marco and Venice. As you know the head of San Marco was given to the Egyptian Coptic Church in return for which the Coptic Church gave up their claim for all the relics so that the rest of the relics could remain in Italy."

Gloria filled in the rest, "If the Vatican announces that neither they nor we have the real relics then the Egyptian Coptic Church will test their own and discover the truth. They will then accuse the Vatican of cheating them and the Vatican will accuse Venice and the Vatican will assert their authority over all of the relics that are currently in the city."

"The pound of flesh exacted from Venice," I said.

"Only in this case it's bone and it's more than a pound. It will serve as a pretext for Lupurelli to expand COPR's powers. He will assert authority over all the relics and be able to control access." Gloria turned and asked Giuseppe, "You said earlier that the Patriarch of Venice does not know that the real relics were never found and the ones that are in San Marco are fake?"

"No. How could one ask a prince of the Church to lie? As I told you earlier, only the Council of Ten and the Doge knew the truth and the Cardinal and his successors were never let in on the secret."

"But all of those people are long dead and buried," I pointed out.

"Not quite. It is only the doges who are no longer with us."

"You are saying that the Council of Ten still exists?" Gloria asked in astonishment.

He smiled and leaned toward us as if he was letting us into a really big secret, "It would be more accurate to call it the

Council of One. We could not disband with San Marco still missing."

Gloria waved her right hand around the shop in an arc, "So all of this is fake, a false front?"

"Masks as a mask," I added.

Giuseppe laughed, "I assure you I am a real maker of masks and all of these are my creations. As you can imagine the Council did not anticipate that it would take five hundred years to recover the bones of San Marco. Because of the many bad decisions made by Foscari before he was deposed as doge, Venice became too weak to resist the Inquisition completely, even though they knew it was a way for Rome to exert its authoritarian rule. They were forced to appoint three inquisitors and the Council of Ten lost its power. The inquisitors were not told about San Marco for obvious reasons but the Council had no official status to continue its investigation nor any funding. However, it continued to do so unofficially. I guess you would say we went underground. After Napoleon's invasion, the members could no longer fund the investigation out of their own pockets. That is when we began to sell masks."

"You said that you have found the building where the mosaic is hidden?" Gloria asked.

"Yes," Giuseppe replied. "I believe a friend of mine who is an architect has located the hiding place of the real mosaic while restoring a building."

"Then, you can easily find out where the relics are hidden after you've seen all of the mosaic. Why do you need me?"

"Because we need someone with your expertise to verify that the mosaic is the one that Foscari made that shows where the relics are hidden. They won't believe me, a mask-maker, after all. Then we can remove the real relics from their hiding place and substitute them for the bones of the pauper. We also have a plan through a fellow Curiosi to secretly replace the fake head in Egypt with the genuine one of San Marco." Giuseppe slipped the two photographs back in the envelope. He then took a camera with a flash attachment from beneath the desk and handed it to Gloria. I recognized it as a Leica M6, a favorite of war correspondents. "It is also important that when after you examine the mosaic and determine that it is authentic you take a photograph of it that shows the hiding place of the relics." Giuseppe then placed two shopping bags on the table, "I have a little gift for each of you as a gesture of my personal appreciation. Each of these bags contains one of the masks that I have made."

***

I stared at the mask and thought that it would be nice to look at but I wouldn't want to wear it. As I wondered where I might display it in my apartment back in Rome there was a knock on my door.

Gloria stepped into my room without hesitation and quickly sat in the only chair leaving me the bed, "I just had a phone call from Father Lupurelli."

"Lupurelli? How did he know you were here?"

"He told me he had called me wanting some advice, and Diego, my research assistant, informed him I was in Venice. I called Diego and he confirmed that Lupurelli had telephoned, but I am convinced that Lupurelli called in order to create a cover story and that he already knew I was here."

"What makes you think he already knew?"

"Because he didn't ask me why I was here. You would think he would be curious, wouldn't you? In any case, Lupurelli told me that the COPR is planning a symposium on religious artifacts and relics that have been lost and wants me to participate, and, since we are both in Venice, he suggested we meet as quickly as possible to discuss it in person."

A half hour later we stood in the Campo San Giacomo da l'Orio looking at the church of the same name. With its austere exterior the church looked like a tourist trap for ascetics. "According to the guidebook for Venice, this area was inhabited by wolves before they constructed this church in the 9th century," I said, placing the guide into my coat pocket. "Maybe that's why Lupurelli decided to make this his base since lupus means wolf."

She smiled. "I see you know your Latin."

"Doesn't every good Catholic?"

"So do a number of not so good ones."

"I'll confess to that much but I'll spare you the details."

"I can't offer you any absolution but I don't think I would be as shocked as you might think. I don't live in a cloister."

Gloria spared me from trying to come up with a response by rapping on the door using its heavy iron knocker and after a short wait, it opened a crack. An elderly face peaked out at us and then the door swung in revealing the nun dressed in a traditional habit. She seemed to struggle to keep her head up under the weight of the large crucifix hanging from her neck as Gloria told her who we were.

"Are you alone?" the nun asked suspiciously and looked past us at the campo. As her head turned the cross swung like a pendulum across the white scapular in the front of her black habit throwing her off balance. Gloria grabbed her arm and held it until the little nun regained her footing. Once recovered, she thanked Gloria. We slowly followed her down a dim corridor until she stopped in front of wooden door with the Roman numeral X carved into it. She knocked and the door immediately opened. A man stepped out into the corridor. He was wearing a black cassock that covered him from just beneath his solemn face to his sandals. After bending over to have a whispered exchange with the nun, she shuffled off into the darkness. He opened the door and ushered us through. Instead of following us, he shut the door leaving Gloria and me alone in a small, narrow room which was crowded with a desk and several straight backed chairs. A desk lamp provided the only illumination other than the feeble light seeping through a postage stamp window set high in the far wall. The door opened again and a tall, thin man entered. Unlike the other priest, he was wearing a black suit with a clerical collar and carried a worn, brown leather briefcase.

"Father Lupurelli, I was afraid for a minute that we'd been sentenced to a life of solitary confinement," Gloria said.

He half smiled and motioned for us to sit down before seating himself behind the desk. "Not confinement but contemplation. However, for a monk, having to share a cell, particularly with a member of the opposite sex, even a sister, would probably be thought of as a form of torture. Of course, I am not a monk."

"One person's punishment might be another's pleasure," I said, as I tried to find a comfortable spot on the hard wood of the chair.

"In that case it would be essential for the torturer to know the difference," he replied with a smile, then leaned toward us, stretching his sharp jaw so that the skin of his face was as taut as a clenched fist. "It is indeed fortuitous that we are both in Venice at the same time, Sister Gloria."

"Quite a coincidence."

"Or providential."

"I suppose that depends on whether I can help you with your symposium. You said that the subject is lost relics?"

"It is a sad fact that the remains, the relics, of some saints are missing and others have even been stolen. Although, in most cases it is only a piece, not an entire body. For the symposium, we are bringing together a panel of experts, such as yourself, to discuss these missing or stolen religious relics." Lupurelli handed Gloria a sheet of paper, "This is a list of the other experts who have agreed to participate."

After looking over the list, Gloria agreed to be part of the symposium.

Lupurelli smiled, "I am so happy to hear that. The symposium will be focusing on first class relics. As you know there are three classes of religious relics."

"Of course," Gloria answered. "The first class includes the body parts of a saint. The second are items that a saint wore or touched, and the third class is composed of objects that have been touched by either of the first two classes. Second and third class relics are relatively easy to buy since there can be no real way to authenticate them, and the supply can be easily increased. On the other hand, it is a violation of canon law to sell first class relics."

"Most people sell the reliquary in which the relic is kept. In that way, the relic itself is given for free so that technically it is not a sin," Father Lupurelli said, "Although admittedly, it exploits the weakness of humans, no matter how pious, to obtain what is rare."

"In other words, they get off on a technicality. I can understand the attraction for a collector. There aren't many things rarer than the remains of a dead saint except the bones of a live saint."

Father Lupurelli's eyes arched at this observation. "As you know, Sister Gloria, the Church does not canonize people who are still living."

"You aren't contending that they weren't saints while they were alive, are you?" Gloria asked with what I thought was a mischievous gleam in her eyes. "In fact, it is a requirement, wouldn't you say?"

"Of course," Father Lupurelli stammered and removed his hands from their prayerful embrace. "But the Church must weigh all of the evidence before it decides who was a saint while they were alive, and they can only do so after the person is dead. After all, some of the evidence for sainthood is only evident after the saint's death such as miracles that occur as the result of praying to the saint. Only then can the correct decision be made. I like to compare it to what is called dark matter."

"You mean the term that physicists use to describe the mass of the universe that they have been unable to detect or measure directly?" Gloria asked.

"Exactly. Just as scientists believe they can learn something about this unseen missing part of the material universe through use of indirect methods and observation, I believe we can discern the properties of the unseen, spiritual universe by examining what we can observe."

"In other words, relics are the opening to an otherwise hidden universe, a dark mass of the soul?" I asked.

Lupurelli glanced at me with annoyance, "We prefer not to joke about these matters, Signor Flynn. In any case, I was only making an analogy. The concern of the symposium is the sad fact that there are always a number of relics that are missing. Some of them have not even been reported. One wonders if those responsible for their care are even aware that they are missing. Or perhaps they are and that is the reason they are afraid to say anything." He brought the fingertips of his hands together forming, with the help of the lamp, a shadowgraph of praying hands on the bare wall to his left. I wondered if this was what monks do by candlelight in their cells to amuse themselves.

"Even in Venice?" Gloria asked.

"Especially in Venice, Sister. There are so many bones of saints here the city itself is a reliquary. There is no question about that. The question is how many of the relics have been acquired through legitimate means. Just take the relics of San Marco that were stolen from Alexandria. Who is to say that other relics that were acquired by theft won't disappear again?" He said as clasped his hands again, "But tell me, what do you think might be missing?"

"For a city that's been disappearing into the sea since the day it was founded, it might be easier to list what isn't missing," Gloria replied.

***

"Be careful," the little nun warned us as she led us back to the front door. "Venice has become a very sinful place and there are signs that the end is coming."

"What do you mean, signs?" I asked.

"For one, the aqua alta is coming. Every year it is higher. Many people no longer live on the ground floor for fear of drowning but that will not save them since the very foundations will crumble."

Gloria turned to the nun, "Remember, Sister, that God made a promise that it would not be a flood but a fire that would come at the end of the world."

"Perhaps, but Venice has always been separated from the rest of the world, so God would have a special end in mind for us."

"In that case, Sister, let us hope God has chosen a Venetian to build a gondola as big as Noah's Ark."

A few minutes later as we stood on wooden planks above the green water that washed over the embankment of the Grand Canal waiting for the Vaporetto, I said, "The sister might be right about Venice sinking into the Adriatic."

"Unfortunately, for someone like Lupurelli, the aqua alta is just another reason to rescue the bones of San Marco and take them to Rome where they can be kept high and dry on the rock of San Pietro. As far as they are concerned, the living inhabitants of Venice, including the little sister, can fend for themselves."

At our hotel the aqua alta had receded leaving behind a soggy welcome mat at the entrance. "Fortunately, it decided not to stay for the night," the desk clerk announced, referring to the aqua alta, and then handed Gloria an envelope that was delivered an hour earlier. Inside were two invitations to a masked party at the Accademia that evening.

"Now we know the real reason why Giuseppe gave us the masks," Gloria said.

***

A man dressed as an 18th-century footman gave an exaggerated bow as we entered the Accademia. Another servant handed us flutes of champagne and we were quickly engulfed in a current of masked partygoers and swept into the large inner courtyard where a white-wigged chamber orchestra played with the vigor of a jazz band. We made our way through the crowded room to the far side and into a gallery where Gloria tugged my arm and we stopped in front of a large painting covering most of one wall.

"It is *Convito in Casa di Levi* by Paolo Veronese," remarked the masked man standing beside us. It was Giuseppe's voice hidden behind a golden mask with a foot long beak. "Of course, as is the case with many things, it really is not that at all. It is actually the Last Supper but the Inquisition objected to the drunks and what look like a group of Germans."

"They probably thought it was a conspiracy by German Lutherans," I said.

"In any case, Veronese made a slight artistic compromise and changed the name so that it now depicts a feast in the house of Levi," Giuseppe bowed slightly. "Please allow me to introduce myself. I am Il Dottore. During the plague the doctors wore masks such as this because the long nose dampened the smell of death." He turned to Gloria, "The volto, or half mask, with the plume of black feathers that you are wearing is called the Temptress."

"I suppose I should thank you for not making me wear a nun's habit to go with it although I am wearing black, which isn't the color I imagine a real temptress would be wearing," Gloria plucked at the fabric of the plain black dress she was wearing. "In any case, now we know that you gave us these masks so that you could tell who we were."

"Ah, but you are not the only temptress here tonight so I have given your mask a particular, but subtle, detail that enables me to identify you. Nonetheless, someone might have followed you and be suspicious of my approach. Therefore, I will pretend to be telling you about this painting and you will pretend to show your appreciation for my knowledge by nodding your heads as I point out various parts."

His gloved right hand reached out from the black cape he was wrapped in and pointed at the upper left corner of the painting and our masks tilted in that direction as if we were marionettes. "Tell me, how was the meeting with Lupurelli?"

After Gloria recounted the meeting, Giuseppe said, "I wish I had been there. It confirms my own suspicion that he believes you might be in Venice because of San Marco. He might even believe you will lead him to the relics. However, as long as he doesn't know that we are working together, we still have the advantage."

"I don't think he knows."

"Good," Giuseppe said. "Now we need you to authenticate the mosaic and take a photograph of it that shows the spot where the relics are hidden."

"First you need to tell us where the mosaic is," Gloria replied. "You said that an architect you know discovered it while restoring a building?"

His arm swept across the painting to the center where a dog looked up at Jesus as he sat behind a table. "My friend, Filippo, discovered it while restoring a palazzo that was originally owned by a wealthy Jew, Jacopo Grimaldi, who built it in the 15th century, fifty years before the Jews were forced by the Inquisition to move into the ghetto in Cannaregio. He was one of the Jewish moneylenders who were the bankers for the nobili. Foscari and his family had become quite wealthy in business as the result of his influence and he had used Grimaldi as his banker. When Foscari concocted his plot to take credit for the discovery of the true relics of San Marco, he turned to Grimaldi. He knew that a Jew would not be afraid of eternal damnation in a Christian hell for being part of such a conspiracy. On the other hand, Grimaldi knew that if he didn't help Foscari he might never be repaid the money owed him. And then there was also coercion. That would have been easy to employ against a Jew who had no rights. They weren't even allowed to be members of the cittadini much less the nobili. So Grimaldi was at the mercy of Foscari."

"Who was not just any member of the nobili but the Doge," Gloria added.

"Why didn't he say anything after Foscari was deposed?" I asked. "After all he would have already lost any chance of being repaid and couldn't be punished by Foscari."

"If he divulged Foscari's plot, he would have had to explain why he'd agreed to participate in such an act of treason and heresy in the first place. As long as Foscari didn't talk, he was safe. Foscari, of course, didn't talk because he knew he would probably be executed once the relics were recovered. As long as he didn't tell the Council of Ten where they were, he had, as they say, an ace up his sleeve."

"Why didn't Grimaldi destroy the mosaic since it would incriminate him?" Gloria asked.

"Grimaldi believed that if Foscari ever confessed and implicated him, he would be able to exchange his knowledge of where the relics were hidden for his life and fortune, or at least his life. Then before he died he left the secret with his descendants. When the entire Jewish population of Venice was forced to move into the Ghetto in 1516, they pretended to sell the palazzo to Lorenzo Gambello, a member of the nobili who was deeply in debt to the Grimaldis. In order to cancel the debt, he agreed to hold it for them until they were allowed to live once again outside the ghetto. Two centuries later Napoleon captured Venice and allowed the Jews to leave the ghetto. The Grimaldis reclaimed the Palazzo from the Gambellos. During that entire time, the mosaic remained hidden in a secret room. After the invention of photography, the Grimaldis had the photograph made so that if they needed to, they could show it as proof that they knew where the mosaic was without having to divulge its real location."

"So that's why the photograph doesn't include the part of the mosaic that shows where the relics are hidden."

"Unfortunately for them," Giuseppe continued, "when Mussolini came to power, the fascists didn't care about saints much less their bones, so knowing where the mosaic was that showed the burial place of San Marco didn't provide the kind of protection they'd hope for."

"You only need to see what Mussolini did to Santa Lucia to know that. Making the trains run on time was of more interest to him than his soul," Gloria said.

Giuseppe dipped his long nose in agreement. "The Nazis shipped the Grimaldis off by those very trains to the death camps. Fortunately, the photograph itself was not lost but was found stuffed in a book that was included in an estate sale six months ago. Ironically, it was the estate of the very same Gambello family who had regained ownership of the palazzo after the demise of the Grimaldis. It was only after discovering the photograph that I was able to learn the full story and where the mosaic is. But I have already talked with you long enough." Raising his voice from the whisper that we had been conversing in, he announced, "I hope I haven't been boring you with my little lecture. Before you leave, however, make sure you look at some of the other paintings. You might find the one next to this of particular interest." He shook my hand, kissed Gloria's and with a swirl of his cape, he disappeared back into the crowd of partygoers.

After Giuseppe left, we followed his recommendation, moved to the left and found ourselves in front of *Messa in Salvo del Corpa di San Marco* by Tintoretto. We turned and looked at each other through the slits in our masks. Gloria opened her right hand revealing a small piece of paper that Giuseppe had slipped her.

***

Filippo was sitting in a café drinking espresso next to one of the many humpbacked bridges that span Venice's narrow, less grand canals. The wheelchair lift attached to the right side of the bridge reminded me that I hadn't seen one person in a wheelchair since I'd been in Venice, as if the lame had all been miraculously cured.

Filippo put down a paperback book with cowboys sitting around a campfire on its cover. We knew from the note that Giuseppe slipped to Gloria that Filippo Castagno would be reading a paperback western. However, it was clear from Filippo's denim shirt, jeans with a large silver buckle, and black cowboy boots that he wasn't packing the book just for our benefit. After introducing ourselves and sitting down, Filippo reached into the breast pocket of his shirt. Instead of a cigarette he pulled out a stick of Juicy Fruit gum and offered it to us. I took one while Gloria declined.

"When I stopped smoking I started chewing gum," he returned the pack to his pocket. "I need to have something in my mouth."

"Even when you are drinking espresso?" I asked.

"Especially then, because I always had a cigarette with my espresso."

Gloria said to Filippo that it was lucky he notified Giuseppe when he discovered the mosaic, "Otherwise, who knows what might have happened."

"Giuseppe didn't tell you the whole story," Filippo replied. "He was the person who got me the job of restoring the palazzo. Don't ask me how because he wouldn't tell me. In return for the job, he asked me if I could look for a mosaic he thought was hidden in the palazzo that showed the discovery of the relics of San Marco. As soon as I discovered the hidden chamber and saw that there was a mosaic inside I stopped everything and told Giuseppe. He swore me to secrecy and then explained the story behind the mosaic. I stopped all work on the palazzo until he contacted an expert who would come and see if it was the real thing. And here you are, the expert. I am proud to be a part of something that will be of service to Venice. You see, I am one hundred percent Venetian underneath this denim." Filippo stopped, looked around and said, "We should be going." He pulled a rucksack over one shoulder.

As we began walking he whispered to us. "There were two men at the café who seemed to be spying on us." I looked over my shoulder as casually as possible and saw the two men in trench coats and wearing sunglasses who we had seen on the motoscafo the day before. When I turned back, Gloria and Filippo were already halfway across the bridge and I had to break into a trot to catch them. On the other side of the canal, instead of following the calle next to it, we entered an opening between the buildings. Once inside the narrow passage we turned left at a right angle and were immediately enveloped in twilight with the sky a strip of blue framed by tile roofs. Footsteps clattered over the bridge we'd just crossed and I sped up, grateful for the silence of the Vibram soles of my shoes. Suddenly, the alley broke sharply to the right, and I almost ran into Gloria and Filippo, who had stopped several yards from another bridge.

"Why have we stopped? I can hear them behind us." Gloria asked.

Filippo pointed to a rowboat tied to the quay next to the bridge, "Quickly, into the boat," and we clambered in as the footsteps behind reverberated off the walls of the alley sounding like a cattle stampede in a canyon.

As the boat bobbed, green water from the canal splashed over its gunwales. Filippo quickly untied the line from the bow and yanked it toward him pushing the boat forward. Just as we were even with the metal ring where the other end of the line was attached, he threw the line onto the quay and we slipped under the bridge. As the boat slid into a barrel of darkness, Filippo raised his arms above his head. Gloria and I followed his lead and our hands clawed the gritty underside of the bridge until the boat came to a stop. There was shuffling at the foot of the bridge then some muffled words, followed by footsteps on the bridge. We pushed against the sweating stone in order to hold the boat as still as possible. The footsteps grew louder and then halted above us at the crest of the bridge. I held my breath, as if they might actually hear it, and stared at the stone above us. It was like a scene from a war movie where the crew of a submarine sweats in silence, listening to the ping of sonar from a destroyer, waiting for depth charges to explode. The footsteps started again and grew fainter as they crossed over to the other side.

We lowered our arms and Filippo pointed at the oars. "Now we must row."

"Row?" Gloria's whispered. "Now that they're gone why can't we walk?"

"Because, Sister, we cannot walk on water, at least I can't and I have my doubts about Signor Flynn."

"Your doubts are justified," I answered.

"I see, we will use the boat to get to the palazzo," Gloria said, not telling Filippo to just call her Gloria.

"And here I thought you stole this boat, so that we could get away from that gang who was after us," I said.

"This is my boat," Filippo replied. "My plan is to row to the palazzo. I know the way so I will navigate and one of you must row."

"I can steer," Gloria announced grabbing the tiller in the stern and wiggling it so that the bow bumped against the side of the side of the canal.

Filippo whispered. "Very good, Sister, you may take the helm."

"I guess that makes me the galley slave," I said, as I grabbed the oars.

I rowed while Gloria steered through a series of canals at Filippo's direction before he told us to stop. I pulled in the oars letting us glide through the water while Gloria pushed the tiller to the right pushing the bow toward a canvas wall that was at least three stories high on which there was a life size illustration of an elegant 16th-century palazzo. Filippo reached behind the edge of the canvas as we approached, grabbed onto something and pulled us behind it. In front of us a grid of metal scaffolding, crisscrossed with wooden planks, rose to the top of the building. The façade had been sandblasted and the light straining through the canvas gave it the pink hue of a baby's skin. Filippo tied the bow line to the scaffold and pulled himself up onto its planking. Gloria and I followed, stepping between the dangling ropes that swung back and forth as the canvas inhaled and exhaled with the breeze, until we reached a padlocked metal door.

"How do we get past this locked door?" Gloria asked.

"Since it is my lock we use a key, of course," Filippo answered, fishing a key from the pocket of his jeans and inserting it into the padlock.

After we entered, Filippo switched on a flashlight he had taken from his rucksack. We followed him down a wide hallway, cluttered with building material, until we reached another door with a padlock. This one had a combination lock and asked me to hold the flashlight as he rotated the tumblers until it clicked open. The room we entered was a large square with a tarp over the floor. Sheets of plywood covered the windows and buckets of paint, brushes, and pans were stacked in one of the corners. The walls were pockmarked with spackle.

Filippo flicked a switch near the door and the room was lit by a bare light bulb suspended from an orange cord attached to the ceiling. "Help me roll back the tarp," he said as he slipped off his rucksack and dropped to his knees.

We rolled up the tarp, exposing a marble floor. When we had rolled it halfway across the floor Filippo told us to stop. He pulled out a screwdriver from his pack and began prying at a seam between two sections of the marble. He slipped it into the crack and pushed down on the handle. The slab slid free and I helped him pull it up.

"It's a lot lighter than I thought it would be," I said, my arms and back sore from the rowing.

"That's because it's not as thick as the rest of the marble floor. You can see how the wood underneath it is raised so that it fills in for the thinner marble. Now help me remove the sections next to it."

Filippo and I took out three more sections exposing a trapdoor with a recessed iron ring. Filippo yanked hard on the ring and the trapdoor opened. He pointed his flashlight into the opening, illuminating a wooden ladder that descended about ten feet.

"It's still dry," he announced and then asked me to hold the flashlight as he descended the ladder. When he reached the bottom he called for us to follow, and I held the flashlight for Gloria and then tossed it to Filippo and climbed down myself.

"Where's the mosaic?" Gloria asked.

"On the floor over there." Filippo pointed the flashlight to the right. As he held it Gloria walked over and examined the mosaic laid out on the floor.

"Even after all the centuries it looks ready to replace the one in San Marco."

"We don't have much time so do whatever it is you need to do," Filippo said.

Gloria bent over with her flashlight and examined the mosaic. Then she took the camera Giuseppe had given her from her bag. The room was lit with flashes. "I hope I got everything," she said.

"Now, we must go back up the ladder. Quickly," Filippo said.

As soon as we climbed through the opening, Filippo slammed the trapdoor shut. I held the flashlight as he took a tube of adhesive from his pack and smeared it on the bottom of the sections of marble and then lifted them into place. "This is in case those two who were following us find the palazzo and search it."

"I don't think they will," I said. "It is sealed like a tomb."

"A watery one," he answered, "because it will soon be covered by the aqua alta."

***

We returned to the boat and Filippo rowed us to nearby Campo Manin. He tied up the boat and we got out and walked to the Campo.

Filippo suddenly stopped and said, "There they are." He pointed across the Campo to the entrance of a calle. A woman holding a closed umbrella above her head was leading a group of elderly tourists through the narrow street toward the campo where we stood. Behind them were the two men who had been following us before we had given them the slip.

Gloria looked quickly at the small canal several meters away. "Do you think we can make it back to the boat?"

"Even if we could, they'd be able to follow us in one of these gondolas."

"We can't let them get the film in the camera that shows where the relics are hidden," Gloria said.

"I'll slow them down while both of you make a run for it," Filippo replied. "I'll get in touch with you back at your hotel and tell you where to bring the film." Without waiting for a reply from us Filippo walked boldly toward the tour guide stopping her and her followers in their tracks and completely blocking the two men from entering the campo.

While Filippo engaged the tour guide in an animated discussion of the history of the Campo, Gloria and I ran up the steps and across the bridge then through the shadow darkened street until we entered the Campo Sant'Angelo. Gloria slowed as we headed toward the bridge leading to the Calle dei Frati. Finally, she grabbed my arm, stopped and gasped, "I'm out of breath."

"We can't stop. Filippo won't be able to hold them up for very long."

"You're in better shape than me," she answered breathlessly as she bent over with both hands on her hips.

"It must be from dodging bullets in the Balkans. Not that I would recommend that as exercise. If we can get to the Campo Santo Stefano just over the bridge we might be able to lose them."

"Okay," Gloria exhaled and stood up straight.

We jogged across the bridge, through the Calle de Frati and out into the campo where we stopped in front of the church that gave it its name.

"We could go inside the church and try and find a hiding place," I suggested.

She looked at the church and shivered, "Santo Stefano has a bloody history."

"Isn't that a prerequisite for a martyr? And San Stefano wasn't just any old Christian martyr. From what I remember, he was the first."

"I meant the church not the saint. It's been deconsecrated more than once so I wouldn't place much faith in its ability to provide any protection," Gloria replied and started counting the streets leading off of it. "There are seven so the odds are in our favor that if we pick one they'll pick one of the others."

"We don't have much time and the closest calle is the first one on the left so let's go with that one."

She looked at me, "But that would be too obvious."

"Since they've already spotted us it's a moot point," I grabbed her left hand and pulled as she looked over her right shoulder at the two men running toward us from the Calle dei Frati.

The men yelled just as we entered the calle. Unfortunately, it was straight and narrow just when we needed one that was crooked and wide. It felt like we were running through a gun barrel with the bullet just behind us. I looked over my shoulder and saw that the two men were walking rather than running toward us.

"They've dropped back for some reason," I yelled at Gloria.

"The reason is right in front of us," she said stopping suddenly and looking at the water that blocked our way. On the wall of the building on the other side of the canal a sign read Rio del Santissimo.

"We may have to swim for it," I said.

"I don't know how to swim and just because I'm a sister doesn't mean I can walk on water."

"Well, we need some sort of a miracle," I said looking back at the two men who were now only twenty meters away.

"Will a gondola do?"

"What?" I yelled and, glancing toward Gloria I spotted the gondola drifting toward us with the gondolier standing in the stern.

"Jump," Gloria yelled and we both leapt over several feet of water toward the gondola as it slid past and landed at the feet of a startled Japanese couple.

"Scusi," we both said in unison as we untangled ourselves and slid onto the bench facing the stern and the two startled lovebirds. The gondola bobbed back and forth as the gondolier struggled with his oar to steady it. Behind him, on the quay one of the men grabbed for the pointed stern and missed and toppled into the water in a gushing belly flop.

***

"Thanks for giving us a lift in your love boat," I said to the gondolier as Gloria and I stepped ashore on the other side of the Grand Canal from the Rio del Santissimo.

We walked across the Campo San Vio to a sidewalk café where we both ordered espressos at the bar. I had a brandy chaser with mine.

"I have to admit it's the first time I've taken a gondola ride with a..."

"Nun," Gloria finished my stutter. "It's a first for me as well," she said then jiggled her espresso cup and looked at me, a smile creeping across her lips, "and I can assure you that our ride together was something I will always remember."

"But not treasure?"

"I have taken a vow..."

I felt my face flush, "I didn't mean, you know, that it was supposed to be romantic."

She laughed, "Vow of poverty is what I was going to say and gondola rides are very expensive. But now that you bring up romance, I hope we didn't spoil the romantic gondola ride for the honeymooners in the gondola."

"I don't think it will be the most cherished memory of their honeymoon."

Gloria stretched out in her chair and looked up. I followed her gaze toward the sky as she said "I must admit, as much time as I've spent inside churches, not even a cathedral's ceiling can come close to the sky itself. No matter how high they soar, they are stopped by something we have made and no matter what is painted on them, it is never more than what the mind can grasp, but when you look at the sky, the mind cannot begin to grasp what the eyes can see."

"I'll leave the comparisons with churches and cathedrals to you, but I can tell you the sky right now looks a lot different to me than it did from the other side of the Adriatic in Sarajevo a week ago."

She didn't answer. Instead, we sat there until the waiter interrupted the silence as he cleared the cups and saucers. Gloria looked at her watch, "My goodness, I need to get the camera to Giuseppe so he can print the pictures I took. Filippo said he would leave a message at the hotel telling us where to bring the film."

After a short walk we were back at the hotel. I decided to go to my room for a minute while Gloria went to the front desk to check for messages.

When the elevator door opened I reached out to flip the light switch that would illuminate the pitch black hallway. Instead of hard plastic my hand struck something soft. Before I could withdraw it, my arm was pulled behind my back, along with my other arm and someone's hand covered my mouth. In seconds, the hand was replaced with tape, then my legs and arms were tied with rope and I was stuffed into something that felt like a coffin but must have been a trunk. Whoever had kidnapped me decided to take the stairs instead of the elevator. When the jolting stopped, I felt the trunk skidding across the pavement. It was then lifted and deposited onto a boat judging from the swaying back and forth and the outboard motor that sputtered to life.

***

"No wonder it was so heavy. This is not the nun."

From the floor where I had been dumped I looked up at the two men who had been chasing us earlier.

The tall man, still wearing the stylish sunglasses, pointed to the squat, broad-shouldered man, "You can call him Silvio." Other than Silvio and the man talking to me, there were no other customers in what seemed to be a small, neighborhood bar.

"And me, you can call me Bernardo. Those aren't our real names of course. You must be Signor Flynn, the nun's assistant?" Bernardo said, then realized my mouth was taped. He looked at Silvio who removed the tape with one swift motion, almost taking my lips with it. Then, he untied my arms and legs.

"I am sorry, Signor Flynn, for the inconvenience," Bernardo said as he shook my hand. "We had expected that you would be the nun. It was dark, and so you are here instead of her."

"Where is here?" I asked, rubbing my sore mouth.

"We have the honor of bringing you to a place that many tourists do not see, a real Venetian tavern. They are called bacari. Have you ever been in such a place?"

"Not that I recall."

"I thought not. Bacari are conducive to conversation. Only for men, however, because women are not allowed."

"In that case, what would you have done if it had been Sister Gloria?"

Bernardo gave me a puzzled expression and then his face lit up, "Oh, you make a joke. For the nun we would make an exception, wouldn't we, Antonio?" He looked at the man behind the bar whose name I assumed was not really Antonio. "Nuns aren't real women, anyway. So now that we are all here we would like to have a little chat."

"I bet."

"Scusa?"

"Nothing."

"Nothing? Ah, if only it was nothing. But you see it is something. Something that is very important for us." He stopped and asked Antonio the bartender, "Can we have something to drink? What would you like, Signor Flynn? Anything you want."

"Nothing."

"Nothing? Oh, that would not be good. Silvio and I would not like to drink while you have nothing. I will buy you a nice glass of wine." He turned to the bartender. "A bottle of your best vino rosso from the Veneto, Antonio, and three glasses, please."

After Antonio brought a tray with the bottle and glasses over, Silvio poured the wine into each of our glasses. I took a sip and put it down. Bernardo pointed at the glass. "You don't like?"

"Ordinarily, yes."

"But not now? I see. You are afraid of us? No need for that." As he spoke he adjusted his sunglasses. "We followed you with the nun."

"I know."

"Yes, we know that you spotted us. It was very clumsy on our part," he looked at Silvio who bowed his head in shame. "So, tell us, how did you give us the slip? The first time when we lost you on the bridge, because we know how you escaped the second time by jumping into a gondola."

"That gondolier looked very surprised," Silvio added.

"That was nothing compared to his passengers, whose honeymoon we crashed." They didn't laugh so I added, "We used a rowboat the first time."

"If you hijacked a boat the first time as well, only it was a rowboat, then you must be a pirate," Bernardo laughed.

"We didn't hijack the boat, it had been left there for us to use. It was part of the plan, although you chasing us wasn't."

Bernardo scratched his chin. "That must mean that the place you went to, where the mosaic is hidden, is on a canal?" He looked at Silvio who was probably rolling his eyes behind the dark shades of his sunglasses. "Of course, that does not help us very much because this is Venice, after all. Could you be more specific as to where you went in the boat?"

"I don't know where we went, exactly. I'm not from Venice."

"Yes, we know you are not from Venice but you could tell us what the building looked like."

"The front of it was covered by a big canvas sheet."

"I see," Bernardo stroked his chin again. "This means that the building was being restored."

Silvio finally asked. "But there are many buildings being restored in Venice so how will we know, which one?"

"Ah, but they always paint on the canvas what the front of the building looks like, or what it is supposed to look like when they are finished restoring it." Bernardo turned to me and asked me to describe what was painted on the canvas. "Please," he added politely.

"You're the good copper? Does that mean Silvio is the bad one?" I asked.

"We are both good!" Silvio finally spoke. "We are working for the Church, for the Holy Father, himself."

"You're on a mission from God, is that it? Does that mean I'll be excommunicated if I don't tell you? I don't know if that would make much difference for me since I'm so lapsed I'm probably self-excommunicated."

Bernardo shrugged. "No, but for the nun it would be another matter. You would not want that to happen to Sister Gloria, would you? Nuns take a vow of obedience. Since you are her accomplice if we ask you then we are asking her and she is obliged to tell us the truth. Otherwise, we will have no alternative but to report this to our superiors, the Holy Father himself, who is also, as it turns out, her superior as well. And if that doesn't persuade you we have methods that will."

I figured they'd get it out of me one way or the other and since we had a head start on them already, once they let me go I'd be able to warn her and Giuseppe, so I described what was painted on the canvas.

"I know the building," Bernardo smiled. "It is near the Palazzo Foscari, which is on the Grand Canal. The building you described is the Palazzo Doloroso. It is on the Rio de Ca' Foscari. It makes sense that Foscari would have hidden the mosaic near his palazzo."

"Can I go now?" I asked.

"Go? Of course. But not until you finish your wine and then have another. Perhaps the bottle? Enjoy yourself. You Americans, even those with some Italian in them, are always in a rush. We insist that you slow down," he nodded toward Silvio. "Also, Silvio, would be greatly offended if you did not enjoy the hospitality we have offered. So, you see, relax and enjoy your private party." He looked at his watch. "We have reserved the bar until 5 p.m. when the owner will arrive. Then, you can leave. But, of course, you are invited to stay, if you are still enjoying yourself. This bacaro's regular customers are quite colorful and can be very entertaining." He then turned Silvio, "Let's go."

"Yes brother," Silvio answered as he and walked quickly to the door, with Antonio following him. They waved to me and closed the door and locked it.

***

As Bernardo said, the bacaro was unlocked at 5 p.m. by the owner. They had taken my mobile so I couldn't call Gloria. I had neglected to ask for her phone number anyway. There was nothing I could do but go back to the hotel and hope she was there. When I arrived the clerk said Gloria had left but gave me a note from her telling me that I should meet her at one of the confession boxes inside San Marco at 6:15. I rushed off to the Basilica. It was closed for the day but following the instructions in Gloria's note I walked around to the north side where the Porta dei Fiori was unguarded and unlocked and entered the narthex. I knew from previous visits that the images of San Marco that are displayed everywhere in the Basilica are always accompanied by a lion, which is also the symbol of Venice. However, looking up at the *Dome of Creation* I noticed for the first time that the lion is shown as not only the first animal that was created, but the first one named by Adam. As I walked under the southern arch of the narthex, the mosaic of the flood also displayed the lion as the first to be invited onto Noah's Ark and the first one to disembark into the new creation. When I entered the sanctuary I looked up at the *Dome of the Pentecost*, the mosaic where San Marco sits with the other apostles. Even at this distance it was clear that San Marco was the real a star while even Peter was relegated to a mere supporting role. No wonder the Vatican is pissed at Venice.

Beneath the dome, the sanctuary continued into the distance following the outline of a Greek cross, with five domes. At the center of the cross, the transept, where the arms of the cross join, was the largest dome, the *Dome of the Ascension*. The basilica's upper walls and ceilings were covered with gold and mosaics that turned the incandescent light into a honey colored dusk that grew darker as it descended into the marble clad lower sections. Even the floor was covered with mosaics. A rack of sputtering votive candles next to one of the massive pillars that flank each side of the sanctuary created a circle of light revealing some of the mosaics that covered the floors as well a row of confessionals that looked like telephone booths. Given the ever increasing number of sinners and the shrinking supply of priests it was only a matter of time before they would allow people to call in their confession. No doubt they would get a voicemail system that would route the call based on the type of sin to the appropriate prerecorded message of absolution and the penitential acts that were required.

Gloria's note instructed me to go to one of the confessionals. All of them had their curtains drawn back except for the middle one, which only had the curtain drawn back on one side. I entered and sat on the bench, the right side of my face a few inches from a screened opening. Still feeling claustrophobic from my time in the trunk I decided against closing the curtain on my side.

"Bless me for I have sinned," I mumbled, omitting the 'Father' from the words I remembered from the distant past when I had last confessed to someone other than a bartender.

"How long has it been since your last confession?" Gloria's voice whispered into my ear through the screen.

"I can't remember," I answered.

"It is my first time," she answered, "on this side, I mean."

"I do have something to confess, though," I stammered, and then told her about the kidnapping. "I confess that I described the picture of the building that was on the canvas covering the front and they were able to identify it as the Palazzo Doloroso. I also told them about the secret room with the mosaic on the floor that showed where the relics of San Marco are hidden. They seemed surprised when I told them that and I realized too late that they didn't know it was a mosaic we were looking for.

I didn't realize they would lock me in the bar until 5 p.m. That means they have had time to get to the Palazzo Doloroso and see the mosaic for themselves so now they know where his relics are hidden. I just hope they don't find them before we do."

Instead of scolding me, Gloria answered as if she were my spiritual counselor. "Don't feel guilty about that because what you didn't know was that where Filippo took us wasn't the real Palazzo Doloroso. Filippo had a duplicate made of the canvas that covers the Palazzo Doloroso and used it to cover the palazzo where the mosaic is. That was the reason he was in such a hurry to leave because as soon as we left his men removed it. I didn't know about this myself until Giuseppe told me. He said he didn't want us to have to lie if we were caught, but I think he was really worried that we might not be very good as liars. Anyway, we immediately developed and printed a copy of the photograph and using it we were able to identify the location of relics. Giuseppe and Filippo went to the spot where the relics were hidden to retrieve them. They said to meet them at the altar at 6:30." I could hear the curtain being drawn back from her side of the confessional.

"Wait," I said, "I haven't finished yet. It's been a long time since I've been to confession, so I've got a lot of sins."

"I'm sure you do, and as much as I would enjoy hearing you recite them, you know the women aren't allowed to be priests – yet – so I don't have the Church's authority to absolve your sins."

"I feel cheated somehow."

"So do I." She was now standing in the opening looking at me with a grin on her face. "In any case if we don't go now we'll be late. They also told me that we should try to be as invisible as possible. I think they want to avoid attracting any attention."

I climbed out of the confessional and followed her toward the front of the Basilica. We passed the entrance to the treasury and finally reached the right transept. Gloria pointed across to the center of the sanctuary. Giuseppe and Filippo emerged from behind the pillars on the opposite side and headed toward the ornate screen of Byzantine iconostasis that separated the sanctuary from the choir and the high altar beyond. They were carrying what looked like a small metal coffin and disappeared through an opening at the far end of the screen.

Gloria tugged at my sleeve and pointed to the place where the screen ended on our side, "That's the public entrance to view the altar. Ordinarily you need a ticket to enter. I don't suppose you bought a ticket? No matter, we'll leave something extra in the poor box."

As we sprinted across the open space that formed the arm of the cross and through the entrance I felt like I was trying to stay out of the crosshairs of sniper rifle. Crouching behind a railing we could see Giuseppe and Filippo. They had been stopped by Father Lupurelli, who was accompanied by my two abductors, Silvio and Bernardo. Instead of trench coats, they were wearing the black cassocks of a religious order. "Now I know why they called themselves brothers even thought there was no family resemblance," I muttered. The coffin shaped reliquary was on the floor in front of the high altar just outside the shadows of the marble canopy that covered the altar, and through the marble columns supporting the canopy, the golden wall of the Pala d'Oro, the altarpiece, glowed in the soft light.

Father Lupurelli addressed Giuseppe as if he were a child caught stealing candy, "You thought you would get away with this? I have to admit this Dante Flynn fellow was a very good liar. Brother Emilio and Brother Carlo were taken in and they convinced me as well." Both of the brothers bowed their heads in contrition as he said this. "It wasn't until we entered the Palazzo Doloroso that I realized we had been tricked. Of course, I knew you would be bringing San Marco here to replace the relics before your trickery could be discovered. Fortunately, we had a very fast boat and the police weren't about to stop a priest. Even in Venice there is still some respect for the cloth."

"Dante didn't lie," Giuseppe answered. "I had Filippo cover the front of the building with the canvas that had the Palazzo Doloroso façade on it."

Father Lupurelli bowed, "A deception worthy of a mask-maker. And you," he turned to Filippo, who was calmly unwrapping a stick of gum, "I salute your ability to execute such a deception but not your piety. Don't you think that chewing gum is disrespectful of San Marco?"

Filippo shrugged, put the gum back in his pocket and crossed his arms. Lupurelli turned back to Giuseppe, "If you are thinking about stopping us from taking all of the relics of San Marco, you should also think about how you have been caught red-handed and would have to explain to the good citizens of Venice that they have been lied to for centuries. Besides, it isn't as if we are stealing, since the right hand of San Marco that your ancestors gave us was a fake. You Venetians, who have never done anything without calculating the financial advantage, should understand better than anyone that you owe the Pope not only the hand of San Marco, but you also now owe nine centuries of interest as well. All of the relics should cover the debt."

"You didn't mention the head?" Gloria said as she stepped into the light. "Won't you have to give the head to the Coptic Church?"

"Ah, Sister Gloria. I thought you might be lurking in the shadows. To answer your question, it is my opinion that we never should have given it to the Egyptians in the first place. Since it is not necessary to expose this ruse of the Venetians now that they are giving us all of the relics as an act of piety and obedience to the Pope, the Coptics will never know that they have the head of some pauper rather than a saint. But before we claim what is rightfully owed to us, how do I know that you haven't removed the relics?" Lupurelli said. He took out a small flashlight and carefully examined the reliquary. After a few minutes he announced "The reliquary is authentic. It is the right age and design and this Latin inscription says it contains the relics of the sacred apostle. The question remains, however, as to who lies behind the cover, or shall I say, inside it? Perhaps

Foscari removed the relics and hid them somewhere else. After all, we know he was a devious man."

Giuseppe responded, "Trust me, the relics of San Marco are inside."

"Yes, but I must see for myself to make sure that it isn't empty." He motioned to Silvio who took out a screwdriver from one of the folds of his cassock and walked over to the reliquary. After a few minutes of prying with Lupurelli directing, Emilio lifted the top. After poking around inside for what seemed like an eternity, he stood up and pronounced, "Just as you said, it contains the relics, including the Apostle's right hand that you Venetians so deceitfully pretended to give to us. Without a relic of San Marco you will need to rename your basilica. Maybe Santa Lucia? After all, she has only your railway station named after her. The patron saint of the blind would be appropriate since you couldn't find San Marco for eight hundred years. Of course, you will need to do something with all of these mosaics of San Marco. I think they would look good in the Vatican Museums, don't you?" He laughed again and waved his hand to Brothers Emilio and Carlo. They stooped and slowly lifted the reliquary. Even though Brother Carlo was taller, his end sagged beneath Brother Emilio as they carried it in a procession behind Lupurelli.

As soon as the echo of their footsteps subsided into the stillness of the Basilica, Filippo took out the stick of gum and popped it in his mouth. Gloria and I stood up and joined them at the altar. She shook her head and said, "Did you tell Lupurelli the relics were in the reliquary because you thought he would believe you and not look?"

"On the contrary," Giuseppe answered. "I most definitely thought he would not believe me and that he would, in fact, look for himself. Which is exactly what he did. However, if I had not protested he would have been even more suspicious and probably looked even closer. But the real reason is that I do not want him accusing me of lying to him."

Filippo laughed, sending a wad of gum onto the altar. "No, really, some bones of San Marco were in the reliquary." He held up his right hand. "Did you know that the hand has more bones than any other part of the human body? I am not lying to you. It is the truth."

"You didn't switch the relics," Gloria said to Giuseppe.

"Not the fake ones in the reliquary, which is what they took with them."

Gloria smiled an nodded her head, "If Lupurelli claims at the symposium that he discovered the authentic relics and is taking them to the Vatican, then I will ask that his relics be tested to determine if they are authentic."

Giuseppe smiled broadly, "Of course, the tests will prove that only the hand is authentic and everyone will conclude, rightly, that the real relics of San Marco are resting under this altar," he turned to Filippo who was vigorously prying his gum from the top of the altar, "that Filippo is in the process of desecrating."

"It's not a desecration. I was just having it blessed by the real San Marco," Filippo replied, then shoved the congealed gum into his mouth.

7

ACKNOWLEDGEMENTS

I want to thank:

My copy editor, Elizabeth Baer, for her excellent work at transforming my often wayward grammar and spelling into a readable book.

Wendy Wintermute, my sister, who proof read and gave me helpful advise on the final draft.

Kiley Grantges for the wonderful book cover and Judy Dean for creating the design concept for the cover.

And, finally, my wife Kathleen Sutcliffe who read numerous drafts, made wise suggestions and encouraged me to "get it done".

8

ABOUT THE AUTHOR

Tim Wintermute writes novels, short stories and essays and is also the publisher of the Prismatist eMagazine (www.prismatist.com). Prior to being a fulltime author and publisher he was the executive director of a charitable foundation located in Detroit, Michigan.

8

ABOUT THE AUTHOR

Tim Wintermute writes novels, short stories and essays and is also the publisher of the Prismatist eMagazine (www.prismatist.com). Prior to being a fulltime author and publisher he was the executive director of a charitable foundation located in Detroit, Michigan.